AMALFI RE-VISITED

A novel by
Adolph Caso

Branden Books,
Boston

Library of Congress Cataloging-in-Publication Data

Names: Caso, Adolph, author.
Title: Amalfi re-visited : a novel / by Adolph Caso.
Description: 1st edition. | Boston : Branden Books, [2016]
Identifiers: LCCN 2016034845 (print) | LCCN 2016041826
(ebook) | ISBN   9780828326360 (softcover : acid-free paper) |
ISBN 9780828326377 (ebook) |ISBN 9780828326377 (E-
Book)
Classification: LCC PS3553.A794 A83 2016 (print) | LCC
PS3553.A794 (ebook) |
  DDC 813/.54--dc23
LC record available at https://lccn.loc.gov/2016034845

ISBN 9780828326360 Paperback
ISBN 9780828326377 E-Book

Branden Books
PO Box 812094
Wellesley MA 02482

Book orders:
branden@brandenbooks.com
www.brandenbooks.com
Amazon.com

Chapter 1
Amalfi: Background

The renowned City of Amalfi is situated south of Naples. It became known as Amalfi around 800 AD; soon thereafter, its people created what became the first quasi democracy in Europe: *The Maritime Republic of Amalfi*. This new form of government evolved out of the need to supply sailing crews for the merchant ships, and the practice of the crews to chose their captains—done through the first of its kind, the ballot box. These practices became the basis of Amalfi's Constitution known as the, *Tavole Amalfitane* (Amalfi Tablets)—maritime codes which were quickly adopted and adapted by all other similar republics and city states, and translated into numerous languages.

As important, Flavio Biondo invented the magnetic compass, thus making trans-oceanic travel more accessible.

In the main square, not far from the port, the Amalfitans erected an imposing cathedral in honor of St. Andrew, their patron saint. The immense structure was connected to its bordering mountains with an undetermined number of deep and multi-directional intersecting tunnels, some of which were used to store both religious and important artifacts. Although the body of St. Andrew is buried in the cathedral, it is speculated that remnants of other important religious figures—captured from Constantinople pursuant to the Fourth Crusade—may still be preserved in those caves.

For a few centuries, all of southern Italy, especially Amalfi, was under Muslim dominion; they had conquered North Africa, Portugal and Spain—their goal being the Vatican, saved only by Crusades themselves. Presently, tourists and residents abound in modern Amalfi; many frequent *Il Tarí*, a restaurant famous for its typical Amalfitan cuisine. The *Tari* was a Arab coin popular in Amalfi

Because Amalfi was situated on the west coast of Italy, it had continuous contacts with all of North Africa, including Egypt, the Middle East, and all the way to Constantinople. Its port was protected by rising mountains to the north and south; they extended inward into the high range, filled with ravines and only a few miles to the highest peak of Mount Lattari. For centuries, these mountains protected the city from within and from without.

Then, unexpectedly, around 1300, a huge cyclone slammed down midway between the islands of Capri and the port of Amalfi. It dramatically pushed immense amounts of water eastward to the top of the mountain, causing part of the mountain to collapse downward toward the sea, practically destroying the entire city. Except for the cathedral and few other structures, everything was destroyed, even the spirit of the remaining inhabitants. Their Port and ships gone, they were unable to make a come-back. Only century later, Amalfi has begun to flourish.

Today, because of its natural beauty embodied in the Amalfi Drive, tourists from throughout the world visit Amalfi; many even become residents of the mythical city. Among the more prominent visitors were: Richard Wagner, composer of *Parsifal,* Henrik Ibsen, dramatist, and Gore Vidal with his friends Mick Jagger and Hillary Clinton.

Yet, private American citizens have assumed permanent residency in Amalfi, two of whom were brothers from the Boston area: the oldest, having been fired from his college position over an affair with a black female student; the younger brother, a would-be scientist; his failed experiments became the target of modern terrorists. Thus, he doomed himself, the woman he loved, and the new Amalfi.

Chapter 2

The Pentagon

About ten individuals were already sitting and waiting for General Miller to enter the secure conference room. They were all dressed in basic uniforms or civilian attire.

Outside the room, the young soldier with a solemn and serious expression on his face stood erect behind the special stand, waiting for General Miller to approach. On the wall, the sign read:

NO MATERIALS OF ANY KIND
ALLOWED INTO THIS ROOM.
ANSWER QUESTIONS
ONLY AS DIRECTED.

As the General approached, the soldier greeted him with a sharp salute. After returning the salute, he stepped in front of the mike, unaware of any other array of hidden scanners and instruments:

"*What is your name?*" the processed voice asked.
"General Miller."
"*Are you carrying items with you?*"
"I am not."
"*What is your clearance?*"
"Top secret."

With the last answer, the guard motioned for the General to go into the conference room.

"Good morning, ladies and gentleman," he said as he took his chair at the round table. Heads of the CIA, FBI, Department of Defense, State Department, Joint Chief of Staff, and other major representatives were all anxiously waiting to learn the nature of the new conflict. The General quickly began.

"We all know that whatever you and I say at this meeting is not to be discussed or revealed to anyone else, other than to develop plans and to execute them accordingly. Thus, I need to reiterate the need for secrecy. You will quickly understand why.

"There is no bona fide source for the information other than the fact we believe a high ranking member of the terrorists in the Middle East has been found dead—not due to any drone attack, or to a specific shooting, or even to his death from poisoning. He is dead as a result, we have surmised, of a rare attack on a specific individual without any prior cancer of any type—of his vocal chords, which brought about a sudden and excruciating death. I cannot tell you the name, nor the age of this individual, not whether he was wittingly or unwittingly exposed to this new chemical attack, or whether this is limited to this specific man singly or with collective ramifications. Worse, we know nothing other than to admit only to speculations which may turn out to be unfounded...

"Coincidental to that is the following, which is based on two separate incidences—one recorded from one of our orbiting satellites; the other from a Military Intelligent unit surveying the Naples area. Both reported two brief, supposedly random radio transmissions with no further intelligence."

"Can you be more specific? Can you describe it so that we can get a better handle on this incident? Do we know the orientations of those two transmissions? Do we have an azimuth?" asked the CIA Director. "How about the timing, other circumstances? Medical reports? Chemical-Biological considerations? Can you tell us more?" he continued, a frown on his forehead.

"What else could have killed the man? Any idea on how it

was transmitted? Mosquito, microwave, radar, radio frequencies. More specifically, what equipment generated the transmissions? Can you verify the transmitter: was it HF, VHF, UHF, SCATTER, SATELLITE, or other?" asked the Army Intelligent Officer. "It would be important to know the type of equipment, to know the place of transmission and whether it is Line of sight or Omni-directional."

An expression of embarrassment on his face, the General, after clearing his throat, began to speak without hesitation. "No pun intended; my voice is raspy because I am doing too much talking," he said. A slight smile caused the others to mimic him ever so slightly.

"I don't know. But I am getting a little paranoid about everything I do, touch and say these days. The reason is simple: this guy was killed and we do not know how. We do not know why. Was he killed because of his high rank? If that's the case, where would we stand—any one of us, if there were such a thing as a line-up?"

"So," interjected another, "What do you want us to do? What do we do in the case of a vacuum—such as this?"

"Can we deploy inter-intra departmental support?"

"No," the General quickly answered. Our courses of actions cannot depend on one another's. There cannot be overlap. We need to discover and to implement appropriate courses of actions—independently one from another, and to bring them here for evaluation."

"Wait!" asked the representative from the Department of Education; "What am I doing here?"

"I don't know," responded General Miller. "I don't."

"As you are the spearhead on this matter: Have you begun to speculate on teams, and other resources?" asked the head of the CIA.

"Yes, but I cannot tell you about any of it."

"Have you become squeamish? Since when?" asked the head of the CIA.

"Well," the General said hesitatingly. "When we came into this room, we were challenged to identify ourselves through devices not privy to us. When I gave my name, I understood the need for voice prints. Now I am wondering whether, in view of the case in hand, if there can be something beyond voice prints for other applications?"

As there were no more questions of comments, the General closed the meeting. On forming a line to exit, each had to wait in line. The General was first to stop in front of the microphone—as before.

"Are you General Miller?" the voice asked.

"Yes, I am," and moved beyond the guard into the corridor full of people walking fast in both directions.

In his office, on the east side of the Pentagon, General Miller sat at his desk, thinking about what and how he was going to say at the meeting. Scanning the various framed pictures on his desk, he waited for the members of his special team to arrive.

Among them was Jody, a special agent with unusual attributes. Unless privy to her background, no one would know or guess that she was an agent capable to love a man as easily as to kill him; and, the one who knew her too well was the General himself.

As scheduled, the six agents, three males and three females, all of different body sizes, looks, and age, sat at the rectangular table, with the General sitting at its end. Because this was a special meeting, no one was allowed to have any recording or writing instruments. Furthermore, the General practically restricted any conversation, and did not allow questions.

"What I am going to say applies to all of you. Make mental notes, being sure you will fulfill your assignments regardless. It is a situation of life and death. Worse, I am not sure that you will all survive. Though it gives me pause, if I were in the field, I would abide by the same mandate." A slight frown appeared on his forehead, showing concern for those present, and a firm commitment on behalf of the imminent mission.

"Your job is to go to Italy as civilians—in connection with someone who is either living there or going there as part of a work force.

"Your challenge: to discover who, how, and why there were two radio transmissions that supposedly killed this high-ranking terrorist. We need to know if the technology used to accomplish this can be used on others and by others. We need to know who the person is—is he or she a zealot—if so, a zealot on whose behalf? Is that person whom we usually define as an idealistic do-gooder is one who otherwise causes only death and destruction.

"As military and special agents, we all know that our recent wars—from the Second War to Iraq, were all confirmed by Congress and approved by the United Nations. The do-gooders have no concern about our lives, or about our innocent civilians, or about the destruction caused by every battle, large or small.

"We need to know that person: what makes him tick. Therefore, your job is not an easy one, by any means, because it's not going to involve just military know-how and techniques. It's going to involve each one of you as if you were private individuals with baggage full of emotions, conditions, limitations, and whatever else you have or are as human beings—all different one from another. Word of caution: as men and women, we all have emotions. In this situation, you may need to depend on those emotions and, at the same time, to be sure you will not succumb to them."

Feeling he may have already spoken too much, he asked to take a five minute break before presenting the details on the task at hand.

"Before I start, you need to know that you have been assigned to a specific detail. Each leader will be in touch with you, and you will have meetings accordingly. Please do not ask any questions about anything at this time.

"Here are the facts as we know them:

"First: there were two radio transmissions, directed to the Middle East. We believe the individual responsible has discovered a means of arming the signal of radio transmissions with fatal doses of something, and to deliver it either singly or collectively on individuals of high standing, especially those in politics and military. We neither know who the individual is nor his politics, nor his zealotry. Certainly anyone who creates this kind of weapon and to use it effectively has to be a zealot. We need to know his range: simply a do-gooder who wants to save the world while watching it being destroyed, or a radical who wants to save the people by turning them into mind-numbing subjects—automatons for their own good, of course. I am afraid this individual can be one or the other.

"That being the background, you will be assigned to a particular location along the coast from the north to the south of Naples. As you may know, we have a large and complex military presence in that region. Once there, you cannot reveal your military affiliation or the reason why you are there even at the cost of your lives.

"Is that clear and understood?" he asked each, individually, as he looked into their eyes. After each nodded in silent agreement, the General continued:

"Several months ago, in a Boston suburb, a person died. The cause of death had something to do with his throat, except that no one exactly knew what. Unfortunately, we do not know any more now than that. But we need to investigate the incident from various perspectives: the most important, and potentially more dangerous, is to send one of you to Boston; the other five of you will be sent to specific military posts in Italy as undercover military intelligence personnel.

"By the way, during this deployment, you will be on TDY (temporary duty assignment) in addition to your regular pay. Knowing this gives me no joy whatsoever.

"Here are your orders," he said. On giving each the appropriate order, the General directed each to leave the office.

"Where are my orders, Sir," Jody asked in a low voice, as she stood up to walk outside the office. She was wearing her running clothes because she had planned to go to the park after the meeting. Now, she was not sure she up to her usual regimen. Nevertheless, she felt healthy, and as strong as ever; more importantly, she understood the seriousness of the task ahead. But, as usual, she trusted the General, having complete confidence in him.

"You have none, Jody. As a matter of fact, you are taking a long leave of absence. You're going to Boston, to be with your mother, because you want to spend time exploring. Later, you will want to go to Pompeii, where your mother will continue to research the ramifications on what might happen to the millions of residents living around Vesuvius when it erupts again. Vesuvius may well be one of several in the Italian fault-line.

"Are you ready to make mental notes?"

"Yes, General."

Both seated at his desk, he began on his outline:

"Some time ago, a married man who was having problems with his wife due to alcohol, died presumably because of his drinking. There was a possibility that he was killed by his wife's lover—Michael Capoverde—a respected local teacher, a would-be scientist. Rumors abounded but never supported by proof from an autopsy which concluded alcohol was the cause of death. With no explanation, he left both the woman and his job to go join his brother—Paolo— living in Amalfi. This older brother, a professor in music at a famous institution, was forced out because he was having a tryst with one of the girls...

"Following, so far?"

"Yes, General," Jody confirmed, a slight smile on her face. She knew how to be patient and responsive at the same time.

"Well, the problem for us begins in Amalfi. Paolo becomes a Deacon at the Cathedral, and Michael becomes an advisor at Pompeii. Guess who he is working with?"

"Please, please: don't tell me!"

"He is on your mother's committee—Professor Jean Villa."

Jody was shocked but not surprised. She knew there would be a connection somewhere. What more and better than that? Yet, she knew she was working big time and with big people, and acquiescing to the possibility of laying her life on the line. Although that realization made her the strong character, she always maintained another side of life—a woman full of emotion, always open for relations with the right men, provided they were not losers. In her prime, she was unabashed in opening her heart.

"What's going through your mind," the General asked.

After briefly clearing her throat, she said matter of fact: "Nothing, just nothing. It's how everything is coming together. How about Amalfi? What should I be expecting?"

"Its geography is as erratic as it is astounding to see. Probably my main concern is that the prominent mountain peak could separate from the rest of the chain. The other tall mountain peak to the east looks like a high connector to the north and a lower connector to the south. What this means is that from Mount Lattari, one can have line communication capabilities to the west beyond Capri, to the north beyond France, to the East beyond Greece, and to the south beyond Egypt."

"How about the Middle East?"

"No problem!"

"Any downside to anything? Jody asked matter-of-fact.

"Yes! The mountain practically encircles the city and its neighborhoods. Since even before the Roman Empire, the place has served my things and many adventurers. The Egyptians were there, the Muslims controlled it for a few centuries, the French were there, and the Spaniards were there, not to mention the Germans. Finally, with the unification of Italy, the new Italians re-enforced the entire coast of the peninsula, with special emphasis on Amalfi. More than any other city, its mountainsides are replete with all kinds of tunnels, even vertical ones. No one seems to know how many of them emanate or return to the Cathedral complex itself. Their sizes vary according to usage: different for storage, different for artillery units. There are also secret passages. At one time, prisoners were kept there. Today, they are mostly blocked, as best we know."

"What has this got to do with anything?" She asked, slightly bewildered.

"There are shafts to the very peak of the mountain. Except for power lines, nothing exists up there—a perfect hideout!

"I don't see the connection," she said, a worried frown on her forehead, mainly because she was not understanding: she was not connecting the dots.

"Not to worry, Jody. Hopefully, we will never have had the need to know. I think we've talked a lot. It's time to go.

We'll see you when you and your mother will go on her Fulbright Scholarship to Pompeii in a couple of months. Meanwhile, take this special cell phone. Familiarize yourself with its features, especially the secret codes. And, be sure to keep this bracelet on you all the time. In cases of emergency, just place the phone on the bracelet—just like this.

"Now, farewell to Boston."

The two walked to the door. As the General extended his hand to the door knob, Jody unexpectedly brought her mouth to his face and kissed him rather passionately

"What is this all about?" He asked incredulously. He was happily married with three children.

"Something to remember me by."

On closing the door, after Jody had left, General Miller walked to the window. On the sidewalk, Jody was already running. Soon, she disappeared altogether.

A somber look on his face, he brought his hand to his mouth. The kiss had made its impact. He moved to his desk, picked up the family photo, and looked at his wife and three children. He kissed them gently, and returned the picture to the table.

He knew that he and his family were relatively safe; he was not that sure about Jody and her colleagues.

Chapter 3
Boston

Upstairs in her bedroom, Jody was talking on her phone with a colleague, when all of a sudden she heard a huge growling commotion by the front door. Tossing the phone on the bed, she ran down the oak stairs, the noise from her hard leather shoes reverberating out of control. She slammed the screen door open. Her mother was helplessly crying on one side of the lawn. On the other side, their neighbor's German shepherd had its paws on Quixi, her mother's white Maltese puppy, barking out of control for fear of being eaten alive. A fierce scowl on its head, the big dog growled. Its sharp canines in its open mouth, they were ready to strike into the helpless puppy.

With no hesitation, Jody moved to the side of the big dog, its eyes following Jody's motion. On getting closer, she lifted her front leg and drove her pointed shoe right into the dog's scrotum, breaking its penis into two parts. Due to the excruciating pain, the big dog released the puppy which quickly ran into Jean's arms, urinating spasmodically over her dress. In agony, the German shepherd hollowed in pain, its cries reaching the owner next door.

"What's happening," he yelled on seeing his dog dragging his rear paws on the lawn.

"He's lucky he's alive," Jody retorted unflinchingly. If that happens again, you'll fare the worst!"

Professor Jean could not believe her eyes. With her Maltese close to her breast, she stretched her fingers into the air to get rid of the puppy's urine from her hands. Her face was still in shock: she couldn't believe that her young daughter was so courageous and so capable of acting without hesitation.

"You're a hero!" she finally said, above her puppy's whimpering.

"Are you OK, Mom? I got to go upstairs… I was on an important call." Then, turning to her neighbor who was carrying his hapless dog back to his house, Jody launched one last threatening harangue, causing her neighbor to move back in a squeamish submissive manner.

Having run upstairs, Jody completed her call. She waited for her mother, whose footsteps were already rebounding in the stairway. She was still holding her puppy close to her chest, making sure she was not dripping anywhere. But her expression of surprise and admiration was still on her face.

"Jody, darling, I never knew you were so courageous. What's happened to you in these last years since you left graduate school? What have you been doing? Come, come here. Help me with Quixi," she asked as she walked into the bathroom. "After we give him a bath, I will need to take a shower—myself—not just to get cleaned, but to calm down. I haven't been under so much stress ever, as best as I remember." Turning reverently toward her daughter, she continued. "I don't know how to thank you, darling. You were always my only and special one, and I haven't loved you as much as I do now."

"Thanks, Mom. I also love you very much. Go ahead and shower. I'll make our usual tea with my favorite crackers. Do you have any?"

"Of course, darling," she assured before closing the bathroom door.

With Quixi snuggled against her side, Jean wanted her daughter to know how legitimately happy she was to know that the three of them were going to spend the summer together in Pompeii. However, she was unsure about why her daughter, without much prior notice or planning, had decided to be with her.

"In the next several days, we're having meetings on up-dates on the status of the San Andreas Faults. In many ways, though dissimilar one from the other, each is similar to one another. In these conferences, I hope to learn more about Vesuvius and its location vis-à-vis one another in that particu-lar fault-line. Would you like to come? You'll be my special guest. And yes, you will be the youngest and surely the best looking of all of us."

"Mom, I have scheduled a few meetings around Bos-ton…"

"Meetings? What kind of meetings?"

"I haven't told you, yet. But, I received a request from some office within the Department of Education asking me to do an informal study—very peculiar to me—of public school teachers who suddenly and altogether leave their professions to go into other fields. Many of these teachers, supposedly, even leave without giving notice. What do you think? Oh, and by the way, I will continue to receive my regular pay, and be paid an additional stipend for this project."

"Don't know what to say. If it were someone else, I would call it a scam."

"Oh, Mom, don't say that. You know I am always on the up and up."

"Yes, dear, I'm sorry. So, where are you headed for, and whom will you be seeing?"

"First I am meeting with our Superintendent of Schools—he's still there, then with Mr. Roto, the High School Principal. Eventually, I will meet with Miss Robin in the language department—I don't know her, then with Mr. Aimon in the science department—the tall lanky guy; I believe you know him. Depending on what turns up, I may call it quits or make additional appointments. Oh, by the way: I also hope to get some dancing in Concord. I used to love that place with its live country music.

"Mom, I hope you don't my asking. You're such a good looking woman. Are you seeing anyone?"

"Oh, Jody, those days are beyond me. You are the only consolation in my life."

Jody was about to say something. For fear of being misunderstood, because she never knew who her father was, she remained silent, adding only in a whisper that she loved her mother very much. In fact, Jody had come to terms with the single reality that she was never going to know her father one way or another. The reality being what it was, she acquiesced to the truth of reality, which she accepted without remorse. Her character did not allow for wishful thinking.

"Now that we've had our tea, I think I should be going on my way."

"Yes, but we haven't established the day for you to come to my office."

"Whatever day you say, Mom; it's alright with me. I can play around with my schedule. Besides, I want to take another look at the Widener Library. I always liked it…"

"…I used to take you to the stacks. I would be working on my projects while you wandered about. You never got tired of the place. To think, you were a young girl, and so pretty!"

Mr. James Gallagher was the superintendent of schools when Jody was a student in high school. Having received a confidential telephone call, he immediately became very amenable to receive Jody, who, punctual to a T, entered his office with a confident open smile.

"Good morning, Mr. Gallagher. You must like golf: So many plaques and pictures.

"Yes. As a matter of fact, I just got off the phone with John Roto, our high school principal. He's expecting you this morning, sometime. My, what a difference," he continued as he stood up to shake her hand. "I'm a bit wobbly," he added in a self-deprecating tone, as he stood on his semi-bold legs, his trousers hanging below his crotch. "Time really makes a difference. Here I am getting decrepit; here you are getting stronger and more beautiful. What a difference since you graduated. I issued you your diploma."

"You are very kind. I assure you, you look much more handsome than you think you are. There are many, many more balls waiting to be hit by your club," she said in a loud smile.

Not knowing how to take the compliment, he sat down as he cleared his throat. "I have a daughter your age. I know what it feels like to be young, like you: But, enough about that. I got a call asking me to allow you to interview a few of our personnel. In view of the call, I immediately said yes. Can you tell me, briefly, what this is about?"

After telling him about her research on teachers unexpectedly leaving their teaching positions, Mr. Gallagher, a slight frown of incredulity on his forehead, was about to ridicule the proposal. "Sounds wonderful," he said instead. "Go see John; he'll take care of you. He's still so young and full of life..."

"He was my principal."

"That's right. That, he was."

On seeing Jody walk through the door, John did a double take. He tried to hide his expression of surprise but to no avail. Jody was too sharp for him.

"Good morning, Mr. Roto. Remember me?" She asked with controlled exuberance.

"Yes, yes," he quickly repeated as he extended his right hand to her. You weren't like this when you graduated. You remind me of Debbie. On her graduation day, all of a sudden, she looked like a woman..."

"It was not I, to be sure," Jody interrupted. Sitting in her chair, she continued: "We all grow up in one way or another and become whatever we are. You, of course, look great. Married life must be conducive to good health, happiness, and good looks."

Jody knew better. She remembered him because she had some kind of crush on him. Physically, he was good looking, full of life, and never lacking in smiles. His bluish-green eyes made him that much more charming. Had she had the chance, she might have made a move on him—but, no such thing. Besides, he was happily married, and Mrs. Roto was a friend.

"How is Mrs. Roto?" Jody asked.

"I gave her a lot of roses. In the end, the florists ran out. I'm only kidding," he said, a wide smile on his face. "We're separated. I'm hoping the florist will bring in a fresh shipment of flowers. So, Jody, what can I help you with? James...I mean, Mr. Gallagher. He told me to help you with whatever you want. How can I be of help?"

"I am exploring the possible theme for a thesis—why do so many teachers suddenly leave the profession for something else..."

"What does that mean?"

"Apparently you don't think this a serious topic."

"I didn't mean to diminish it."

"Then, what do you mean? You are certainly not giving me much encouragement..."

"No, no, Jody. Never mind. Do you have specific names?"

"I thought you might provide them. For instance: what teachers left in the past few years. If you can give me the list, I will look it over and chose a suitable name."

"This is the strangest request."

"If you can't, no problem; I have contacts with other high

school principals," Jody said, moving her hand down to the chair in order to get up and leave.

"No, no! Just because it does not make sense to me does not mean this cannot be a go. Sit down; relax. I am here to help you, regardless."

"Great! How can I access the list?" She asked. "Wait, please," she said, fumbling for her phone. "Hi, Mom, I can't talk with you, right now. I am with Mr. Roto. I'll call you later," she said and immediately hung up. "She said to say hi to you."

"That's quite a phone, you have. Is it an Apple?"

"It's one of those weird, low-cost phones that only illiterates like me could understand," she observed as she restored it into her bag… Now, where can I see the list?"

About 30 minutes later, Mrs. O'Brien, his secretary, came over with a master list of the entire staff. In looking it over, Jody made it a point of not knowing she was looking for a specific name, she being well aware that she was a simple private citizen even if possibly misguided in her endeavors.

"Whatever happened to Jack Johnson? She asked of Mrs. Obrien.

"He died many years ago," Mr. Roto intervened, a mischievous look on his face. "He was a Black heavyweight champion of the world—the first Black!" he enunciated.

"Are you showing off?"

"Yes, Miss Villa, let me answer in reference to a specific name on the list: Mr. Johnson left due to family problems. One of his sons was dying from a drug overdose and he had to leave the state. He never came back even though he was a good teacher. We don't know where he is now."

"Can I interview some of his colleagues?" she asked of Mr. Roto."

"Certainly," Mr. Roto quickly acquiesced. "Mr. O'Brien, just go ahead and make the arrangements. As a matter of fact, just go ahead and let Jody meet with whoever she wants."

"Thanks, Mr. Toto, You're very kind."

"No need for *Toto*. I am not Hispanic…" Just as he was about to ask for clarification, he decided to be the wiser, and stopped.

With Mrs. O'Brien by her personal desk, Jody asked her for a personal favor in identifying those teachers, making sure she would not let on that she already knew the name. Actually, her goal was to lead Mrs. O'Brien to suggest the name on her own.

"How about Mr. Sestito? He was a chemistry teacher."

"Give me a few more names."

Finally, Mrs. O'Brien suggested Mr. Michael Capoverde, and then Jessica Smith.

"That's it; just these two names. First Jessica: Why did she leave? And, who was she?"

"Anglo American, gorgeous woman, promiscuous, and pregnant."

"I can guess why she had to leave. How about this *Capo…*something? Who is he? He is a white man?" Jody asked with a serious frown. "Oh, by the way: I wanted to ask if you your family is from County Cork. You remind me of so many women—you know—the ones who dance and play the violin on the Public Channel."

"Oh, Jody, you're so kind. Do you have Irish blood in you?"

Jody had not anticipated the question. Slightly awkward, she hesitatingly replied: "I don't think so. May be some generations ago. I believe I am fully Italian…

"So, what's with this Capoverde? Why did he leave? Who did he work with that I may interview? ETC."

"Well, word was that he was seeing this married woman whose husband was an alcoholic. Very conveniently, it seems, the husband died—due to his drinking. Word was that Michael—Capoverde—was going to marry her. All of a sudden, he leaves, without a regular notice, and goes to live with a brother in Amalfi."

"To do what?"

"I don't know."

"Was he close to any of his colleagues?"

"It's hard to say. Although I didn't care for him personally, he was considered a bright man with interests in languages and in science. How can that be, I don't know. But, you cannot depend on me, on these matters. I am only a secretary and my information is superficial."

"But: Are there no efficiency or grading reports of some kind?"

"Yes, these reports are at the Office of the Superintendent."

"Mrs. O'Brien, this is very important. Please give me names of at least two of Mr. Capoverde's closest colleagues. Not just related to work, but socially as well."

"Socially, I cannot be of help. But, the two individuals stand out. It seems they were very close. They are still working and doing well. They are Mr. Aimon in the Science Department, and Miss Robin in the Language Department. She taught Latin."

"How about Mr. Capoverde: What did he teach?"

"He dabbled in science and languages, that's all I know."

"You've been very helpful. And, you're also very smart. Should I get through my thesis, I will be sure to mention your name."

"You don't have to do that," she answered with an ingratiating smile. I'll call both of them and tell them you'll be up to see them. Best wishes," she added and walked Jody to the door.

Outside, Jody made a quick assessment on how things went with Mrs. O'Brien. Except for the inquiry on her fatherhood—which she had already filed into the deep end of her mind, she felt satisfied with the interview. But the best-worst was yet to come. She was now ready to do some social activity with her mother, and possibly go to Concord. Learning that her mother was busy the next day, Jody decided to head for Concord around eight in the evening.

A host of young to mature people had already gathered at the famous saloon—southern style and everyone dressed accordingly: namely, jeans with matching shirts or blouses. Almost all sported long hair, especially the women. The head guitarist, with three others, backed by a drummer, maintained continuous eye contact with the dancers who shifted from one side to another in the directions suggested by the vocalist. The secret to their success lay in the fact that the combination of the music, choreography and rhythm caused a special collective bonding to the dancers all of whom were full of smiles knowing they were executing to the command of the caller. In this case, he was an older gentleman—light baritone, flexible body, himself swaying according to the flow of the music. There was hardly a couple amidst the crowd mostly of single men and women. In addition, there were always expectations on who might appear, either to the side of, or across each dancer.

Jody was already in her glory as she exhibited her deliberate moves, her breasts deliberately moving up and down rhythmically.

"Hi, there!" the voice shook her out off her trance. She looked to her right and there was John Roto. "What a surprise to see you here. You look gorgeous," he continued as he clutched her hand in passing her to another dancer. "I will see you in a few minutes."

In exactly four minutes, he appeared from her left. "I see you're enjoying it very much. Join me for a drink after this turn?"

The two separated, each in the opposite direction. Jody never said a word either to confirm or deny. As the music stopped, John sprinted toward her. "Are we on for a drink? They serve everything here,"

"Sure," Jody answered with hesitation. "I'll have a Coke."

John looked quiet debonair in his outfit; furthermore, his slim body made him a very good dancer. He was not humble in knowing he was good. Jody felt an attraction, but was unable to pinpoint it.

"I'll have a Scotch on the rocks," he ordered from bar tender. "Sure you only want a Coke?"

"Yes, thanks. Just a Coke, if you don't mind."

Drinks in hand, they moved to a corner in the crowded and noisy room. There, they sat next to a few other couples perchance there, just like them.

"You're a great dancer," John commented in sincere words.

"Thanks. I don't do much dancing these days. I am enjoying it very much, though. Thanks for the Coke."

In a few minutes, the Caller announced the next round. John took her glass and walked to the bar, not remising in telling her that he would meet her on the floor. With the rhythm of the music elevated, the two met as before. In taking her hand, John pressed it more than just gently, holding to the last moment. Jody, still, did not know what to make of John. After all, though separated, he was still married. What could come out of this? And what was there for him—a single one-night stand? Somewhat perplexed and so untypically unsure of herself, Jody decided to accept the invitation. At his suggestion, they went toward Route 128 to a popular bar at a secluded hotel. John drove his red Mustang.

"Couldn't help seeing your bracelet; it looks beautiful. Where did you get it? No, no: who gave it you—one of your boyfriends?"

"I wish it were true. No such luck. My mother sends me money at Christmas, and here is the result. I am glad you like it."

John was driving south on 128 in the middle lane. As he was approaching his exit to the right, and while passing a slower car on the inside lane, a large raccoon spurted across from the left side of the highway. Skillfully, he brought the car to his right, slamming on his breaks to avoid colliding with the car on his right, thereby saving the life of the wild animal, and a near fatal collision with the other car.

"Great con-tr-ol!" exclaimed Jody—her joyous outburst quickly ending on seeing flashing blue lights which brought John to a screeching halt. Simultaneously, the driver of the car in front also stopped.

"License and registration," demanded the officer.

"Officer, please!" interrupted Jody.

"I am not talking to you; you're not the driver," the Officer said, commandingly.

John handed over the documents. At the same time, the driver of the other car accosted the officer.

"Officer, I saw the whole thing. Let me explain…"

"No need to explain nothing. Go back to your car and leave, unless you want to be ticked for interference."

At that, Jody insisted: "Officer, please give me your badge number."

"Who do you think you are? One more word out of you

and you'll end up in jail, for obstruction."

"We'll see about that…"

"What did you say, bitch?"

"Nothing…" she said in a low voice, looking into the bewildered face of John; he was frustrated in seeing things get out of control so fast. Without letting John notice, she brought her cell phone and hooked to a special knot on her bracelet. In a moment or two, she resumed her normal stance. "I'll see him in hell," she muttered to herself.

Typical of the traffic stops, it always took a few minutes for the officer to trace the license and registration, to be sure that all the information was legitimate. Finally, after a time that seemed like an eternity to John, he waited with his hand holding his wrinkled forehead, and in complete silence. Finally, he saw the officer approach.

"Here are your documents. You may go. Case closed."

On hearing those words, Jody was about to shout to the officer to go fuck himself; instead, she kept her cool. Instead she looked at John to assure all was well.

On leaving, the officer raised his hand in a salute to Jody, and walked to his cruiser, his tail between his legs.

After gaining control, John drove to the exit. At its end, instead of going to the bar, he made a U-turn back onto 128. In a few minutes he was back at the dance hall.

"I am sorry things didn't work out," he said. "Maybe another time: You're something else. I wouldn't know what to do with you. I saw a florist up the street. My bet is to go and see if he has some fresh roses... Good night, Jody. I will keep you in my heart."

As she walked to her car, Jody felt disappointed, not in her behavior, but in bad luck with men. "Someday, I will meet the right man!"

In the morning, her mother, with Quixi on her lap, and breakfast on the stove, she waited for her daughter. Finally, she appeared at the door, stroking her hair with a brush.

"Good morning, sunshine. We've been waiting for you. How was your evening?"

It was not the question she was expecting, especially because of Mrs. Obrien's query. The thought of having no father made her uncomfortable. She wanted to talk to her mother about it, but decided to postpone it. Instead, she mentioned the name of John.

"You mean, Mr. John Roto? John *the rotor rooter*—you mean, Mr. Roto, the principal? What do you have in common with him?" the mother asked, puzzled by the revelation, but glad she did not pronounce her thoughts aloud.

"Sure, by pure coincidence, we met on the dance floor in Concord last night. He was very nice. And I think I may have made him nervous…"

"Nervous, over what?" she asked with a terse *what*.

"No, mother, nothing happened between us. We went to this place for a drink but never got there. We were on 128 when this cruiser stopped him for speeding—which he was not. Actually, John did an incredible job is saving the life of a wild raccoon and possibly the lives of those in the adjacent car, not the least our very own. Well, that asshole, pardon my French, wouldn't hear of it. Besides, he was rude. I intervened on behalf of John, and the officer finally gave him a warning."

"And, that's it!"

"Except that instead of going to the bar, John decided he had had enough and opted to take me back to Concord. His plan was to buy a dozen roses for his estranged wife. He simply dropped me off and took off in his red Mustang."

In semi-silence, interrupted only by Quixi's squeaks, the two women ate their breakfast, each waiting for an opening for a new topic of conversation. Finally, the mother spoke. "Were we to do an activity together?"

"Not to your office, today!"

"No, we'll have to do that another time. No, we talked about Concord, you know, the Minute Men Park. We said we might like to go there. It is still a significant place of historical importance. I still like early American history."

"Yes, I would like to go: How about this afternoon?"

"Sure, for you going to Concord on two consecutive days..."

"...And for two different reasons. Oh, well."

Off of Route 2 there lies the Minute Men National Historical Park. On a splendid sunny day, the two women—her somewhat disobedient Quixi in tow, began their tour—on their own. It was the chance for the mother to talk a little about the significance of what happened on April 15, 1775. In her confirmed opinion, this was the date in which the new nation was conceived. The shot heard around the world was not necessarily a shot from a musket, but shots fired by about 400 outnumbered Minute Men—all volunteers sporting their private weapons—any male ages 16 to 60, standing firm to accomplish two things: defend their families and homes, and, defeat an enemy bent on negating freedom and independence, using not only their personal defensive weapons, but assault weapons as well.

They leisurely walked by the Bridge, then went to the Obelisk, then walked along the Battle Road trail. They spent some time admiring Chester's Minute Men Statue by Daniel Chester French. Adjacent was the Memorial Obelisk. "Reminds me of Egypt and Rome," the mother commented with a sigh." Julie obviously wished she were in Italy. Finally they stopped at the Hartwell Tavern.

"I wouldn't mind having a beer," Jody quipped.

Finally, they were awed by the Muster. The men in the original uniforms with flares, and those on instruments with their tunes just added to their satisfaction. To a point, they were happy.

"Is there a single lesson you learned, Jody?"

"If it were not for the Minute Men, each one ready to sacrifice his life on behalf of his fellow Americans, there would not be an American nation today, let alone American people. To think, we represent all the races in the world. Once citizens, we receive every right earned by the Minute Men. As I think about it, I find it hard to believe this happened. It was a man-made miracle the likes of no other. They are the one who created the Revolution that impacted the world. Think about it: up to that time in global history, but specifically for the West, in every nation the people existed for the governments—mainly monarchies. Then suddenly, these guys in Concord and Lexington started saying that governments have to exist for the people and not vice-versa. They went against every vein of popular history of their times, including historiographers who hadn't even understood the principle behind our Revolution…I better stop. I'm getting wound up."

"No, go on, mother; you're making a lot of sense."

"The thing that ticks me off more than anything is the Second Amendment. Our Founding Fathers understood all too well what happens to certain individuals once they gain power. They try to increase their power by decreasing that of the people. We've seen it times and times again. Our natural right first: as people we have to have the right to bear and carry arms. How better to control would be tyrants! Our Fathers understood it; our modern politicians are discarding it—at our expense…"

Her mother's pride was no longer a secret, she added:

"Think of all those Americans who are still in Canada…"

"…And, how about those who are joining the terrorists: How do we allow ourselves to be so brainwashed?"

For lunch at the local restaurant, Jody took advantage of Chef's Special. She ordered a small serving of Neapolitan *cozze*.

"How did you like the clams?" the mother asked.

"They could not have been better. But they were good," Jody added. "I gave one to Quixi. He ate it."

Satisfied with their meal, the three got in the car and headed home, delighted with the whole outing.

"We have to do it again," the mother suggested. "Do you like rabbit stew?"

"Yes, we will," answered Jody, a slight sign of disgust on the reference to rabbit. A slight shadow appeared on her forehead.

"What is the matter, darling?" the mother asked.

"Nothing, mother—really, nothing."

"Come on, Jody. I wasn't born yesterday."

"You know Mrs. O'Brien, the school's secretary? She asked me whether I had any Irish in me. Though I felt uncomfortable, I said that may be, a long time ago, I may have had."

"Jody, I wish I could tell you about your father. The fact is that I don't know. When young we make all kinds of mistakes. We do foolish things. I was very lucky to overcome them and become a decent human being. We can consider ourselves lucky. I am so grateful to have you, you cannot imagine. And you are as strong and beautiful as you are wise. One thing I can assure you: I could not tell you a fib because I really do not know, and there is no need for me to provide details that are embarrassing to me."

"You do not have to, Mom. I love you so very much."

With that positive statement, the two women reached

home. By the front door, they stopped to unleash Quixi and he quickly began to squirt around the green lawn.

"Any more problems from our neighbor?"

"Not since you fixed it; you know what I mean," the mother added—a great laugh on her exuberant face.

Miss Robin met Jody in the housemaster's office. On learning why Jody wanted to talk with her about Michael, she decided to take Jody to her desk, on the stage of the theater. There was her desk and those of the other language teachers.

"I don't know why you've come to talk with me about Michael," Miss Robin said defensively. Besides, he's been gone a long time."

"I know you've been given the reasons why I am here with you. I cannot tell them to you. You have to trust in me. I am here for an important cause; but I cannot tell you anymore. I do not have to interview; I have others. But I believe you may have answers that could be very important. Would you bear with me for a few minutes?"

A bit reassured, Miss Robin, a rather tall, imposing woman of a certain stature, her head slightly bowed, agreed to proceed.

"On one important condition," Jody insisted.

"What is that?"

"That what we say remains confidential: Agreed!"

"Agreed."

"Why did Michael leave without saying anything to anyone, including you? You were close colleagues, sharing professional information on so many things, including linguistics…"

"Linguistics: This is not about his relation with that woman… You know: the one whom he was madly in love with?"

"If you don't mind, I would like to deal with linguistics first. Did he talk with you about the alphabet system and his theory on how to create a system of organizing alphabet sounds into a system having a strict one-to-one relationship between letters and corresponding sounds? A phonemic system—not phonetic: something like that."

"Yes, he was fascinated by the Latin alphabet. He always asked why the Romans developed such a system for writing when none else did, including the Greeks. That's right: he wanted to streamline the alphabet for the computer age, to create a code to facilitate cross linguistic and cultural differences in this age of instantaneous global communications. He talked about a system that prescribed the following, as an example: the letter *a* in the English language can be pronounced as many as 16 or so difference ways when appearing in words. Depending on the previous letter to it or the letter following it, the letter *a,* at times, is not even pronounced. Well, he was looking to create a system that would allow for the letter *a*—used in whatever language, to have only one sound represented by one letter. Likewise, if it were a consonant, each to have a distinguishable sound—unlike the *c* which is pronounced both hard as a *k*, and soft as a *c*. Am I making sense? Rather, is he making sense?"

"Are you making these connections because you know Latin?"

"Those who teach or know Italian make the same connections. That is why, in Italy, learning to read is not a problem while it is a challenge in England and in America. Do you understand me?"

"I am just enjoying your explanation. I wish I had been your student."

"Why weren't you?

"I took French," she admitted, causing both to laugh.

All of a sudden, the two women had gained the confidence of one another. Each felt there was an understanding of what they were saying; more importantly, each felt that the subject at hand was enhancing their own grasp of this new field. Although Jody wanted to continue talking about linguistics, she wanted to be sure not to get carried away with that esoteric discussion. She had to ask about the basic character of Michael, especially his relations to the woman whose husband had died so un-expectedly. However, she needed to broach the real question behind it all: could any extraneous intelligence be piggy-back to that potential system?

In other words, could this be like harnessing a rocket to deliver chemical warheads?

"Woe, you are now out of my range. If you wish, we can talk about Michael, the man."

"You're right. I am over my head in simplistic speculations."

After a short pause, to clear up their slight artificial smile, both felt awkward on how to and where to begin. Jody suggested describing Michael as a teacher, as though she were his supervisor rating his professional performance.

"First, he was always neatly dressed, healthy looking, with a rather optimistic attitude. He was hardly sulky; rather, he smiled frequently. He was fun to work with and to be with. He was never abusive in any way. I liked him for his politeness..."

"He sounds perfect..."

"...No, no: Don't get me wrong. Morally, he made many errors such as to have curtailed if not diminished his intellectual potentials. He fell in love with this woman. She was the wrong one on two accounts: she was married, and, she was a whore. Her husband was a wretched alcoholic. Word was that too many times he didn't make it to the bathroom; he ended up in the closet. He was also a curser and always in and between jobs. Luckily for Michael, I thought at the time, unexpectedly, the man died—of natural causes.

"I recall, thereafter, Michael had a sudden conversion, a type of apparition wherein things suddenly cleared up—as though he had had a vision—because, he changed. He became somewhat of an introvert. Not that he stopped talking, but he was pensive… something heavy on his mind, as though he was shouldering a heavy burden but did not know the source of that burden or pain.

"What a shame. He was a real nice man, intelligent, prac-tical—full of talent. He was good with tools, and told me about his handling stone as though he inherited the art of a stone cutter. He was also a carpenter in many ways. Unfortunately, he fell in love with the wrong woman. Can that really be love? He was the product of an arranged marriage. Can that really be love? I would go for the latter."

"You seem to know a lot about him."

"These are our desks—next to each other. We spent a lot of time together, here behind these curtains. The language lab is right there across the hall. He always liked to fidget with the various controls. Of course, I never understood the first thing about electronic matters," she added, pushing her hands outwards to put a distance between her and the lab.

"Didn't you two ever socialize?"

"No! Besides, I am married. I have children. I hope to be-come a grandmother."

"Is there anything special or peculiar, anything you re-member him for?"

"Yes, very much: It is a secret; but I will tell you. One morning, we were talking about tests and testing—he hated standardized tests. He wasn't loud or anything like that. At a point I put my head down to pause. Suddenly, he brought his face to mine and he kissed me ever so gently. "Why did you do that?" I asked—the sweetness of his kiss still on my lips.

"You are so beautiful; I could not resist", he answered in a low voice. After apologizing, he left to go teach his class.

"So, you remember his kiss," Jody reiterated, but silently begrudging not having had a similar moment in her life. "I have to go now; Mr. Aimon must be waiting for me in the Science Department. Many thanks for your time. You're very nice. I wish I had taken Latin."

"Don't forget, he is Dr. Aimon."

Jody had not known Dr. Aimon; she had already graduated when he was hired as the Director of the Science Department. Tall, rather thin, full crop of hair down to his ears, he exuded confidence in his colleagues and in his students. Having earned an Ivy League Ph.D. added to his aura as a prominent teacher and scientist. Furthermore, he made no bones talking about the various scientific researches he had conducted on his own.

"Good morning, Miss Villa…or shall I call you Jody? James—I mean Mr. Gallagher directed me to answer all of your questions. He tells me you are gathering information on the backgrounds of teachers who, without so much as giving advance notification on leaving their positions, the simply take off and never seen again. Personally, I don't give a damn. No need for me to know why one does one thing or another, or why one does not do the one thing or another. Do you know what I mean, Jody… By the way, I like to have seen you when you were a senior. You are very attractive…"

"Thank you, Dr. Aimon. I can see why you are so esteemed by your colleagues," she answered, leaving a modicum of sarcasm not picked up by the Doctor. He was taken up more to find Jody so poised and mature-looking.

"So, what can I help you with?"

"I understand that you knew a couple of recent teachers who left the school practically without giving notice, disappearing altogether from society and without any trace of them. I find these situations very strange."

"Once you gather the information, what will you do with it?"

Careful not to lose control of the interview (the Doctor was asking the questions rather than allowing her to ask the questions and for him to give the answers).

"I've been given a couple of names of teachers who simply quit. One was Michael Capoverde. He was not a scientist. But, apparently, you and he were friends. So, if your relationship was not based on science, was it social?"

"Social, social?" he repeated, a smirk on his face. "Michael liked women! Ours was strictly a relation based on scientific topics. For a guy having linguistic background, he surely knew how to draw and to establish scientific methods to his work. Michael was much smarter than he appeared. He…"

"Can you be specific on the scientific discussions you had?"

"Speculations on phonemes…"

"What's that?" she asked as if she had never heard the word before. "I know about phonetics. I always look at the words in parenthesis to learn how to pronounce them. You know, typical Webster…"

"Because of Michael, I learned about phonetics, graphemes, phonemes, allophones, etc., etc. He was on to something, but no one understood, except for me. The fact is that I was curious; I understood very little of what he was talking about."

"What were his speculations—practical applications, I mean—about his conclusions?"

"He had none. He was too smart to think he could come

up with any system that has not been discovered or invented by someone else. Actually, in many respects, he was very humble—unlike *moi*, for example."

"Oh, you speak French?"

"*Pas de rien*," he answered, smiling in self absorption. "Well, do you have anything else to ask me about?"

"All this stuff about phonemes, etc., of which I know nothing: did he ever talk on harnessing this information to another system—such as piggy-back one discipline onto another. What I am trying to understand is this: was he trying to discover a means of getting one's voice print and be able to manipulate its DNA as to affect it—either to enhance it or control it to the point of destroying some given human being?"

"Woe? Stop! What the hell are you talking about?" he challenged, raising his voice. "There were never any such discussions. There were never any hidden agendas or intentions. You are off your rocket, Jody!" His slight vehemence more than apparent, Jody decided to retrench.

"Didn't mean any disrespect or insinuations; I had heard about that, but nothing concrete. In any event: Why did he leave so suddenly?"

"I have wondered about that so many times. I know about his misbegotten relationship with that woman…"

"Excuse the interruption. Does anyone know her whereabouts?"

"I don't know. I heard that she may have gone to Capri after the insurance settlement—she got a lot of money; but I don't know. As a matter of fact, I don't want to know. She practically destroyed that man, and he, he was too stupid to understand. Love is one thing and I can admire it; stupidity is another, and we can legitimately and seriously criticize it as not acceptable—just to reject it."

Such candid and true observations made an impact on Jody, less so in her role as an investigator, but more so as to her persona. There were moral considerations, behavior that impacts on a positive or negative future. She felt good about her behavioral tendencies.

"As I look back, I am glad I listened to my mother, and to so many other people—like you, for instance."

"That's very kind of you, Jody. But I don't know what else to add. I miss Michael very much, and I wish him well. Should you ever, for whatever reason, be in touch with him, give him my best. Tell him I located an antique limited edition 1963 Buick Riviera in blue. I am enjoying it very much."

As she began asking her last question, she instinctively knew she should not. Nevertheless, she did ask the question to her great regret: how many children did he have? Here she was, a professional steeped in transactions and negotiations, and asking a question for which she did not know the answer.

"I don't have any," he said dryly. "You, on the other hand, are wasting your time and your beauty. You should be having children—many of them. I wish you had known a person like Michael. He would have done well by you. He would have turned you into a great woman. "Best wishes. I have to go; I have a class coming up."

Disarmed, Jody brought her eyes down. It was not the interview she had expected. The outcome was anti-climactic, with a lot of private issues bandied about without resolve. Feeling disappointed in her performance, she headed home to be with her mother, with hope of getting some authentic tender loving care. For, in the morning, she would be going to Harvard to spend time with her mother in the Archaeology Department.

Having parked the car in the garage near the Divinity School, mother and daughter made their way past the Anthropology

Department; then finally, to her office.

On the wall on the front of the conference room there hung a large world map with charts on the various known volcanic defaults on the earth. The one that extended from the Middle East into Sicily, up towards Naples, into France and then westward toward the Atlantic Ocean bore special markings.

"We're going to be discussing both the potential re-eruption of Vesuvius, the impact it might have on the people and countryside of Pompeii, and other repercussion on the fault line especially to the north, there, around Monaco. The picture that is emerging is very disturbing."

"Besides you, who else is involved? It cannot just be Harvard!"

"No, dear: There are about six of us going—you're the seventh except that you don't count. You're only my daughter piggybacking on a freebee," she said happily laughing.

The problem with Jody was to see how she could inject herself in the project and be seen as a credible researcher on causes that made teachers leave their jobs. Certainly, being in Italy, there was no way she could continue that story. Her rational had to be that she was taking advantage of her mother's Fulbright grant, wherein she was getting free vacation time.

"Do you actually have a list of your fellow researchers? Who's going to be there with you offering expertise on whatever...?"

"You're already focusing on the details. You should have been a scientist."

"Yes, Mom: I should also have been a great author like Thomas Mann, a great artist like Leonardo, a great poet like Dante, a great dramatist like Shakespeare, right!"

"Of course, Mom: Meanwhile, I will struggle with my

present, boring, and useless thesis."

"Don't say that. Everything has value."

"Mom, can we go to the Weidner Library? Remember when you would take me with you. You did your thing at your booth, and I wondered about all those rows of books and boxes. I don't remember ever seeing so many names I had never heard of—from all over the world. You used to tell me that the library was the depository of Western Civilization, and to a certain point, World Civilization."

"I always love the fact that you were never so present in asking questions about everything, and making appropriate commentary as well. You were such an angel."

The Library, with its imposing Roman columns, dominated the Harvard Yard. Coming from her office, mother and daughter passed by the Fogg Museum, then into the Yard, walking by Emerson Hall, and, immediately in front of the Library. Jody's heart pumped a little. She hadn't seen it in many years.

"I get goose pimples," she admitted, realizing she was too mature for such emotions. "Let's get some lunch," she suggested, and began to walk around the Library, and crossing Massachusetts Avenue. After consuming a couple of hamburgers, the two made their way back to the office.

"Let's look at some demographics around Pompeii: This part in deep red represents the higher population density. These parts—in lighter red—represent lower densities. That doesn't matter as much if we look and consider the landscape. Because, all lava will flow through this area toward the sea, everything in its way will be destroyed. I would predict, conservatively, that lava will kill a couple million people."

"Wow, Mom, that's awful. That's much more than any similar 'Yes and no, dear'. An explosive from Vesuvius may be contained or localized by the volcano itself—just look at

Pompeii and Herculaneum. The people killed would be the same except that now there are that many more inhabitants. With a man-made vector as a missile, no one can predict what could happen in any direction of the fault line. We could have more than an Armageddon on our hands!"

"Mom, what are you saying?"

"Yes, my dear. I know. Don't be agitated. These are only would-be scenarios; like so many studies, they never materialized during World War II itself and thereafter."

"Do you guys have any predictions? The Muslims, in large numbers, are on the march everywhere in this world, as refugees and-or as terrorists. Do you guys discuss these potentials?"

"We don't deal much with current political events. We're academics."

At that, Jody was able to control herself. She knew, in her heart, that her mother was more than aware of the world situation: that efforts were being made to establish a New World Order replacing the present—now considered Old. In her debriefings, the scenario had un-mistakenly described what was actually happening. The media reported it everywhere. Despite the acridity of those reports, both the people and their government representatives continued unaffected.

Jody seemed confused over the massive coverage on world affairs. Nevertheless, she clung to her principle that there was a right and a wrong across the board, that the only equalizer was the dagger to the throat of another human being. In that respect, the equalizer has remained constant in every culture and civilization.

"By the way, Jody, if you wish to see more literature on volcanoes, I have several volumes in my office at home."

"Thanks, Mom: I'll take a look. It should be interesting."

Noticing the half-hearted response, she pressed her

daughter. "Did I say or do something to offend you?"

"No, Mom, there isn't any."

Now, she was convinced there was something wrong—that it had to have something to do with Jody's personal life. For the last few days that they had been together, Jody had never talked about any romantic relationship. A woman, as good-looking and vivacious as her daughter, couldn't be without a significant half; it was not realistic.

Unbeknown to either, mother and daughter, each seemed stuck on parallel lines that could not meet. Yet, the relationship between mother and daughter defied logic, because they were engaged in two separate worlds that were not intersecting. Jody was aware of the chasm; yet, she had no choice but to stay the course. Her mother, on the other hand, did not completely understand what was driving her daughter, except that there was more than met the eye.

For example, everywhere she went, in the Yard or in the Square, people of all ages, especially those of her daughter's age—they were always on their cell phones. Not Jody! Worse, Jody was never without her phone. It didn't make sense, but she was not about to inquire, one way or another.

Having prepared supper, with Quixi on her lap, Jody thanked her mother for another great meal. It seemed that the two women were at peace with one another at supper time—sort of idyllic moments. The reality of making preparation for their imminent trip to Italy, however, was uppermost in their mind.

"I wonder how Quixi is going to take it—first time in a foreign country. Maybe we should talk Italian," the mother said, as she stroked Quixi's face."

"*Ciao*, Quixi, *come stai*—how are you?" Jody said with laughter.

"Oh, Jody, you're so funny. I am taking two bags. How

about you? We're allowed three bags each."

"What, we have three days before we go to Washington," Jody said. "I will be ready. By the way, I meant to ask you: Do you have a list of colleagues that will join you? As important, do you have the list of your Italian committee counterparts?"

"Jody, I think the lists will be coming tomorrow or the day after."

"Can I look at them when you get them?"

"Certainly, darling: If the lists do not come here, they will be given to me in Washington."

Chapter 4
Washington D.C.

Candidates from all over the United States met in the auditorium of the main Convention Center in D.C. Those admitted to the Orientation were those appearing on the master list; the awardees were Fulbright, Rhodes, Marshall, or Truman recipients, and covered various fields of studies. It seemed the planners had gone out of their ways to assign not more than three individuals to each category. A cursory glance also showed that there was no specific grouping either by age, sex, or race. Professor Villa, however, was probably the oldest and stood out for her Ivy League credentials. In fact, she was very well known as shown by the number of scholars stopping by to give her their warm greetings. Typically, she returned the greetings always with open smiles.

"Thanks, Mom," Jody said to her mother before being admitted to the auditorium. "I'll see you later at the banquet. I will dress appropriately."

A long line of cabs, their engine running, was waiting for Jody across the main entrance of the Center. As she made her way to the sidewalk, a cab from across the street pulled up, picked her up and quickly disappeared. In less than half hour, she was standing at the door of Brigadier General (BG) Miller. On entering, Sergeant First Class (SFC) Brodeur stood up to welcome her. On showing her ID card, the Sergeant quickly obliged her to hand over her phone and bracelet, that he would give the two items back to her at the end of her meeting.

"Welcome back," the General said as he approached. He extended his arms, giving her a very appropriate gentle hug. "How was your trip?"

"Really great: We have a lot to talk about."

The General placed his hand to her side and directed her

towards the entrance of the conference room. He walked first.

"*What is your name?*" the processed voice asked.

"General Miller."

"*Are you carrying items with you?*"

"I am not."

"*What is your clearance?*"

"Top secret."

Jody stepped up.

"*What is your name?*" the processed voice asked.

"Jody Villa."

"*Are you carrying items with you?*"

"I am not."

"*What is your clearance?*"

"Top secret."

At the end of the short entryway, they entered the door to the right. Inside, there were ten chairs--*Chiavari* so called as they were similar to those in the White House Dining Room-- known for simplicity in style, sturdiness, and light weight—not easy to hide anything in them. Nothing else was in the room, except bare walls. The General placed two chairs side by side, sitting down after Jody was seated comfortably.

"The most important news is that Michael Capoverde is on the list as the Coordinator of the Radio Alert Network for the Pompeii Region…"

"…What does that mean?"

"The little I was able to garner from my mother, Michal is the inventor of an instrument which, when installed at specific locations, if there is any vibration in the earth's crust of any kind, the signal is picked up at headquarters and its charts immediately reveal both the coordinates and the type of volcanic action."

"That sounds great, especially if there were to be an earth-quake. I can imagine if this really works, it might help save an untold number of lives. However, this is not our preoccupation. We have to find out what and how else he is using this communication expertise. Certainly, we have more proof that he has more than just passing knowledge in this field. You know how to go about uncovering the secrets. Do you have any questions about this part? I note, with pride, on how well disciplined you are in using your phone. I gather things worked out well on Route 128…"

"Yes, thanks. It feels good to know that I have back up— even in a foreign country, I gather."

"Of course, Jody, you do! What else of interest?"

"Lots of weird stuff, almost all disconnected but needing consideration. For instance, this woman by the name of Connie: Though married, she was having a serious affair with Michael. Word has it that her husband felt something was going on. In one of his jealous tirades against her, he threatened to kill her. Speculations surfaced that he tried to do that through phony car accidents. Connie asked Michael for help, but he refused. Then, all of a sudden, the man ends up dead. The coroner said from alcoholism, and he was quickly buried. She made some money from his insurance, after which, she took off. She went back with the hope of patching things up with Michael, but that did not happen because he had taken off to Italy.

"I did go visit the grave site—not far from where my mother's house. And I found it in its original condition, both unattended and in disarray. No flowers, no nothing."

"In view of Michael's expertise on linguistics and physiological radiation—where's the connection?"

"I wish I knew. Nothing so far: Sorry. I'll keep a close eye. One more thing: Michael had a brother—also not married. He was Professor of Voice at the Conservatory—highly respected in his field. A serious man, in his younger days, he had considered the priesthood. Opera got the better of him. To make a long story short, he was fired, upon which he left."

"Why was he fired?"

"He was having an affair with one of his students. That's all I know. "

"Very well: We have to go now. I think Mrs. Miller—Maryann—my wife may be outside. We're going to lunch…"

Both got up. Having placed the chairs in their original positions, he walked to the door on the left. Outside, both stopped as before—a cloth on the wall above the microphone.

"Are you General Miller?"

"Yes, I am."

"What time is it?"

"Eleven forty five."

"Are you Jody Villa?"

"Yes, I am."

"What time is it?"

"Eleven forty six."

On approaching the desk, the General asked SFC Brodeur if there were any messages. "Yes, General, Mrs. Miller is in our office, Sir."

"Come in, Jody. I want you to meet her."

In the office, General Miller immediately approached his wife, giving her a very large hug. He then presented Jody. "Maryann, this is Jody. We've been having a conference on some very important matters."

"I am very happy to meet, you, Mrs. Miller. Your husband is very proud of you, and I can see why," Jody complimented her in extending her hand.

"Thank you, Jody. What kind of work are you doing?" Mrs. Miller asked in earnest. She had never met any of her husband's colleagues.

"As strange as it may seem, I am doing research on personnel who quit lucrative jobs without as much as giving notice. However, I am joining my mother in Europe for several weeks, mainly for vacation—at her expense," she commented, a big smile on her face acknowledging the fib.

"Yes, yes: I think I understand," Mrs. Miller said. "Would you like to join us for lunch?"

"I cannot. I have to make an appearance at my mother's." She extended her hand to Mrs. Miller and left, not without a warm glance to the General.

"What a shame, she not married," commented Mrs. Miller to her husband."

"Not everyone can be lucky like me," he answered as he glanced at the family picture of himself in civilian clothes, his wife, two sons and one daughter.

Jody stopped at the desk. SFC Brodeur quickly got up and went to the file cabinets; on dialing the code, the drawer opened. He picked up the bracelet and phone and handed them to Jody. Assuring her that the equipment had been calibrated, he gently handed the pieces over.

"Have a great day," he said with a smile.

"Thank you," she answered with a smile of humility.

In the cab, bringing her arms around her body, Jody felt somewhat envious of Mrs. Miller, and not too happy about herself. Her brain began to stir: In her quest for job security and advancements, she had gained an advantage over what— not having a family of her own? Yet, unlike her mother, who had acted irresponsibly but at least had a child, Jody truly felt that in the long run, she was going to have neither love, nor children, nor a satisfying professional career. Furthermore, the stakes had gotten un-ambiguously high, and inherently fraught with danger.

Out of the cab and into the hotel suite, on not seeing her mother there, she went into the bathroom and took a long hot shower. She was still in the shower when her mother returned.

"I am home, darling," she yelled into the bathroom.

"I'm almost done," Jody answered.

In her robe, Jody looked rather ravishing. "I used to look like that," the mother bragged on her daughter's behalf. Jody got close. In giving her a hug, all of her negative thoughts went away.

"Jody, darling, we have 45 minutes before our group will meet for dinner downstairs. What would you like to do?"

Caught off guard as that was the last thing she was thinking about. "Yes, yes. I guess we could get acquainted with your colleagues."

"How so, Jody?"

"You have the list. Let's see what they're all about."

With Quixi to her side, Jody spread the pages on the kitchen table. After a brief, inquisitive glance, she said: "Woe, Mom, they're all over the place, and in every direction. But, I already looked at this list. Most will be going to other institutions all over Italy. I'd like to look at the list of your colleagues that will be working with you. Do you have such a list? Or, will you get it when you get there?"

"No, darling, I have it. Here it is."

Jody couldn't believe her eyes. The biographical information on each individual was incredible. But, of course, the name of Michael Capoverde was there in alphabetical order, and had no problem hiding from her mother the specific reasons for her inquiry. Instead, she skimmed over the names, asking her mother to comment with the hope of gaining information which she would not get from a direct inquiry. More important, she could not raise suspicion of any kind. Her task, now more evident, was to feign disinterest.

"Do you know any of these personally?" Jody asked.

"I know some of them in passing. Information back and

forth you know. I am looking forward to meet them all once we're in Pompeii."

"Does anyone stand out to you for any particular reason?"

"They all have intriguing backgrounds. I have to wait to meet them. Then, when we start our interactions, I will be able to make assessments of one kind or another. Looking at biographical information that's made public can only give indications but nothing more."

Jody was not surprised at her mother's expressed sincerity. "Well, I'm curious. Do you mind my looking at it over the next few minutes?"

"Not at all, honey."

Her attention fell mainly on two entries: Michael Capoverde and Captain Domenico Fracastoro. Purposefully avoiding mentioning Michael, Jody commented on the Captain's name, in passing.

"Did you see the Captain's last name, Mom?"

"Yes, I have. What about it?

"Fra cas to ro…"

"Technically, *Fra ca sto ro*. Were you checking the syllabification?"

"I guess so, Mom. Thanks."

Jody was impressed by the man's background. He was the Captain of the port of Naples, one of the larger ports in Italy, probably the largest port for immigrants—always full of ocean liners and expensive yachts. More Italians left their country from Naples never to return than any other European port, especially those headed for Ellis Island in New York. As Jody perused his background, she discovered something she was not aware of: the Captain was a graduate of the Naval Academy with strong roots to La Spezia, the birthplace of the underwater guerrilla warfare that had seen the destruction of the Austrian Fleet of World War I. He had also compiled the history of naval action during World War II. At this point, Jody made the connection between the Italian Frogmen and the US Navy Seals. Also unusual were degrees in Social Science. The single, more startling biographical information, however, was the fact that he was not married.

"Mom, did you know that the Captain is not married?"

"I think I read it: So what?"

"It seems peculiar. He is the chairman of the committee."

Soliciting no further comments from her mother, Jody continued looking at the list—at Michael Capoverde. He was an American, also not married, lived in Amalfi, had been a teacher of languages, had background in radio communication systems, had received two patents relating to instruments designed to predict earthquakes...

"Jody, are you about ready to go? She asked from her bedroom. Please bring Quixi to his quarters."

Matching each other up as two teenage girls do standing tall in sizing themselves up, the two laughed as they left their suite for the cab outside.

At the Center, a guide in full uniform escorted the two women to the banquet dining room—almost full with the special guests. The PA technician was doing his final check on the efficiency of the system. Jody was already on her way to co-mingle with her mother's colleagues, especially those of her age; her mother did the same thing, drawn to those having the same background as well.

The menu was all Italian:

> *Aperitivo*: *Campari*
> *Antipasto: Bocconcini*
> *Vino: Aglianico, Pinot grigio*
> *Primo piatto: Fettuccine Alfredo*

Carne: Bistecca fiorentina
Pesce: Salmone a la Adolfo
Insalata: Verdura locale
Dolce: Tiramisù
Brindisi: Prosecco trevisano

After about 30 minutes wherein the guests were feasted with drinks and Antipasto of various origins from the Italian peninsula, the representative of Fulbright representative called the group to order. Having achieved silence from the guests, Mr. Derek Hamilton opened with the first lines of St. Francis' poem:

> *Lord, make me an instrument of your peace,*
> *Where there is hatred, let me sow love;*
> *where there is injury, pardon;*
> *where there is doubt, faith;*
> *where there is despair, hope;*
> *where there is darkness, light;*
> *where there is sadness, joy;*
>
> *O Divine Master, grant that I may*
> *not so much seek to be consoled*
> *as to console;*
> *to be understood*
> *as to understand;*
> *to be loved*
> *as to love.*
> *For it is in giving that we receive;*
> *It is in pardoning that we are pardoned;*
> *And, it is in dying that we are born to eternal life.*

Having read the verses to a very receptive gathering, Mr.

Hamilton brought his glass of *prosecco* foreword onto the guests, and wished them all a wonderful dinner, reminding them, however, that he would end the evening festivities with a few additional remarks.

"Mom, that was fantastic. I had no idea that St Francis was a poet."

"He wasn't. He was true to his word, however. We can see it in his, *Cantico delle Creature*. You should read it. It appears as the leading poem, in the original dialect of his day, in every anthology of Italian poetry."

The meal was extraordinary, and everyone agreed. Encomiums to the *chef de cuisine* were heard at each table. Perhaps the most popular was the *tiramisù*. Few knew about it, thus the surprise. As it was served with *prosecco*, it brought additional smiles of approval. Jody was extremely happy, thus bringing more smiles to her mother's face.

At the podium, Mr. Hamilton brought the attendees to order. With the last chatters down, he began.

"How about a round of applause for the chef," he said in a loud voice. The guests answered with an extended enthusiastic applause. After thanking them for support, he continued.

"First I bring with me kind words of support from our President. He is very much in favor of these cultural and scientific programs. He wishes you all well." Everyone applauded. "Now, just a few remarks on two or three themes on why you are going to Italy, and, what may be expected from you. We hope you will bring back the kind of information we can disseminate for the benefit of our American brothers and sisters.

"As you know, our earth has always had earthquakes of one type or another. As devastating to life and things are the ones produced by volcanoes. We have rifts of all kind on the

West Coast, especially. We can never forget Mt. St. Helen! The devastation was widespread, here on the surface of the earth, and in the atmosphere with its pervasive pollution. Notwithstanding the damage, the loss of life, though elevated, was not as bad, compared to the fatal results from other similar quakes. Can you imagine a situation wherein we can better predict these eruptions? We may not be able to control the damages to the environment; we can certainly reduce, significantly, the loss of life. To this extent, I am pleased to tell you that Professor Jean Villa will be working with her counterparts in exploring the feasibility of new units designed to give us a better heads-up before a volcano explodes. We are especially interested for Hawaii, our West Coast, and others places such as Colorado. Needless to say, this kind of research can bring lots of benefits to everyone…"

Because of the large applause, he stood back—his hand aimed at the table of Professor Villa.

"Although the world keeps talking about slavery from time immemorial, in this our 21st century, we have not come to grips historically. We know that slavery was a common practice. It was also so in Israel. Certainly the Greeks took slaves, and the Romans did no less, with one exception: though rare, a slave, regardless of provenance or race, could become a citizen of Rome anywhere in its empire. It took a couple of centuries or so before American slaves gained freedom, and much longer in gaining citizenship. In addition, America held on to slavery as an institution longer than any other European or Latin American nation. Our Ph.D. student will do comparative research on how slavery was made possible, how it was managed, and how it ended in Rome vis-à-vis America. Our hope is that through this thesis, we will all be informed of what actually happened so that we can close the divide that keeps our races from gaining the means to the rights enjoyed by the population at large…" Mr. Hamilton said, amidst an extended applause, as he pointed to Mr. James Harrison.

"For this one, we're back in Rome—ancient Rome. Around 161 BC, Greece, under Seleucid Dynasty, made power grabs in the Middle East, especially Israel. Under siege, a group of Jews were sent to Rome to ask for help. The story goes as of that event, Jews established themselves as a community in Rome and they have maintained their presence across the centuries to the present—un-interrupted. During the height of the Empire, there were as many as 13 Synagogues within the city of Rome, and as many as two Roman Senators who were Jews. These Jews have survived in Rome, as a dynamic community, and nowhere else, including Israel has that community been replicated. Having survived Hitler, this community has produced diplomats, generals, scientists, and impresarios such as Olivetti. While Venice established the first Ghetto, in Rome Jews have enjoyed practically continuous liberty.

"Jerome Dershovitch, at the table down there, will develop the theme at the University of Rome…"

Interrupted by the applause, Derek Hamilton stepped back until the hall was quiet.

"We're still with the University of Rome for the next recipient.

"We know—or should know that World War II came to a brutal end as a result of two US-built atomic bombs having been dropped on Japan. We should also know that each of the belligerent nations had established very aggressive programs to achieve the goal of building the bomb. The reason why those nations were not successful was due to the fact that Enrico Fermi ended up in America and not in Germany or Japan. He achieved the first chain reaction, which was the basis of the bomb. We should know that much of the experimentation took place first in Rome and then in and around the athletic field of the University of Chicago.

"The speculation: Had either Germany or Japan won the war, would the conquered nations, including America—would we as a conquered people—as present Americans, be enjoying a level of international prestige and well being as the Japanese and Germans are enjoying as our intimate and respected Allies?

"This task is assigned to Helen Francis…"

Maybe because Helen was a woman, the crowed gave a roaring ovation, startling Mr. Hamilton.

"Oh, my," he commented. Then a smile of pride covered his face.

Jody, of course, was full of smiles. "What a group, Mom; you're at the very top with this group."

"Yes, now we have to make sure we bring ourselves to Rome without incident."

"Why do you say that? I have never seen anything as uplifting as this."

"Yes, you are right."

"No, Mom: tell me what's going through your mind."

Closing her face toward Jody's ear, she said, to her daughter's astonishment: "You know how much I love music. I went to see Guido Cantelli direct Verdi's *Requiem Mass* at Boston Symphony. It was magnificent. I shall never forget it. Also, I shall never forget that soon after, Guido with his whole orchestra crash-landed near the airport of Milan. I guess what I am trying to say is that things should not happen as accidents. These things are worse when they are man-made. I don't feel at ease going to Europe at this time. There are terrorists all over the place. Too often, they are among us and we only know that even as migrants, they're not even vetted."

"Oh, Mom, not to worry: Airport security is pretty effective."

After chit-chatting with their counterparts at the table, mother and daughter walked around saying hello almost non-stop. Professor Villa was that popular, and, therefore, in demand.

"People have great expectations of you. I am sure you will not disappoint them," Jody said.

"Mom," she then added with a twinkle in her eyes. "To-morrow is our last day—here, I mean, in Washington! Why don't we go to the National Gallery? There are many master-pieces from Italy. Although I would like to see the *Jesus* of Dalì, I would also like to see the *chiaroscuro* of Caravaggio, *The Taking of Christ—Saints and Sinners.*"

"My, my, Jody: You're talking about some big names. Caravaggio, especially. You know he was a master painter and a *farabutto* at the same time."

"Mom, enough already with these Italian words. 'Farabut-to!' What does it mean?"

"Rascal!"

At *The National Gallery of Art*, mother and daughter showed mutual admiration for Dali's Jesus dramatically suspended from wooden beams of the cross—*The Sacrament of the Last Supper*. In their view, Jesus commanded all their attention notwithstanding Dali's artistic ability to move the viewers as he did. Jody was really taken back by the artist's virtuosity. Not so with Caravaggio's Jesus.

In *The Taking of Christ...*, Jody was struck by the artist rendition of the Christ on the cross. There he was, waiting to die, and being the only one with the light clearly shining on his face.

"He's receiving all the light," commented Jody to her mother.

"While the bewilderment of the others is wrapped in the powerful *chiaroscuro* of noteworthy power," the mother added, reflecting on the relationship between art and content. "Where does Caravaggio come into this scene? Remember that in real life, he was a rascal. He is purported to have killed one of his critics, and that he, himself—he either died of natural causes or was killed. And we still do not know the circumstances."

With those thoughts, Jody was prompted to think about the imminent future and her having to face Michael, wondering whether he was a Caravaggio full of talents or a rascal full of mischief.

At the International Airport, the passengers were processed and safely in their seats for the impending takeoff. Quixi was placed in a special cage in the back of the plane. The Boeing 777 was filled to capacity. Jody sat in her preferred seat by the window. Her mother cuddled up to her, her left hand joined firmly to Jody's. The thought of flying—her feet off the ground—was bad enough. Seated in a plane about to takeoff was worse. Besides, she could not hide that fear. Psychologically—knowing she was going to fly, in retrospect, she should not have gone to the Museum. Seeing images of Jesus was of no comfort to her during these moments of anxiety.

"Mom, easy: There's nothing to worry about. There are thousands of these flights all over the world…"

"…Yes, and the one that comes to mind is that of Guido Cantelli, not to mention all those planes that have mysteriously gone done without plausible causes. I do not know what to make of it all. I'm afraid to fly to begin with. This other terrorist stuff is making it worse.

"Here, hang on, Mom," Jody assured her as she clasped both her hands. "Not to worry; I will take care of you."

As the plane took off in a burst of speed, Jody placed her

arms around her mother's shoulders. When the plane finally finished its ascent, Jody released her clutch.

"I am so grateful. Thanks, Jody. Now, Jody, what were we talking about…?"

"We'll be landing in Rome, take a chartered bus to Naples, and continue on to Pompeii. I am looking forward to seeing all those ancient pines along the road. I always liked them."

"Is it because of Respighi?"

"Yes, Mom, you introduced his music to me."

The flight over the Atlantic Ocean went rather smoothly. Professor Villa was happy except for the landing at the *Leonardo Da Vinci Airport* in Rome. Once again, she gave her hands to Jody.

"O.K. Mom," Jody said, to reduce her mother's fears. "What is Leonardo's particular achievement when it comes to his paintings—never mind the fact that he was a master in *chiaroscuro?* As a young girl, you told me that several time."

"I am glad you remember, darling. You tell me."

"The smile, the smile: The smile is dynamic. You look at his *Mona Lisa.* She is smiling with you. She smiles back at you no matter the angle you choose to look at her. 'Forget the perspective.' You used to tell me. 'It's the smile that keeps on smiling,' you used to say. Oh, I don't know how to repay you for all the joy I have gained as a result of so many wonderful things you taught me, especially about music and art…."

Her hand clutching those of her mother, the plane came to a smooth stop, to which the passengers gave the pilot a loud round of applause.

Puffing loudly with a smile on her face, her mother thanked Jody once again.

In no time, they were off the plane; and, for some un-known reason, mother and daughter passed through customs without the slightest inconvenience. Jody, especially, and her mother didn't even have to show their cell phones.

On the way to the street, Professor Villa recognized an old friend coming into the terminal. "Hi, Elvira, what a surprise: You must be going back to the States."

"Yes," confirmed her heavy-set friend. "I just wish I didn't have to fly!"

"I know how you feel. My daughter, here, helped me through it. What a burden to be like this. Bye, Elvira. We'll see you in Boston in a few weeks."

"Who is that?" Jody asked. "You didn't even present me to her."

"I just didn't want to waste time. She is a petulant friend who made my life miserable on a flight to Italy a few years ago. I think she put the jinks on me with this unreasonable fear of mine."

Except for the break at the *Autostrada* Grill whose facilities crossed the six lanes—as though it was a covered bridge, the bus ride was not that comfortable. At the Grill, however, everyone's spirit picked up after ordering either *espresso*, or, *espresso lungo*, or, *espresso macchiato*, or, especially, *cappuccino*. In retrospect, they had as much fun in pronouncing or mispronouncing the Italian words as in tasting the various types of coffee. However, they had no problem pronouncing the French word, *briosch*—the special Italian-type doughnut.

Chapter 5
Castellammare di Stabbia

In arriving in Italy, Jody's challenge was to discover whether Michael Capoverde was the person with the know-how on a new type of warfare that could have similar impact as its biological-chemical counterpart. This consideration was critical because such an attack could be imminent. At the same time, she had to show concern on behalf of her mother about a probable eruption from a volcano that has been dormant since about the 79 AD. Her deference to her mother was well calculated because all indications pointed to the connection between her mother' role and that of Michael. The challenge for her was to keep her mother from being harmed in any way, and for her mother to be the conduit to Michael.

Jody's subconscious concern was emotional in nature. She had not been able to square her findings thus far about this man Michael, whom she had never met. Yet, he seemed smart, if not unusually intelligent; he may have killed or was the cause of a man to die; he seemed to have the means or know-how on how to save the lives of millions of people and at the same time to be the potential cause for the death of as many millions; he could be a man of virtue on one hand, and one of treachery. Yet, she could not forget the expression on Miss Robin's face in remembering Michael's kiss. She was finally in Italy, and the truth about Michael had to be finally discovered. Did she have the intelligence and the fortitude to fulfill the commitment to her mission as an agent of the U.S. government, for which she had placed her hand on *The Bible*.

Having arrived in the center of Castellammare di Stabbia, Jody and her mother were impressed by the beauty of the place; for, in looking due west, they saw the Tyrrhenian Sea extending westward towards Ischia and Capri, with the two tall remnants still standing; in turning their heads northeast, they looked directly onto the top of Mount Vesuvius. Luck would have it, that a light sliver of the moon was traveling into the western evening sky.

"My, *che bello!"* Jody exclaimed, as she looked at her exuberant mother. "Who would have thought it?"

With Quixi under her arm, Professor Villa began to walk toward the entrance of the residence. She was quickly met by two porters who, after a brief but resounding welcome, they went to the back of the bus to retrieve the baggage. On seeing the white puppy, one confided with a motion to his eyes that another dog had come not too long ago and they had to clean after them. At the desk, the *Signorina* welcomed the two Americans with a broad smile.

"*Che bel cane. É un maltese?*" (What a beautiful dog. Is it a Maltese?) She asked.

"*Si."* Jody answered.

The building was spacious, with a large restaurant, and several conference rooms, including an auditorium. Their suite had two bed rooms facing the water, one bath with shower—inclusive of a *bidet*, one small living room, one small kitchen, and one place for Quixi. In all, the two women were happy with their accommodations.

While Jody went to her room to check on phone messages, her mother was already unraveling the paperwork spread on the living room table. She had to prepare herself for the first 10'o'clock meeting the next morning; and she was a little nervous even though the meeting was informal—over coffee and pastry, so the members could meet one another.

The roster called for 20 individuals both from America and Italy, all bilingually proficient in English and Italian, and all very bright in their given fields of expertise. The chairman of the committee was listed as Domenico Fracastoro, Captain of the Port of Naples, as noted on the list.

Although Professor Villa had looked at the Captain's credentials and found nothing out of the ordinary, it was Jody who scrutinized the significance of that background: he hailed from La Spezia, a sister city, equal to Genova in many ways, except that La Spezia had a special port and a special naval history. It was the birthplace of the modern underwater guerrilla warfare, better known as America's Navy Seals. Among their many naval feats, the one of two-man details sunk more navy and civilian vessels than anyone other team. By sinking Austria's Mediterranean Navy, the Italian frogmen brought an end to World War I. The Allies, especially England, suffered huge losses in World War II. Captain Fracastoro, a retired officer, was a member of that distinguished force known as the Decima Mas.

Jody had read William Schofield's book about those frogmen, and was more than aware of their accomplishments. But now, with world wars being thankfully absent from the world scene, it did not mean that everything was just fine. She had to find out just who this man was. While Jody was sitting at a coffee shop at the tip of the port, her mother quickly got to learn the persona behind the Captain's white uniform.

In calling the meeting to order, and after his warm welcoming remarks to the members, reminding them that there would he future sub-groups meetings, he called out the name of each attendee to get up to be recognized.

On hearing her name called, Professor Villa stood up, raised one arm; and, with a large smile, she thanked the Captain. On seeing her, he turned his head to the right to avoid being heard. But, to no avail. "*Maronna!*" (Madonna) he exclaimed, barely audible, causing many to snicker in wonderment.

"I didn't mean it to start things off this way," Fracastoro whispered to his assistant.

In no time, the formal meeting closed and everyone grouped around the various stands full of all kinds of pastries and finger sandwiches. Espresso, tea, *cappuccino* and other beverages were served at separate stands.

"*Buon giorno*," said the Captain on approaching Professor Villa, who was chatting with a group of colleagues.

"Ah, yes, Captain Fracastoro. *Buon giorno*," she replied somewhat flirtatiously. "How are you?" she added, almost at a loss for words.

On turning in a way to keep their colleagues from hearing his conversation, he began to whisper into her ear:

"*Rosa fresca aulentissima...*" (Fresh new rose of Spring...)

"What are you saying, Captain?" she asked naïvely, knowing too well she had gotten to him. Was he the typical *Latin lover* famous-infamous as known all over the world? "I am not understanding what you are saying. I think it is Italian," she said, purposely using the present progressive tense. "But you must be *napoletano*."

"Ligurian! You know: we discovered and revealed new routes to wherever"

"Columbus, is that right?"

"Of course, the one that did so much for human beings across our world..."

"...And what did it get him?"

"Obscurity, criticism based on ignorance. The fact is that in the Americas, he caused the natives from committing human sacrificial beheadings, and from Cannibalism. He also introduced his Christian God, who brought their redemption.

"...If you don't mind, I would rather finish on the theme I

began. Yes, yes: It is one of the earliest form of modern Italian, first used in Sicily. Let me recite it, with the hope of meeting with you soon so we explore the greatness of Ciullo's poetics."

"*Poetics?* She said to herself. "What a hell of a way for a come-on. "Yes, yes, please do…"

Rosa fresca aulentissima
ch'apari inver' la state,
le donne ti disiano,
pulzell' e maritate:
tràgemi d'este focora,
se t'este a bolontate;
per te non ajo abento notte e dia,
penzando pur di voi, madonna mia…

"Well, what do you think?"

"I didn't understand a word of it. In any case, this is hardly the place for *poetics*. We'll do it another time… Oh, ciao…" she turned in giving salutation to another colleague passing by. What is your name?"

Left to one side, the Captain, both his hands stretched out, he expressed a feeling of having been had. He quickly moved on to engage other colleagues.

Meanwhile, Jody sat by herself at a table by the water, sipping another *cappuccino,* thinking less about her mother and more about her mother's colleagues, wishing she were there to meet Michael face-to-face, then admitting to herself that there would have to be a better, more propitious time. Deep down, however, being alone as she was, knowing that her mother was so involved with so many people and having a good time, made Jody feel even more alone, to the point she thought of herself as an *isolate* despite knowing that in looks she was no slouch. The combination just was not there for her. It wasn't there for her mother either; yet, her mother had made something—of and for herself.

Her shoulders, somewhat bent inward, she walked home, almost oblivious to the various activities of life around a vibrant sea port.

"Mom," she called on entering the apartment. Her mother not being present, she went to the study. Perchance, she looked at the table full of paperwork. The schedule of participants lay open on the table. In addition, a schedule of meetings for the various subcommittees was also open. Her eyes quickly went to her mother's meeting, which included Captain Domenico Fracastoro, Chairman; Michael Capoverde, General-Selective Alarm System; Professor Jean Villa, Demographics surrounding Vesuvius, Luigi Pascoli, Colonnello Stormo Incursori, and two others. Jody's eyes remained fixed on Michael's name. "Alarm System! What did that have to do with anything?"

In no time, she was on her phone scouring the Internet. Having gotten very little if any reliable information, she decided to go on her encrypted line—her cell inserted into one of the notches on her bracelet.

Getting close to meeting target
Keep posted
Developments?

Return message:

"C (Connie) phoned M (Michael); husband grave vi-olated; body stolen; M chastises her harshly; orders not to call again; hangs up."

Frustrated, Jody disconnected from the line. She neither knew who committed the action nor the reason for such action. She wanted to know if any part of the body, such as the head with its vocal apparatus, had been singled out. Were terrorists involved? Did the police finally put two and two together? Or, did a foreign entity have the need to acquire the same information? Could Michael be the key? Could Michael have been responsible? Or, was it just happenstance? Worse, was the death of that man just a hoax? Jody's mind was full speed ahead to the point she had a headache. Luckily, her mother was on the way back home. A little motherly *tlc* might be what she needed to calm her down—just as it did when she was a little girl.

Her mother walked into the apartment with a funny grin on her face, in full contrast to Jody's somber expression. Jean quickly picked up on her daughter's unhappy mood.

"Jody, what is the matter, darling?"

"I had hoped to be with you. I guess being alone does not make me happy," she answered. The words had come out of her mouth as thought she had the whole thing thought out. She was surprised, because she had unconsciously devised her plan of action right then and there. She immediately knew her mother was going to ask her to go with her without having to ask her to do so, and run the risk of divulging her strategy.

"Sure, darling. In the next couple of days, we're meeting with a few subcommittee members. Would you like to come? I am sure there will not be any objections. I got to know the chairman. I am sure he won't mind.

"Who's that? Is this the one with that funny name—*castoro*—beaver, something?"

"Don't get smart, now, Jody. Respect will get you everywhere."

"I'm sorry, Mom. I didn't mean to be disrespectful. I apologize," she said, her head bowed.

"His name is Domenico Fracastoro, Captain. He knows a

lot about literature. You will like him, I am sure. By the way, he is actually the Captain of the Port of Naples—a prestigious position with lots of responsibilities. He has a lot of power and influence, and I believe he's one not to mince words with. That is my impression; I could be wrong. Here, let's look at the list," she suggested, and went to the table to look at the lists having the information she was looking for.

"Pretty good," Jody said. "He's not *napoletano*."

"He's Ligurian, like Columbus."

"So, what's he searching for?" Jody asked with a slight smile on her face. There was no pun in her question; she was literally referencing Columbus without ulterior motives; she derided those who place quotation marks around his name as though he were a man of fiction or one of questionable achievements.

"Our concern over a potential volcanic explosion is the maritime traffic of the region. You can imagine the havoc from the confusion in surviving traffic let alone the destruction. Domenico seems like the right leader both to develop and to implement appropriate plans."

"I thought you were also looking for better ways to predict volcanic actions as well."

"Of course Jody: That's as important as anything else. Imagine, for instance, if we can tell the exact spot of explosions. Mt. St. Helen comes to mind. It exploded not from the very top, but on the weak side due west direction. That's the side that carried the brunt of almost immeasurable destruction. So, it would be great to have that kind of information, don't you think?"

"Of course, Mom: But, how can you get that information?" Jody asked opportunely.

"An ex-patriot, from the Boston area of all places, is a member of our committee. He has some experience with communications—I have zero knowledge in this field, and he will be making a presentation. Would you like to come? I am sure Domenico will not mind your being present. I will let you know."

Jody was almost beside herself with the outcome. Things were falling into place as if predestined. She never imagined that this captain, Domenico, would actually facilitate her introduction to Michael.

Unexpectedly, her cell phone vibrated. After moving to one of the pre-determined notches, she read the code

(prefettura, center,
tomorrow. Bag, 9:30).

In a few seconds, the message disappeared.

"Mom, do you mind if I go to the port. Yesterday, I had the most delicious *cappuccino* with the best *sfogliatella* ever. Do I have to come with you, or can I come later?"

"You can come anytime, darling. By the way, no one makes a better *sfogliatella* than the Neapolitans."

At the *Prefettura* Police Station, Jody went to the main desk. After showing her ID card, the government official made a phone call. In good English, the woman said: "A gentleman will be over in a moment."

A middle aged man in uniform arrived from the corridor to the left. "*Buon giorno, signorina. Mi chiamo Federico.* Good morning, Miss. My name is Frederick. You understand Italian?"

"*Si, signore. Ma preferisco parlare inglese.*"

"Yes, of course. Please come with me."

They walked to room 8. After a clerk checked out Jody's credentials, she followed Frederick to a secure room. Inside, he told Jody to sit at the table with him across on the opposite side. Another man in uniform quickly approached, placed a pistol on the table, and left.

"This is your weapon: Beretta sub compact, especially designed for you to carry in your bag. Please empty your bag because I have to place it in its special side pocket."

"Why is that?" Jody asked.

"In case you need to use it directly from your bag. See this patch here? By pressing it, you will be able to fire the pistol— just like this," he continued. On pressing the patch, he activated the trigger, and the pistol would have fired if loaded. Note that the pistol cannot come loose. To take it out, you have to open the pocket. By the way, before I forget, when in hand, remember this: you are the only one who can fire this pistol. What do you think?'

"I'm stupefied. You guys think of everything. *Grazie.*"

After a few more minutes of instruction, Jody was escorted out of the building. Wasting no time, she returned to her mother's conference, already underway. After making eye contact with her mother, she received a nod to come. Her eyes subdued, she scanned the faces of those in attendance, recognizing the face of the Captain. On seeing that of Michael, she felt a shiver in her spine.

"I've been waiting for you, darling," her mother said cheerfully, but in a low voice.

"Thanks, Mom," Jody answer, sitting down.

Across the large table, Captain Fracastoro took over the microphone. "This morning, we're having a very special meeting to learn more on how to better predict volcanic eruptions in general, and those of Vesuvius in particular. We know what happened the last time—61 AD. The place was practically destroyed and the inhabitants decimated. Studies done by Professor Villa and others show that, if the people had received better prior warning, more would have escaped death.

In addition, if the cities of Pompeii, Herculaneum, and others had developed better urban plans—that, too, would have helped. Today, we're going to discuss a plan we hope to implement first in our general area. If it works as I believe it will, then we can bring it to the volcanologists around the world. Remember, this is a very informal presentation. We need to listen and then ask questions. We are also obliged to express reservations or give criticism.

"It give me pleasure to give the microphone to Michael Capoverde, a long standing friend of mine who lives a few kilometers south in Amalfi. He lives, by the way, with his brother, a Deacon, at St. Andrews, a beautiful place we should all visit…"

Somewhat shyly, Michael cleared his throat. "My name is Michael. I do live with my brother—it's easy to get absolutions, this way," he commented, generating the hoped-for laughter. (Jody nervously held her mother's hand.). This is the unit I am recommending. It was my idea, but developed over the years with a few friends. How does it work?

"There are basically two plastic cylinders: the outer is 12 inches round, 12 inches high; the inner is 10 inches round, 10 inches high. The idea is that one cylinder floats within the other with an even space between the two walls of about an inch, as you can see," Michael inserted the two cylinders within one another. "But, notice: the larger of the two has a bottom and a top cover with a small hole in the center of each cover. The inner cylinder has a line that keeps it from collapsing on either the wall of the outer cylinder or from touching the top or bottom covers. In other words, the inner cylinder needs to be floating and at the same time and not moving. It moves only if the some kind of force causes the inner cylinder to shake, thusly…" With the two cylinders one within the other, with the inner one clearly suspended within, he shook the instrument causing the inner cylinder to bang its bottom rim against the wall of the outer cylinder. "So far, so goo?" he asked his audience whose eyes were fixed on the instrument. Clearly, no one had seen the experiment before except for the Captain. "Now, notice the following copper wires running horizontal around the bottom rim of the inner cylinder. The out cylinder, however, has vertically placed single wires running from top to bottom. So, when there is a tremor, the wires of the inner cylinder touch the wires of the outer cylinder. The point of contact creates a pulse that is processed through an electronic board which pinpoints the geographical coordinates which are then transmitted to wherever. And this is a potential radio transmitter," he added picking it up from the table."

"Mom, is this science fiction or real?" Jody asked. The expression on her face was in line of sight of her mother only. As guest, she did not want to offend anyone let alone reveal she had a direct interest in knowing and understanding what that man was talking about.

"This is truly magnificent, Michael," the Captain chimed in. So, where would you place these instruments? And, I want to be sure that I understand what you are saying: The signal generated reflects the direction in which the volcanic energy and sound waves are traveling? In addition, we will know the epicenter of the eruption?"

"Yes, we should, as soon as we have these units installed, we can begin testing."

"Do you have recommendations on where these installations should go?"

"Yes, we have two within the area of Vesuvius, two within the area of Monte Carlo and France. There are always tremors in these areas. To the South, we should have two in the area of Aetna."

"How about outside Europe?" asked Professor Villa.

"Yes, for sure: California, Jakarta, and elsewhere where earthquakes are recorded."

"Wait!" Captain Fracastoro interjected. "Your system is not limited to volcanic eruptions only; is that right?"

"No, it should be as effective with any other type of earthquake."

There was no doubt that Michael had made a convincing presentation. He had also generated admiration, especially from Jody.

"Have the sites been established, and are they open to the public?" Jody asked, somewhat meekly. She had to show her ignorance about the subject matter.

"It's not up to me; it's up to the Committee, to the Captain, here."

"I see no problem with that, do you, Professor Villa?"

"Not at all," she answered, her eyes directed onto her daughter. She had not expected any openly reaction from her daughter.

"One last question," said Captain Fracastoro. "Will the installation be in the soil or in solid rock?"

"Great question: Rock is the best conduit of vibration. We would drill a perpendicular hole a few feet into a specific rock, build a steady base, then install the unit protruding several feet above the surface, being sure that the cylinders, with the transmitter with the antenna, have a clear line of site path to the receiver of the main radio station somewhere near a headquarter."

"Perfect," Captain Fracastoro injected. If there are no more questions, the meeting is now closed. Many thanks, Michael. You've done a great job!"

While standing to one side, Professor Villa and Jody approached Michael. "How does your system differ from the Richter scale?" the Professor asked.

"It probably doesn't. However, the Richter scale tells the magnitude and the amplitude of the seismic waves. We are trying to make better predictions when these are about to happen."

"How do you measure the intensity or the magnitude of the movement?" asked Jody.

"My, you guys are really into this. What a pleasant surprise! Very quickly: the higher the shaking or the movement, the greater the movement of the inner cylinder against the wall of the outer cylinder. The more contacts between the horizontal wiring circuit and the vertical wiring circuit the greater the intensity of the quake. The information is projected on a grid from low to high, and is printed on a chart, much as in other similar applications."

"Great!" Jody commented. You must be very familiar with the terrain leading to the top of Vesuvius."

"Yes, pretty much."

"I would love to see it."

"Sure. If you wish, I can take you there."

"Do you live around here?"

"No, I live in Amalfi. But that doesn't matter. We can arrange it, no problem."

Again, things were falling in place without even trying. Better still was the fact that it was happening under the awareness of her mother, who was giving silent approval of the whole thing. Jody understood and felt confident.

At that moment, Captain Fracastoro approached the three, but spoke to Michael specifically. "*Michè* (Michael in Neapolitan), next week a few decrepit old men will be having dinner in Naples. Would you like to join us? There will also be a show. Someone will be singing, mimicking a very famous tenor. You will like it."

"I am not sure. I will let you know. Excuse me," Michael

added. "I do have to go now." His eyes reflected reservation through frowns on his forehead.

"Hope to hear from you," said Jody on extending her hand to him.

Michael was not entirely himself. The unexpected call from Connie had made him anxious. From now on, he had to be careful whom he dealt with. Spies, in his assessment, came in all kinds of forms. And, he knew he didn't know how to identify them. Though intelligent in so many ways, he was naïve when it came to human relations, especially when it came to love. He had fallen in love and paid a high price on discovering that true love can exist only if love was true on both sides.

His big problem, now, was that he may have left himself open to all kinds of misunderstandings, including retributions. Did Connie's husband die as a result of the car accident, or from an application of his experimental transmission? He had been satisfied in learning that the autopsy had shown the man had died of natural causes brought about mainly by alcoholism with the accident being only the trigger of what was bound to happen sooner than later.

Compounding his worry was the speculation on the international media that a high ranking terrorist had been killed from conditions supposedly similar to those of Connie's husband, that is, that the man's vocal apparatus had received a jolt of cancer-causing radio transmissions that somehow had a specific print, as with finger prints which are particular to specific human beings, only.

His brother, Don Paolo (Capoverde), was the Deacon of St. Andrew Cathedral. In the recent years in Amalfi, Don Paolo had made a name for himself as a very serious man of the cloth. Because of his background in music, he had developed the Sunday High Mass into a production of high quality such that the church was almost always filled to capacity. What would happen to his brother should word get out about the relationship with Connie?

Now, he had to go back to Amalfi and check out his secret laboratory with all his experiments, being sure that his communication system was intact and that nothing had been jeopardized.

Furthermore, he had to walk the many tunnels connected to the Cathedral, making sure that no one had penetrated their security, especially those that served as depositaries of documents, books, reliquaries including those that had been taken from Constantinople; these were body parts being preserved for future identification, and no one but him, except for his brother, knew anything about.

It was rumored that at the time of the Fourth Crusade in 1204 to Constantinople, the city had been completely plundered. Important religious relics from Israel and other parts of the Middle East that had been brought to that city had now been confiscated and brought to various parts in Europe. The body of St. Andrew, of course, was the most important relic for the Maritime Republic of Amalfi, which built the famous prestigious cathedral. Special caverns with camouflage entrances were also built throughout, from the north, to the west, to the south of the mountain ridge around Amalfi. Although these tunnels and caverns had minimum use during World War I, they were extensively deployed during World War II. The Italian Army first built those gunnery positions; but, it was the Germans who extended those positions—all aiming at destroying naval Allied units from piercing the Axis perimeter of defense. All of which, however, was rendered useless when the Allied successfully invaded Salerno.

Michael was also aware of the many reports on the

Knights Templar for having built the tower in Newburyport, Rhode Island. He had not heard a word about, let alone having any idea whatsoever about another claim about the body of Jesus.

Having inherited the last remains of Jesus—to free the cross for another victim to be crucified, they took the remains to Constantinople, thereby allowing the possibility for Jesus' remains to have been transported to Amalfi by those Knights—these were not in his mind. The results of World War II were.

Those were not really the thoughts of Michael, although he knew, too well, what the ramifications of World War II had on Italy specifically, and on America. In his mental assessment, he concluded that America, through Roosevelt, and to a lesser degree through Churchill—that America had saved Western Civilization if not the world. The more than 110 million people killed through the actions of individuals the likes of Mussolini, Hitler, Stalin, and Mao Zedong just blew his mind.

Michael was now concerned about his personal future. Being involved with Captain Fracastoro, Professor Villa, and others, in being such an active participant on the project—was he exposing himself personally as a man, and as an experimental scientist with one secret wish only: to eliminate those individuals the likes of Hitler who had brought havoc to the human race. The facts of random, suicidal, indiscriminate terrorist attacks that were leaving thousands of victims all over the world was inconceivable to him; he felt that he had the moral responsibility to do something to reduce or to stop the wanton slaughter as best he could.

His idea was to single out only the blatant leaders responsible for their incomprehensible carnage. But, he thought: What if something he himself did or was doing went wrong, and instead of reducing the dangers posed by the terrorists, he, Michael, did he increase that danger?

He sat on the balcony of his apartment, his eyes overlooking the Tyrrhenian Sea. Every thought in his head made him more depressed—typical symptoms of a recluse, of an *isolate*. He continued sitting, in deep silence, unaware of his neighbors, of his surroundings, not even of his brother inside the apartment. Then, suddenly, the voice of Giulietta, their beloved permanent housekeeper, called out to come in: Supper was ready.

"*Stasera: Fettuccine Alfredo, Salmone a la Adolfo,*" she said proudly.

"What's that?" Father Paolo asked—an expression of curiosity on his face. "Never heard of the second, have you, Michael?" On seeing his brother slightly despondent, he continued: "*Michele* is there something wrong?"

"No, Paolo, there is nothing wrong. I am looking to taste this new dish. Where did you get the recipe, Giulietta?" Michael asked, defraying the question.

"From the Internet," she answered proudly.

"How do you like that?" Michael asked his brother as a commentary. "Even in Italy women are empowered these days."

Having noted his brother's evasion, Paolo continued in a different direction as both began eating the first course. "What did you do, today? I know you had an important meeting."

"Yes, Paolo, very important: You know, I have been working on this alarm system. Today I actually showed them how it works. My only reservation is about the inner cylinder. They may not have completely understood how it works, that the bottom rim of that cylinder is free floating—meaning, if there is a tremor, the rim bangs against the outer wall according to the strength of the tremor. If it is weak, the contacts are light and few; if it is strong, the contacts are heavy and many: The higher the number of contacts, the bigger the tremor.

"The other thing they may not have understood is that the signals received at headquarters—if few and mild, the warning would go to the local district only; if many and heavy, the warning would go to the general area headquarters."

"It sounds pretty clear to me. If I understand it, then the others for sure have understood it; believe me," he confirmed, not letting on that he was still curious on why his younger brother seemed troubled. "So, who was there, at the meeting?"

"I don't think you know them. The two main ones were Captain Domenico Fracastoro; he's in charge, and very smart. Then there was Professor Jean Villa, from Harvard. She is also very smart. Then there were a few more committee members with special scientific backgrounds none of whom asked questions, except for one. She did so while we were having refreshments."

"Who was that?"

"Jody, the daughter of Professor Villa—she asked me about the topography of Mt. Vesuvius. She said she remembered the song, *Funiculì, Funiculà*, by Pavarotti, and always wanted to take the *funivia* to the top."

"So?"

"I said yes jut to be nice. If she calls, I might make an arrangement."

"Is this what's bothering you? It must be... Wow, this salmon is delicious... Giulietta! Congratulations! You know, Michael, it seems a bit drastic taking a woman with you to Vesuvius, a woman you just met by coincidence. Did her mother say anything about this? In a sense, you work for her."

"I know; I know! I'm not really comfortable."

"Is she coming on to you?"

"It didn't feel like she was. We'll see."

"Do you know what I would suggest?" Paolo said, "Take her out to dinner first..."

"Hm… I have to think about it," he answered, satisfied that his older brother's concern had been deflected."

However, while sugaring his *espresso* and getting ready to eat his dessert, Paolo spoke again, causing Michael to shake his head in surprise. "What!" he said in a controlled by louder voice. St. Michael? What's he got to do with anything?"

"Why are you getting so excited? I just wanted to tell you that the other day, by pure coincidence, I was taking a perfunctory inventory of items held in a small obscure part of the church, and we came across a portrait of St. Michael. Remember when you were a young boy, you were always fascinated by the image of your name-sake patron saint—an angel in full armor, sword in hand, foot on the devil's neck, about to slay the Devil under his foot."

"Yes, yes, I remember. It's the story of my life…"

"I thought you only liked the imagery, Michael."

"Of course I liked the imagery; but that's all. So, have I seen this piece? I don't recall."

"I don't believe you have. It might be a Guido Reni…who knows. It's a great work of art, and I thought you might like to see it. You know, you were named after him. Our late parents, my God rest their souls, must have seen some connection between you and St. Michael."

"I'll be there first thing in the morning."

"I will be serving communion…"

Saturday evening of that week, Michael picked up Jody at her apartment and drove to Naples. He had made reservations at the *O Sarracino*, a night club made famous—many people believed—by the late Renato Carosone. His song in Neapolitan became a big hit in the 50s. The owner of the Club—a close friend of Michael—also lived in the same complex in Amalfi. Umberto Saracino was himself of *pure* Neapolitan blood, going back to the time when the Muslims were in control of all of southern Italy, with their main headquarters in Palermo, Sicily. Michael had made sure not to tell Umberto that he would be at the Club that evening, because he knew that Umberto would have made a fuss on behalf of his neighbor.

Unbeknown to Michael—for he and Jody were somewhat ensconced in a secluded corner booth, was the presence of Captain Fracastoro, already there at a large round table filled with about ten of his *Octos* (short for, octogenarians). He and his friends were immersed in their own things, one feeding off the other about every ailment in their precarious existence. Whatever the conversation, it always ended with egocentric conclusions on the importance of each. Nothing really was about anyone else but oneself. The good thing was that each made fun of the other, and always either being the target of a joke or creating the joke at the expense of another.

"Giuseppe, ask Franco why his face smells of perfume?" asked the Captain, a mischievous smile on his face. Franco had been out on a rendezvous' with a hooker, and was trying to eliminate the odor on his face. The wig on his head made his caricature come alive.

"Franco, why are you putting so much perfume on your face? Is it because you ain't had no little amount of pussy these days?" As important was the manner he asked the question. To which, they laughed more on how he had asked the question than on the insinuation in the question—their broken dentures a sight to behold. All of these idiosyncrasies added to their never-ending ribaldry. "Hey, Franco, how's it going with your wife?"Another asked mischievously, insinuating he was unable to deal with one woman, never mind two.

"You know, she has a problem with me. She's always telling me that either I have severe body odor or malicious bad breath. I check myself out and I don't smell myself none. I even check my mouth… Wait, tell me if I smell…" he said, standing up. Bringing his mouth to Franco's, he let out a big burp.

"Get the hell out here," Franco yelled, pushing him away to the delight of his buddies.

"*Sporcaccione!* Dirty pig," cried another, his fingers wiping the tears from his eyes.

Everyone laughed except for Vico. Diminished in size, he remained silent and pensive. He had had a bout with his wife, who felt that he hadn't left enough for her to survive, should he die first, that to be sure, on the recommendation of one of her sons from a previous marriage, he should make her the sole owner of the house now owned jointly.

"What's the matter, Vico?" the Captain asked, knowing his friend was down in the dumps.

"Nothing, nothing: we all have our ups and down", Vico answered in a feeble voice.

Just as Vico's, the Captain's private life, especially his divorce, was off the table, even though everyone knew that his wife had left him for another—maybe, two to three men. The fact was that having fallen out of love with the woman he had truly and deeply loved, he made it possible for his Ligurian wife to leave the impression that she was the one who had initiated the action.

The second thing off the table was his deep infatuation with the Professor from Harvard. He made it a point not to say anything about her without exception. But, his *Octos*, though feeling something was happening with their *de facto* leader, each respected each other's emotional privacy—almost.

"Hey, Francesco, how long has it been since your wife…?"

Almost all in unison, their eyes lit up with wicked smiles, "… *dieci anni* (ten years and maybe more…"

"Last night, for me, you buffoons. Come on, tell us, which one of you can still get it up?" he challenged with a sarcastic smile. "Even you, *petrosino* (parsley), we know you have your eye on the American professor from Harvard…"

Before the Captain could say anything, the would-be Casanova continued. "…She needs a real man. Will you introduce her to this real Casanova: at your service, Madam!"

"You're so full of *merda* you have to flush twice each time!"

They all laughed in unison—so much that the guests at next table began to laugh as well even though no one knew why. "Hey, *capitano*, is that the guy, down there, isn't he the one who likes to dance?"

"Who are you talking about?"

Bringing his hands to the side of his eyes, squinting, he exclaimed: "*Maronna mia!* (Holy Mother of God!) It's Michael with the professor's daughter. We're in for fireworks, tonight, dear friends. Just don't let on we're here. I don't want them to see me, O.K.," he warned them all. "Hey, *cameriere*—waiter: come here," he called the waiter with a whisper. In no time, Umberto Saracino came to the table. "Did you see who's at that corner table?" the Captain asked.

"Yes, I do now. I am glad you told me. I'll call the musicians to gather."

Mainly guitar players, slowly each made his way to the platform.

At their table, Michael and Jody were enwrapped in their own conversation. It seemed that not even the noise from the other clients reached their ears.

Michael wore a light green silk sports coat over a whitish shirt and silk grayish trousers. His brown hair was slightly long and fluffy. The expression on his face was not jovial, but very attentive to his conversation with Jody. He was not sad, however, in any form or shape.

Jody, on the other hand, wore a bluish silk jacket with a wide bottom rim over a white shirt somewhat *décolleté*, her full breasts well covered but very, very visible; her skirt—tight around the waist but flailing down to her upper knees, gave her a lilt when walking. She also wore leather shoes with low heavy heels. She told Michael she had shopped at the local *bottega* at the Port. She did not smile much either, but seemed more engrossed in the conversation than he was.

A bottle of *prosecco* on ice was on the table, they had already toasted: she with *cheers* and he with *salute.*

"You surprised me when you ordered the bluish clams as your appetizer," Michael commented. "It's a great choice, especially the one with wine garlic sauce. Very few people order this dish; usually they order *vongole* (small clams)."

"Do you mind?" She asked, a slight frown on her face."

"No, not at all. Actually, for some unexplainable reason to me, I get a kick watching how people eat those *tasty* clams. I get turned on, for some reason."

"That's a great start," she answered with an open smile as she picked up one clam, opened it with both hands, and, sucking the morsel drenching with sauce, she noisily put into her mouth. Michael looked at her in awe. Jody's eyes were fixed on his face as she repeated her motions—the juices dripping from both sides of her mouth down to her chin. Suddenly, Michael got up from his chair.

"What!" she exclaimed with a naughty expression on her face, not knowing how to react.

Standing over her, he bent down, placed his arms around her, and kissed her. Before he knew it, Jody was responding with one continuous prolonged kiss of her own—her oily hands clamped on his sides. They stopped only because of the loud and boisterous clapping from the Captain's table. The *Octos* stood on their feet to be sure their attention spread to the other guests.

Neither believing what had happened, Michael stood up, looked around at the noisy crowd, and quickly sat down.

"Are you embarrassed?" she chided.

"No, I am rather liking it," he answered in a wide smile.

"This one for you," she said as she took another clam, placed it into her mouth, and noisily swished it down her throat.

Michael brought his glass of *prosecco* up. "May we have many more of these," he said boldly and proceeded to drink the full glass.

"I shall never forget you," Jody said in a low and serious voice.

It seemed coincidental that as soon as the two finished their *antipasto*, with Jody wiping her full mouth and chin, the orchestra leader, now that all of his musicians were in place, began to ask his welcomed guests to give him their attention.

"*Signore e Signori*," he began—a full smile on his face, accentuated only by his slim black mustache. "Ladies and Gentlemen, this evening we're introducing our newest light tenor. He sings in the tradition of Pavarotti and Bocelli, except that he is Neapolitan—the young *Roberto Spaccacuore* (Robert Heartbreaker). With his rendition of, *Il diavolo e l'angelo*, he was backed by our full special guitar section."

His *bacchetta* (baton) aimed at the guitars, he dropped it dramatically. Amidst the wild cheers, the guitarists began as the singer made his way to the microphone. Before handing the mike to the singer, however, the conductor urged all: "*Tutti a ballare!*" (Everyone on the dance floor).

Not soon after the initial blast of the guitars with a heavy rhythm supplied by the drummer, the dance floor was almost entirely full of dancers of all ages. When the singer began with the lyrics from, *Il diavolo e l'angelo*, everyone responded positively. Michael, especially, was captured by the title itself—the devil and the angel. He had had a conversation with his brother about just that, and the subject was vividly in his mind. He stood up, took Jody by the hand, and, on saying, "May we?" he led her to the floor. In an instant, he picked up the beat. With her chest firmly into his, he drew her tight. Their feet secure in their steps, he twirled her outward and quickly back into a solid embrace. Without paying attention to the other dancers, Michael and Jody danced flawlessly and with full energy. On tightening her breast to his chest, she tilted her foot backward. Then holding her by the hand, he pushed her body out for about six twirls, the bottom of her skirt making undulating patterns as its rim lifted more and more upward, as if she were the dancer in *Sleeping Beauty.* They were so tuned into each other, that they did not realize the other couples had left the floor altogether. Toward the end of the song, the guitars with the full orchestra came to a dramatic *crescendo*, wherein Michael once again spun her foreword and back, with a final burst that brought her back into his arms, to a thunderous applause. Holding Jody with one hand, he waved to the guests with a thankful gesture, as both returned to their table.

"*Grazie, Michele.* By the way, the song was written by Andrea Bocelli himself."

Bedlam broke out at the Captain's table. Even Vico stood up and applauded.

Franco, on the other hand, having remembered Boccaccio's placing the devil in Hell, commented with a smirk: "If Michael is the Devil, I would like to be him tonight."

Having had their *second piatto* (sole), with a *tiramisù* without comparison, after their last glass of cold *prosecco*, they scooted out the back door without being seen.

It was a glorious evening for Jody. Ironically, she had expected the opposite.

On their way to her apartment, as Michael drove his *Alfa Romeo Veloce* on the *Autostrada,* she confided in him that she had had a great time and that she was grateful with the hope that they have many more such evenings.

"I hadn't predicted anything—one way or another. The evening—or, our date, turned out to be exceptional. You were also stunningly beautiful and refreshingly sexy."

"Wow, Michael. Does that mean we may have a second date?" she asked as she clutched his hand."

"Did you not want to go to the top of Vesuvius?"

"Of course: But I believe I want much more. Do you agree?"

"There's a great hotel near your place…"

"I know, darling. I am sure we'll get there."

Chapter 6
Amalfi

The city of Amalfi is surrounded by a mountain chain that leads from the north, due east, then south, and due west. It is a conclave made possible by the landslide pursuant to the hurricane of a few centuries go. The city is connected to the main road that leads north to south. No automobiles are allowed in the square, however.

The *Duomo* (Cathedral) stands on the right. A road-path leads west toward the far mountain chain. It leads to the oldest still-operational paper-making factory of the Western Civilization. On the north side of the road is a lemon grove famous for its super-size lemons used especially for *limoncello.* On the left of the road, among the many stores, *botteghe,* and other businesses, is *Il Tarì,* a restaurant that goes back to the time when the city was under Muslim rule. There are also many other kinds of buildings including apartment complexes.

Across the Cathedral, there is also an array of sundry businesses, with a large number of private and public apartments, mostly to the rear abetting the grove. The more prestigious and expensive ones are to the front with a view west to the Capri islands.

Michael and his brother lived in the sixth apartment, with a two-car garage below within walking distance. It had two bedrooms, one ample living room, one study, one convenient kitchen, and two bathrooms—one with bidet and shower, one with tub. The study was used mainly by Giulietta (she had her own apartment on the upper part of the city, and lived there with her retired husband).

His neighbor, Umberto Saracino, with his wife and two toddlers, occupied the fifth apartment at an angle; its front door had a clear view of the Cathedral. Although the apartment was about the same size with the same configuration inside; outside, the differences were in the stairway from the sidewalk to the apartment, and the size of the front deck. Umberto's apartment was much larger and enclosed with gates—more suitable of children. Whereas Michael's was on the other side, one could not see one deck from the other. In addition, due to maintenance needs, Umberto had to replace two vertical rods of the railing next to the stairway leading to the main door. He had a repairman cut the two rods in half and connect them temporarily with one rod joining the half-way up, leaving a rather large opening to the top of the railing. The repairman strapped some tape to keep the children from possible injury.

At the Port below, Michael rented a slip for his 14-foot outboard boat.

Whereas Michael had a standard Alfa Romeo, Umberto had a Lancia four-door sedan and a dilapidated-looking old 124 Fiat for his daily use. One would not know, however, it was a special car made to look old. Under the hood, it was a different story: special bullet-proof glass all around, four-speed synchronized shift box, special opening for firearm usage, a front and back fender designed for ramming, emergency light system, and more. Going back and forth to Naples every day, and having to go back home late into night always exposed him to danger. The notorious *ndrangheta*, and other similar underground criminal organizations, was still alive and well. Being a Neapolitan himself, and a Night Club owner, Umberto knew too well the need to protect his family. In addition, whereas Michael looked physically fit, Umberto kept in shape; he was a Black Belt holder.

Because they were neighbors, Michael spent a lot of time with Umberto. If not drinking *prosecco*, they drank *aperitivo*—always in his studio. Umberto amassed a large collection of antique books, especially illuminated manuscripts. He was probably one of very few, Catholic Italians, who had original illuminated editions of the Quran going back to the 11th Century.

Although their meetings were sporadic, the two enjoyed their companionship because they were able to discuss the affairs of the world without fear of repercussions or hostility between one another. Among their favorite topics were the comparisons between the Koran and the Bible, issues such as Communism and Democracy, way of life developed in the Western and Eastern Culture. He strongly resented the media's opinionated stand against the use of the word 'Crusades', as being evil and racist, to the point that a president of the United States was forced from repeating the word in public. "Why were the Crusades activated in the first place?" Michael would practically yell out. "Why, my dear Umberto, have millions and millions of non-Jews world-wide become followers of Jesus as a result of their free will. How does that contrast with the followers of Muhammad? If you are forced to follow, can you call yourself a follower? If your free will is denied, can you still be a man? We can put an image of Jesus in a urine jar. Draw a cartoon of Muhammad and all hell breaks loose! You can be decapitated!

"Many people project an attribute of enlightenment on the part of the Muslims who invaded North Africa, Portugal, Spain, Southern Italy, and many other places; yet, the same individuals would project an attribute of depravity of the European Crusaders who brought about the liberation of the West. The fact remains that neither Humanism nor The Renaissance was the product of Islam; when Gutenberg invented the printing press, books were prohibited from being printed or imported into the world of Islam."

Michael was in one of his moods. Umberto understood and agreed with him at the same time. "Umberto, how can anyone educate people that are oppressed, people that are subjugated? Shouldn't our goals have proprieties? It seems to me that we should first free the oppressed from subjugation, and, secondly, educate them. Please tell Malala, if you can!"

They even discussed the various types of dictators—this one of significance to Michael, who became excited when the likes of Stalin and Hitler came up. In their discussions, however, Michael never let on about his secret dream to eliminate these kinds of individuals from the face of the earth. And Michael did not know that, by being friendly with Umberto, a descendent of the Moors who had dominated Southern Italy for centuries, because at one time his father professed—secretly—the religion of Islam, that he had become a target of recent Caliphate leaders.

Aside from their personal and private encounters, they did not do much in public. That is, they did not frequent public places, nor, for that matter, go to church together. Instead, Michael enjoyed talking with Fafa about her two boys—the older almost seven and the younger about five. Often, Michael played with them on the deck. From the first time Michael shared a few *Baci* (kisses made of chocolate and hazel nuts) with them, they always expected Michael to bring more. It became evident that Michael enjoyed playing with them.

"By the way," Umberto asked of Michael, "Who was that woman? You two seem to make a great couple. Is she someone new in your life? And, why didn't you tell me about her?"

"That was an unexpected date. She is the daughter of my boss. Literally, she has appeared from nowhere. I never knew that Professor Villa was married let alone with a smashing-looking daughter."

"And what a hell of a dancer," Umberto added. "Well, did you get any place…?"

Michael quickly interrupted. "She wants to go to the top of

Vesuvius, and to walk some of the paths up there. I said yes. But I am not sure about the whole thing. I know the topography of Vesuvius from a cartographer point of view, not from a tourist point of view."

The two were sitting on the patio furniture, just talking, when Fafa with the two children arrived.

"Hi, Michael, how are you," she greeted with a warm smile.

"I am fine, thank you... Hey, kids, come on over. I want a hug."

The two boys rushed to Michael, both hugging him at the same time.

"Umberto, you haven't offered your friend a drink. What kind of a host are you? Michael, may I get you a cold beer?"

"Yes, Fafa. Thanks."

It was late afternoon, and the air was just perfect. She went in and returned with two *Peroni Nastro Azzurro* beers to the delight of the two men. She then turned to the children playing to one side. "Come on, kids, let's go inside. We need to prepare supper."

"I don't know what I would do without them. I am so blessed to have had Fafa bestowed upon me—yes, I mean just that, and the two boys. I don't know what I would do without them," he repeated.

"I don't have any children; so I don't know. But they were conceived. Were you aware of the potential outcome, or was it just the sex that dominated your actions?"

"How can one tell?" Umberto answered shrugging his shoulders. Sex must have driven us together. In no time, however, love must have taken over. Michael, ultimately, it is love, because we are aware of what we are doing, and of the consequences of our actions. Reproducing ourselves! What a miracle? How two individuals come together? Think about it!

We should all aspire to it; that is the love emanating from it."

To a certain point, Michael was flabbergasted. He had never heard any man talk this way about love.

After having finished his beer, Michael bid his friend good evening, and walked to his apartment. Giulietta had already prepared supper. She was just waiting for the brothers to arrive.

After having had another great dinner, the two brothers moved to the deck. Sitting on chairs by the table, they sipped on their *Espresso lungo* (twice the amount of water) with distinct pleasure.

"What did you do at church today? Anything of interest?"

"Yes, Michael, an amazing thing happened down at the parking lot," he answered, while adding a bit of *Sanbuca* to his coffee. "This car was stopped. The wife, somewhat frantic, got out of the front seat. Rushed around the back, and opened the color to a screeching baby. She immediately sat on the seat and pulled her blouse up. Then she picked up the baby whose shrills were louder than ever and placed the baby on her breast. In no time, the crying diminished, replaced by a series of moans, until I heard nothing more. The husband got out of the car. After making sure that everyone was well, he got behind the wheel and drove off."

"Except that she may have taken her blouse off, what was the big deal?" Michael asked.

"No big deal in anything!" His brother retorted. "First, the human concern of the mother and the father; secondly, the phenomenon of the human voice…"

"Phenomenon! We all cried…"

"And many of us still do. But that's not what I am talking about. As babies we just make noises; then we make sounds. Then we begin to attach meaning to the sounds. In a way, we go from darkness to light, from noise to sound, to meaning…"

"I still don't know what you are getting at. I'm sorry."

"I just thought that the scene in the parking lot could be the genesis for a choral symphony to be as background to a Sunday Mass, wherein the priest says the Mass and the worshippers sing the lyrics as directed by the *Maestro d'orchestra*."

"So, the idea is to begin with noise and slowly and gradually bring instruments and human voices, singly or in groups, at one level or another, reaching various *crescendo* with *sotto voce*, until the climax wherein every voice, every instrument and every drum beat and cymbal clash together to a perfect and loud end. Am I reading your mind?" Michael asked incredulous of what he had just made up.

"Yes, Michael. Thanks... So, Michael, you've made me understand you're dating someone from the States."

"Yes, I mentioned it in passing. Jody—she's the daughter of Professor Villa. I thought I told you. Now I remember, I told Umberto instead. Anyway, she's never been on Vesuvius. When I described the installations I have recommended for the project, she asked me if I could take her along. I said yes. What else could I say? I am surveying part of the crater this Friday, and I'll be picking her up late morning. I hope she can handle the trails; they're pretty rugged."

"Be sure to carry backpacks."

Having come to a stop in the highest parking lot on the south side of the crater, Michael parked the car closest to the main path. On stepping out, Jody unexpectedly shook her head.

"What's the matter?" Michael asked as he was passing his arm through the straps of his pack.

"What is that odor? I never smelled anything like this."

With back packs securely tied—hers the heavier of the two packs, Michael took the lead with Jody behind. "This is the *ginestra*, the broom flower, especially important in this region.

You see, with its explosion, Vesuvius was to have destroyed everything, including all life forms. The crater, with its stark remnants of bleakness, continues to be a reminder of that destruction—as though death was to reign. But, as we get closer to the top, we will see this bush flower growing there where there is only death. So, this vulnerable flower represents two challenges: gentle as it is, it is defying brute force into eternity; its perfume, as odorous as it is, replaces the stench of the deadly gas that keeps on bellowing from its throat."

"Oh yes. The 'throat'," she repeated inaudibly. "Your explanation is so beautiful. Did you just make this up?"

"No. Every Italian boy and girl in middle school knows Giacomo Leopardi, the poet adhering to a pessimistic way of life; he wrote the *Ginestra*—the broom flower. It seems to me that he showed optimism over pessimism by describing a flower blooming in full life at the edge of the crater in standing in un-assuming defiance. The flower is not collapsing; the volcano is."

"I have to read him…"

"You should. But, remember one thing: as a man, he was not that good-looking, and he never had a girl friend—nowhere nearly as beautiful as you. And, the only caress he may have received from a woman must have been from his mother. Yes, it seems to me, he was always in love, yearned to be loved but never loved. Yet, he truly appreciated those individuals lucky enough to be in love—especially when love was consummated.

As they walked the several paths meandering to the top, Jody asked all kinds of questions, showing receptivity for his knowledge as never before. They walked for about two hours before stopping for a break by a quick food stand. On ordering one *aranciata* each, they sat down on a bench with a wide panorama unfolding before their eyes. Jody had never seen anything like that before.

"I am indebted to you, Michael. I never thought this site ever existed. Nature can be very cruel…"

"I don't want to go there, only to observe that the earth itself continues on its path without awareness of our emotions, or, for that matter, of God, or for that matter, of science, or of numbers, or poetry, of love! These are man-made things belonging to the world of man. How or why we love leaves no awareness in nature; how we live and die, likewise, leaves no trace on nature—only on us: on you and me."

"I never thought about these things."

"Have you ever loved someone and loved by that person at the same time?"

"Would not they be our mothers or fathers?"

"I know you know what I mean."

Pursuing that train of thought created a slightly somber mood which was not what Michael had planned to talk about. He felt something special about Jody, and wanted to be sure that his feeling was authentic. More important, he wanted to be sure that her feelings toward him were as authentic.

"Jody, we have to go to two places: there by the crater at the top of the very edge where other flowers are blooming, and then, if you wish—because that is the basic reason why we're here—for you to see my prototype. Are you in agreement?"

"Yes, of course…" Her cell phone rang. Pulling her hand-bag from her backpack, she looked at the screen: "coordinates". With the phone resting on her bracelet, she pressed a couple of buttons, and placed the phone back in the bag. As she was putting the bag into the backpack, she said in passing: "That was my mother; I will call her later.

Unbeknown to Michael, by pressing a specific key on the keyboard, she automatically revealed the coordinates of her whereabouts. Michael thought her placing the unit on the bracelet was just an awkward gesture on her part.

"Sorry for the interruption. Where do you want to take me first?"

From the very top of Vesuvius, they looked directly into the wide caldera. Rock slides from the upper walls filled the circle with no fixed order. Evidence of destruction was visibly pervasive. Jody couldn't quite come to grips with what was in view. Yet, if she felt an ounce of consolation was the presence of that yellow flower blooming around the more precarious edges. Michael could not help commenting on the sight in front of them.

"Do you see, Jody, when it comes to life, we should understand certain basic things; for instance, we are told that there may be life on the moon, or elsewhere on other planets or other bodies within a single universe or in an infinite number of universes. What they mean is that there may be life forms there equal or similar to those on the earth: animals, fish, trees, and worms—on and on and on. This kind of reporting especially from scientific communities around the world that there may be life out there similar to ours makes no sense. Life forms—your body and mine, are the result of certain chemical conditions that came together in the past, which resulted in generating a specific self-reproducing biological form, with a specific DNA as its basis, and accordingly evolves to completion at the time of its death—as that specific, non-interchangeable form only, which is never duplicated in nature. For as long as the specific DNA exists, those forms will exist. Once the DNA dies, the creatures—singly and collectively also die…"

"Michael, darling, we're looking at the broom flower. I love its smell. Get a few petals and rub them on my breast. This I can understand, and might well like it."

Michael got the hint: he was talking too much. He walked

towards the yellow flower, clipped a few blossoms, and returned to Jody. "These are for you," he said. "Here, let me put this one in your hair. You're more beautiful than any flower," he added in a low, serious voice. He placed his mouth on hers. Feeling his tenderness, she prolonged the kiss until she heard a grunt. Two other couples were looking with approval laughter.

"One other piece of trivia: do you mind?"

"Please go ahead." Jody got to understand how much Michael liked to delve into the significance of things.

"Being you are staying at Castellammare di Stabbia," he commented with special emphasis on pronouncing the port city, "few people know that the popular Neapolitan song, *Funiculì, Funiculà* was first sung to the public at Castellammare di Stabbia. You know, every famous tenor, from Caruso, to Gigli, to Pavarotti and Bocelli—they all sing it. The song is part of a universal repertoire..."

"You're not going to give a lecture on music?"

"No," he answered with a patient smile. He also knew he had to have patience with himself. "No, I just thought you might like to observe that the song—like the flower in your hair, is a happy and cheerful song, one that allows great singers to show their virtuosity: All done on behalf of joy and in defiance of death. We're standing on the caldera of destruction. I look at you, and you embody that song."

"Michael, whatever I may have thought of you was wrong. You are a poet," she confirmed. Subconsciously, she hadn't yet discovered the man.

Finally, after an exhaustive walk, they reached the transmission site, full of signs: "OFF LIMITS Transgressors will be Prosecuted". Jody was impressed, and she made it a point of her admiration.

The unit was built on a huge solid boulder connected deep underground to the rocky wall of the volcano. The idea was to be sure the Instrument rested on a direct connection, to better record any tremor, however small; and to transmit the information to the central station. The construction was rather simple: a drilled twelve-inch round hole eight feet into the rock, fitted with a sixteen-foot heavy duty two-inch thick plastic pipe, it contained hermetically concealed electronic transmitting instruments connected to an FM directional antenna. Within the tube, there hung another suspended pipe rigged with specially designed wiring, hanging through a mechanism that kept it from touching the inner wall of the outer pipe (except when there were tremors). In that case, the wired base of the inner pipe would make contact with the wires of the outer tube. The instruments would then measure the frequency and strength of each contact and transmit the information foreword according to protocol.

"This is very interesting. I have a question. In transmitting the data, can you add to that data?"

"What do you mean *add*? What can you add, other than the information recording as a result of the vibrations from the single or continuous tremors?"

"I know, Michael, I don't understand much about these things; but, please, don't be impatient. In college, I took basic science courses, and was impressed by Nicola Tesla, from Serbia. He seemed to be more of a mystic than a scientist. But he always tried to piggy-back things and never succeeded..."

"Are you driving a *Tesla*?"

"I am not. Please be serious. He built huge antenna networks through which he tried to transfer energy from one point to another; it never worked. Then he was against building skyscrapers and bridges made of steel because steel could be inducted to the point that it would disintegrate—turn to rust.

He applied electric currents to a few bridges, if I recall, but the steel in those bridges never corroded to cause them to collapse…"

"So, do you drive a Tesla?" Michael continued—a slight smile with obvious sarcasm.

"No, I drive a *Fusion:* No, no, an *Alfa Romeo* in Italy. Need I say more?" she asked mimicking his smile and sarcasm. Having understood one another, they embraced with a brief and open kiss.

"So, now, can you answer my question?"

"About cars?"

"No, about these transmissions: Has anyone done what Tesla was unable to do?"

"All kinds of people have made experiments, but without results— much as Tesla. But the question you are trying to ask is this: What intelligence, meaning information, can one piggyback onto radio energy signal and transfer that information from one location to another? Is that right?"

"Yes, for instance, can one transfer such things as chemical or biological—not information such as *informatica* or formulas—but microbes themselves. Is it possible? Has it ever been done to your knowledge? There was talk about something similar to that had taken place in Boston some years ago."

"No, Jody, no: Not to my knowledge. And I would know. I have been conducting experiments for many years on radiological propagation—different applications—to see what could be transmitted onto a given signal or frequency or on series of signals or frequencies. I was not successful."

"How boring!"

"Me, the experimenter, or, me the blather?"

"Not you. I just do not understand these things. Please forgive me. By the way, are we stopping for supper somewhere? I am dying for *cozze* clams," if you know what I mean.

"I'll never forget that kiss!"

"There is a place less than half hour from here. No fish, however. Actually, the restaurant is famous for not having a menu. It serves whatever its chef prepares. It can be *capretto* baby goat, *braciole* rolled meat, *stufato* stew, *agnello* lamb, and many more. The problem is: they don't ask you what you wish to eat. You have to pay for what they serve you to eat.

"Do you want to take a chance?"

"What if they give you poison?"

"No one's been reported dead."

"How do you know the food is good?"

"The last time, I waited in line half hour."

"You surprised me the first time. Let's go for it!"

As predicted, there was a line at the restaurant. Michael opened the trunk of the car to put the two back packs on the seat out of the view of potential thieves.

"What do you have in this thing—lead?" he said, on pick-ing it up.

"Now I know you're not married."

"What does that mean?"

"If you were married, you would know, from the amount of stuff in the bathroom for the use of the wife only—that the wife always needs much more than the husband. Thus, mine is fuller than yours."

"Jody, I'm not complaining."

"I know; I'm just having a little fun with you."

They sat in a corner outside under this very large *pergola* canopy of tree branches thick with leaves, sipping on the *aperitivo*. Jody wondered about the meal.

"Do you know what is being served?"

"No. But from the looks of those leaving the restaurant, I would conclude the food must be good. If you wish, we can ask any of these or the waiter himself. Do you want me to ask, or would you dare an unknown future."

"What's so unknown about the future?"

"I think about the kind of food. I know that whatever, its quality is going to be good. When it comes to you, I have no such concern..."

"I love you, Michael."

He hadn't heard those words in decades. Now more than ever, he felt re-assurance and comfort. Had he finally found the woman of his life, perhaps even the mother of his children? Typical of Michael, he kept his thoughts to himself when it came to his emotions.

The waiter finally called them to their table, once again in a more private and less noisy part of the dining room. Michael pulled the chair out, and Jody sat comfortably down with a smile projected at him.

"What would you like for drinks?" The young man asked. "Drinks are *à la carte*."

"Do you have *Lacryma Christi*?" Michael asked.

"Our most famous wine," the waiter answered with enthusiasm. "Shall I bring a bottle?"

The two sat at the table as though they were on a honeymoon. Nothing, either said, had any references to their past personal lives or to commitments they may have had in relation to their work demands. They sipped on the white wine as though they knew the evening was not going to end there, with no thought to the loaded Beretta in her special handbag or to the special cell phone that monitored her every move. On the other hand, Michael had exposed himself to the international scene of spies and terrorists—men and women who believed he had discovered the means of piggy-backing biological toxins and bacteria to radio transmissions. Both friendly governments and those at war wanted to secure those means for themselves.

Unwittingly, because of their intimate relationship, both had become potential targets with potential fatal results. No thoughts either to the possibility of pre-emptive military action that could bring major catastrophe to the earth itself. Neither could imagine these outcomes.

"Here's your main course," the waiter said politely. "I am sure you will like it. It really is our very best."

"I recognize the ingredients," Jody volunteered: "Chicken, I think, vinegar peppers, potatoes, all fried in simmering vegetable oil for about 15 minutes, with a good cup of white wine blended and stirred into the content. Slow cooked for another twenty minutes, it was then served with an *insalata mista*—vegetables from local growers. The bread, in the form of a *panella* was place on one side of the table. Jody was tempted to ask for butter, but did not.

Having enjoyed the main course, in turn each expressed complete approval, on everything, from the wine, to the main meal, to the service. Everything was perfect. Next was the dessert: *zabaglione* with house *prosecco*.

"Michael, do I have time to go to the lady's room?"

"Of course, darling." He hadn't pronounced that word in such a long time, and Jody was particularly pleased to hear it.

In the stall, she quickly placed the phone on the bracelet. With one finger, she printed:

not this one

The screen gone dark, she replaced the phone into the bag and quickly returned to the table.

"Just in time," she commented on seeing the waiter with the dessert.

The *zabaglione* was magnificent, and the cold *prosecco* couldn't have been a better companion.

Both were very happy. Having paid *il conto* the bill, Michael asked Jody: "Would you like for me to take you home?

"Why, did you have something else in mind?

"There is a small hotel down the main highway with balconies onto the Bay. We could stop there."

"Yes, Michael, I would love it."

Michael was finishing his shower. "Where are you?" Jody asked. She was in bed with a sheet covering her body. On seeing him come, she lifted the sheet. Michael became momentarily mesmerized. Probably due to the present moment, so charged with emotional energy, he became incredulous. The most beautiful woman in the whole world was right there, her arm stretched to receive him.

He bent foreword, his face on her belly; he brought his mouth to her breast, and quickly to her mouth. Her legs open, he fell between them, pressing into her.

"A bit more gently, Michael," she said as she pulled him further into her. "Yes, like this," she said in an almost inaudible voice. She continued as he settled in. "Yes, just like this…"

Feeling that he may have been overpowering, for, he knew the consequences of coitus whether as a result of love or sex, he began to pull way.

"What are you doing, Michael?"

"I just want to make sure this is what you want. Babies usually become the byproducts of these things."

"Yes, Michael, I want a child—your child. Yes, come deeper, and stay longer: the longer we stay this way, the greater chances of quintuplets. Yes…"

Michael placed his mouth on hers to keep her from talking. He was already beyond the point of no return. Nothing could stop him now. Her receptivity was such that she herself could not stop. Moaning, she spoke again: "Gently, gently, let these moments fill with eternity…don't come yet, Michael, Michael!" she almost screamed.

As he was trying to catch his breath, he brought his face on top of her and Jody began to kiss him once again. "Michael, I love you so much!"

"I love you, Jody. Please don't move. Let's stay this way a while longer.

His body fully relaxed in her arms, she drew her fingers in his hair. Before she knew it, Michael had fallen asleep. A small smile of acceptance, she drew the sheet over his body and waited. Several minute later, he awoke.

"Did I just come back from Paradise?"

"Yes, we were both there."

General Miller had called a meeting of the Special Committee members already in session. The report from Jody—wherein she disclaimed the potential in connecting Michael to enriched radio-propagated transmission—that Michael should no longer be the target—came as an astonishing surprise to those in session. Several immediately began to suggest a romantic involvement gone wrong. A few even intimated the possibility of treason. One requested an update of what supposedly happened to the other woman who died unexpectedly from wounds connected to a car accident.

"According to a final report, Michael had nothing to do with. The incident had nothing to do with anything," the General reiterated. That case is closed.

"So, I need to put that to rest. Did the husband try to kill his wife so he could take up with the lover—the wife of his friend? It doesn't matter any more.

"As I said, there is no connection. Let's move on.

"We cannot cast aspersions on Jody. We have to keep on assuming that she is a bona fide employee of our government, that her oath to her office is valid, and that she will continue to accomplish her mission…"

"Which is?" asked the CIA Director.

"To be sure, one way or another, that Michael really has no role in this new potential weapon system."

"What are the implications for her?" asked the Director of National Intelligence.

"We have to assume that, just as America has national defense interests, other nations—friendly and otherwise, are engaged in getting a handle on this. Whoever captures this system would gain an enormous amount of power. It would make a big difference on the world scene: tantamount to having been the first in creating the atom bomb."

"Assuming everything is on the up and up: is she in harm's way?"

"Assuming she is doing everything by the book, and that this man has been wrongly targeted: both are in harm's way."

"With that," General Miller added, "we need to deploy appropriate countermeasure systems to protect her. Please come up with your department countermeasure options. The meeting is adjourned."

Jody was home talking with her mother about Michael; but, she gave no details about her feelings toward Michael. Although she felt the urge to tell her she was in love, she resisted sharing that important aspect of her happiness. Down deep, she had found the love of her life, the father of her children. As soon as possible, she would render her letter of resignation, resolute that before that date, she would fulfill all that was required of her. She was fond of General Miller, whom she admired very much, and would not disappoint him.

Nevertheless, she thought about her behavior and considered the possibility of having acted as a juvenile.

With that, she became more resolute and sure about her feelings toward Michael, and she was sure there was reciprocity from Michael as well.

In her bedroom, she opened the phone pursuant to a priority signal:

Continue
photos, back

The screen turned black.

The message was clear to her: She had to continue with her investigation no matter what. She had to take photos of installations, especially the antenna field above Amalfi. She had to be circumspect in her actions and behavior, being sure to have the means to protect herself. The implications: counter terrorists may want to abduct her when she least expected it. In addition, she had to be more than vigilant, now that the man whom she was pursuing was no longer her target but her lover.

She was sure of her feelings and of her emotions. She considered the possibility of having gone through a juvenile period and concluded that what happened with Michael was legitimate, that she was truly in love for the first time in her life. She was going to give meaning to her feelings at all cost, except, of course, her commitment to her mission.

Convenience couldn't have come at a better time. Michael, with the approval of his brother, invited the following: Jody, her mother, Umberto, and Fafa for the Saturday evening dinner. The occasion was not to celebrate, or to announce, or to share his new relationship with Jody, but to introduce Jody and her mother to his neighbors. Michael, however, did not do any of the cooking. He asked Giulietta, together with her husband, to handle it all. He did manage to bring together a list of good wines, however.

There were two surprises that came during the wonderful dinner: Fafa's ancestry was Ethiopian-Italian. As a young woman, she was a practicing Muslim. Umberto was a collector of rare books, having often made inquiries to Houghton Library at Harvard.

"My, o my!" Professor Villa exclaimed. "Two things: my name is Jean. Please, and, no *Professor* stuff. Fafa, what an unusually beautiful name; I like it very much. Did you ever wear headgear? Either the *Hijab* or the *Burka*. No, the reason I am asking is this: your beauty would have been wasted in a world wherein beauty is appreciated and not denied. Your face and hair—Umberto, you are a lucky man to have such a beautiful wife."

While her mother was dominating the conversation, Jody and Michael sat next to each other without much regard with one another. Unless one were privy to their inner emotions, no one would have gathered, from their demeanor, that they were lovers—passionate lovers. Likewise, aside from having blessed by the Lord in the prayer before the meal, Michael's brother— the Deacon, said hardly anything.

"What kinds of rare books do you have, Umberto?" Professor Villa asked, in genuine interest.

This being the first time anyone had shown any interest in him other than as a restaurateur, Umberto's eyes lit up. "I have a Boccaccio's edition of Dante's *Divine Comedy*. It is the edition in which Boccaccio called the epic poem "Divine". I also have a 1559 Venetian edition of Petrarch' *Canzoniere*. In addition, I have an early edition of *Don Quixote...*"

"The man who could not distinguish between the woman who served as an inn-keeper and Dulcinea," added the Deacon.

"Appropriately so," added Umberto. "Lastly, among others, I now have three illuminated editions of the Quran."

"Why do you say three?" Julie asked.

"Because, I bought the third book a couple of weeks ago—very un-expected."

"What do you mean, 'unexpected'?" Julie interrupted loudly.

"This guy walked into the restaurant, sought me out, it seems, and asked me to look at his book. You should have seen this guy: about 220 pounds, muscular, tall, huge wide back, with four or five thin sausage-like layered muscles from one side to the other of his neck. 'How much?' I asked, without further consideration. '500' he said. I pulled 500 Euros. 'Thanks', he said. 'I'll see you soon,' and took off."

"That's weird," Michael added. "Had you known this guy before?"

"No."

"Did he know you?"

"I don't think so."

"That's really weird," interjected Jody. She was openly disturbed by the incident. "Was he Neapolitan?"

"Hard to say."

"Regardless… Can I take a look at the book?" asked Julie.

"Sure. We're having dessert at my house; I'd love to show them to you."

Sitting at the table on Umberto's deck, they waited for the dessert to be brought out, while each sipped on cold *prosecco*. Michael, seating at the chair near the ramp to the house, on seeing the railing still needing repair, he asked Umberto what was the status.

"There, see the rods? The guy was supposed to come this week; but, nothing doing. He'll call me as soon as he can come."

As assessed by Michael, that part of the rail represented a potential hazard, to any adult who might be falling, and especially to the children who might get their heads trapped in the openings. "Umberto, please get back to him and fix the problem."

In no time, Giulietta brought out the dessert: a multi-layered *mille foglie*—cake of a thousand leaves, with strawber-ries.

"What a beautiful cake," Julie remarked. I can't wait to taste it."

"I'll have a large piece," the Deacon interjected to show his approval.

After several minutes of more drinking and eating, Profes-sor Villa asked Umberto if he would show her the books.

"By all, means, Professor Villa…"

"Never mind the Professor Villa stuff. Remember, I am Julie…"

In Italian, and this is still prominently practiced, the pro-nouns *lei* and *tu* (*thou?* and *you*) are used to address individuals according to their social status. Therefore, Umberto felt uneasy addressing the Professor by her first name—the equal of *tu*. If they had been on an equal social footing, each would have used the *tu* form. In this situation, to show courtesy, custom demanded the formal third person singular form. The professor, to show equal social footing, if not humility, chose to be considered no higher or lower than Umberto.

"By all means," Umberto obliged. He walked to her seat. Extending his hand, he pulled her up. "We'll be right back… Jody, would you like to come. The books are really worth-while. You will enjoy them."

Umberto was honored to show a Harvard professor his small but significant books. Secretly, he also sought reassur-ance from a professional that he was not off course.

The first book he took from his shelf was a 1555 edition of the *Divina Commedia*, published in Venice, and bearing the word *Divine* on the cover as given by Boccaccio.

"I can't get over this," Jean exclaimed. "May I?" She asked. "I will handle it with care... I know you have three copies of the *Quran*. Do you know that the first edition of the *Quran* was published in Venice and that it had lots of problems?

"What's interesting, Umberto, is that Mohammed died in 642 AD; Dante died in 1321. Gutenberg, the inventor of moving type died in 1468. The only books available during that time were in the form of illuminated manuscripts. How Dante was able to get information on the *Quran* is beyond belief, because, you may know, Dante placed Muhammad in Canto 27 of the Inferno; it is the abode of individuals responsible for schisms, such as Muhammad's son-in-law who caused the emergence of the Sunni and Shiites. The Muslim world has never been the same since then. The question: how did Dante predict in the 11th Century that which has become evident in our present century?"

"How do you know these things? Your field is archeology," observed Michael.

"We delve into history all the time. Besides, today, every person has a library at his finger tips if he or she has a computer, or a smart phone, or pad. I dare to add, however, that I have never seen such an important—though small collection of great masterpieces. Umberto, you made my day!"

With that, they joined the rest outside, and continued with their drinks and dessert.

Don Paolo, who had said hardly a word, asked if he could speak. "In the next several months, we'll be rehearsing for a High Mass, which we are composing. I am hoping all of you will come to the first rehearsal next Sunday. I would love to receive your input, just as you did today with Umberto... By the way, Umberto, I want to congratulate you. One of these mornings, I hope you will show them to me as well. I studied the *Divine Comedy*, and admire Dante as a poet. I also admire him as a judge. He placed so many people on the proper slopes of the 100 cantos without making an error in judging the culpability or innocence of each individual. It's amazing! Who thought his renderings would stand the test of time."

"I'll be happy to come to Mass on Sunday," Jody quickly volunteered. "Michael, would that be all right with you? Could you pick us up?"

"Sure, sure."

"This could be another adventure for me," the Professor added without second thought. "You know, Don Paolo, I always wondered about the remains of St. Andrews. By the way, he is one of my favorite saints. The others are St. Francis, St. Anthony, and Padre Pio, in that order."

"Very good," answered Don Paolo.

"How about you, Fafa, will you be coming? I am sure the kids will enjoy themselves."

"I wouldn't miss it for the world," she answered.

In his office, at the Port, Captain Fracastoro had received two confidential reports. One dealt with the City of Naples with its plans to host a convention on how to better integrate into society people having different lifestyle and sexuality. In some way, Umberto Saracino would be involved because of the prominence of his restaurant. The second was a head's up on potential infiltration of the port itself. This meant his crew had to be on alert of the vessels coming in and those leaving. A few days earlier, he had also received word that a gam of sharks had appeared in the waters surrounding the volcanic islands of Procida and Ischia.

He was concerned that the sharks might be a threat to bathers on beaches and on boats. He also knew that people, from time to time, had gone beyond Procida in rented boats. On occasions, bathers dove or jumped into the warm waters in the nude: more as a result of impromptu pranks than odd behavior.

It seemed that a school of fish had made its way toward the island, their visible direction made possible by flocks of pelicans diving into the water.

Having received reports that private boats full of adventurous bathers were sailing in the same waters, Captain Fracastoro immediately sent a fleet of high-speed hydrofoils to that location, and none too soon. The sharks, which were feverishly feeding off the fish, created some frenzy among the pelicans diving from above. Unfortunately, two swimmers had gone a bit far with their little boats. On capsizing, the sharks made mince meat of them, with scraps remaining for the birds. Luckily, Fracastoro's diligence backed by action saved the day in that some 50 swimmers could have become fatalities.

To recognize the Captain, his usual group called for the typical dinner at Umberto's restaurant. The surprise: the captain was bringing a date. The condition: everyone was to be on his best behavior, meaning: no references to sex, no vulgarities, etc. After all, an American professor from—of all places—Harvard—was there, and they should show respect.

The last to arrive was the Captain. His right hand guiding Julie to the table, he directed her foreword with gentle pushes to the left or right. On coming close to the table, his friends all looked up at the same time, their mouths wide open, their eyes full of expressions of disbelief and mischievousness at the same time. Vico, of course, was the first to stand.

"Welcome, Mrs?..."

"My name is Julie, very glad to meet you. You all must be friends of Domenico."

"Yes, these are all friends of mine," the Captain intervened. With expressions of patience on his face, he quickly introduced her to the group. Vico, however, did not sit down.

"I must say, our friend, Domenico—excuse me, Captain—did very well. He's never brought, to our reunions here, anyone as beautiful as you. Did he tell you, you are beautiful?"

"O.K.; lay off. We're here to have a good time," the Captain said.

"But, Domenico, could there have been women, just as 'handsome' as I—that you could have brought here, among such prestigious and handsome group of elderly..."

"Decrepit gentlemen..." interrupted one with mocking laughter...

"Gentlemen..." Julie picked up, a great smile on her face. She had passed the test, and she knew it. Before long, everyone was having a ball, even Domenico in his own quiet way.

The dining room was packed. Convention members were everywhere, and were more than visible and distinguishable by either their outrageous costumes or by high fashion *haute couture*.

"Who else but they can afford such extravagant clothes!" exclaimed interrogatively the oldest of Domenico's friends.

"They certainly are not paying for child support," interrupted another.

"Now, listen here..." Domenico tried to interrupt...

"They have an additional benefit," interjected another.

"What's that?" asked Vico, in a full of voice loud enough to be heard.

"They don't spend money of contraceptives," responded another," in great fanfare.

"One thing's for sure: what and how they do is their business," offered another.

"I'll drink to that," Julie added as she lifted her glass. On drinking, she forced a conclusion to that single aspect of the conversation. Domenico wondered what was next.

He came to realize that he liked Julie. Actually, he may have fallen in love with her: At his age? The pensive look on his face, despite the festivities within his group and the obvious celebrations in the restaurant, betrayed his state of mind.

"What's the matter?" asked Julie, pulling her face to his ear.

"I think I'm in love with you."

"Couldn't have found a better place myself for this declaration…"

"Sorry, Julie: I mean it."

She brought her mouth close to his, and kissed him gently, but not without commentary from each of his friends.

"Enough of this…"

Under different circumstances, they would not have given in. Unexplainably, Vico came to the aid of his comrade. "Do you know…" he began to ask.

At that point, each brought his hand to the ear gesturing he wasn't loud enough. That was the signal they were going to sit back, enjoy their meals with wine, and watch the orchestra play Neapolitan music.

"If only Michael and Jody were here now," Vico commented.

"Jody!… My Jody?" Julie repeated incredulously.

"What's wrong with that?" Vico asked.

"Yes, Julie, Jody and Michael were here. They danced the likes of no one I know on this earth. I hope they will have a complete, joyful, wonderful and happy relationship. Here's to them, Domenico concluded raising his glass.

"Here's to us," Julie said, raising her glass and looking softly into his eyes.

Because he was the chairman of the special committee, Captain

Fracastoro continued to receive reports from various committee members as well as reports from other agencies. Among the more specific concerns was the status report on the huge mountain-side rock protrusion due north of Monte Carlo, but sloping down toward the city of Monaco. He wanted to know whether Michael's system had been installed on that rock and whether the system was operational. Nothing had been made public on any and all of Michael's installations, including that on Vesuvius. Captain Fracastoro was more than pleased to know that their efforts had paid off, notwithstanding his new relation with Julie. Nevertheless, despite the fact that Michael was romantically involved with Jody, he had more than a legal and moral responsibility to be sure that nothing of the personal stuff interfered with the committee's mission. What he did not know, including Julie, was that Jody was a secret agent—not just a research student-scholar working on personnel relation-ships and motives for employment for a potential research paper.

Now that the Captain had come into her mother's life much as Michael had come into hers, Jody asked herself whether she was up to the challenge. "I have to be," she confirmed to herself.

The following message appeared and quickly disappeared from her screen:

vigilance.

It was a beautiful Sunday morning, just right for a High Mass at the Cathedral. Michael was proud that his brother was on the Altar with the Bishop saying Mass.

Captain Fracastoro went to Michael's house where Julie and Jody were already waiting. Umberto, Fafa and their two boys were also ready to go to church. Once assembled, they walked to the square and up the massive stairs to the main entrance. Inside, the ceiling shot upward as though it was making contact with the stars. The main floor was completely jammed, and each lateral altar was filled with people involved in special activities of their own. Michael noticed the placement of the orchestra and choruses, also noting the placement of other musicians scattered about.

"We're in for a treat," Michael promised his group. "This is the first live rehearsal of the new work-in-progress. If it goes beyond the first movement I will be surprised. My prediction is that it will be more challenging than Verdi's *Requiem*."

"Have you seen the text," Julie asked. "I would love to see it. By the way, I meant to ask: What is the difference between a Requiem and a High Mass. Which one is it?"

"I have a good idea what's it about; but, the text is evolving still. I cannot tell you because it hasn't been determined."

Meanwhile, Fafa was busy with the boys; they were interested in the images of men in armor with swords scattered around the walls.

"We'll come back another time when the church is empty," interjected Umberto impatiently.

The small bells ringing, the Bishop brought his followers to stand. After his initial words of solidarity and faith, he asked for the faithful to participate in singing the specified parts assigned to them. With silence achieved, except for scattered screeches of babies and little children—which was the genesis of the mass in the first place, the drummers began beating one at the time at first, and then joined by others as the noise increased to a high pitch.

"So much noise," Fafa commented, bringing her hands over her ears.

"That's the idea, Fafa. First there was noise—literally. Then there was sound. Man turned noise into sound. We added meaning to sound. Through sound, man began to speak…"

"Silence, please!" shouted an old man intent on hearing the music.

"Sorry," Michael replied, and spoke no more.

The choirs, also spread in groups around the church, came in, their crescendos growing in magnitude as each person enunciated the prescribed lyrics. As it stood, by the end of the first movement, the music was more than astounding, considering that it was the first attempted rehearsal. Secretly, Michael was in his pride and joy because he was seeing his brother's concept translated into a work of art.

The Mass continued for about an hour—a bit too long for the boys. "Mamma, when can we go?" They knew that they would all stop at the local bar where they would be given their favorite donuts with a light *cappuccino*. The adults, of course, would have *espresso macchiato,* or, *corretto.*

"I'll have *Sambuca*," the Captain said to the waiter. "And you, *amore?"* he asked Julie, who said yes while lowering her head. It was the first time that Domenico had referred to her lovingly in public.

Jody, meanwhile, kept a slight distance from Michael. He knew that Michael was just being discreet.

"I don't understand why so much Anti-Semitism in the world while Muslim terrorists are targeting Christians, Sunni, Shia, Wahhabi, Jews and others at the same time," commented Umberto. He was reading the Quran and could not understand the rationale behind actions of so many Muslims. It was harder for him to understand so much in-action on the part of the "regular, everyday" followers of Islam: "Because, in the end," he reasoned, "havoc was incurred on specific targets and on their own brothers and sisters as well. The whole of the human race became the target. Like so many members in the *Jews for Jesus* movement," Umberto observed, "what these Muslims need is a similar movement for themselves…"

"That way, they would be in tune with Judaism in that so much in the Quran proceeds from biblical traditions…

"The other thing I do not understand, for the life of me, is this *trojanism* in broad daylight."

"What are you talking about, Umberto?"

"You know, it was the Greeks who successfully launched their Trojan horse. As a result, the Greeks conquered their enemy. Today, millions of mostly Muslim refugees are being welcomed into Europe and in America without any resistance of any kind by the local citizens. In fact, the western governments are facilitating the arrivals of these, supposed, refugees through all kinds of western subsidies. Yet, they are all bypassing empty refugee camps in their own lands. It seems to me, this is nothing more than a Trojan horse in broad daylight. This phenomenon is a plot to bring about the destruction of our way of life, from within. We know they are not being vetted.

"What is even stranger is this: before going into war with Iraq, the President received approval from his Congress and the UN. In pulling the American troops out of Iraq, was a similar protocol of approval followed? Yet, whereas the issue of refugees was negligent during that war, it has become a big issue some six years after America pulled its forces out of Iraq. I still do not understand why there were no refugees then, and so many refugee now."

For Jody, those observations were on target, except that she needed to find her way to the secret passages and tunnels connected to St. Andrews.

"Captain Fracastore, I would imagine the entire coastline of Italy is replete with tunnels, especially in the mountains that descend into the various seas," Jody commented, soliciting a response to an observation for which she already knew the answer.

"Of course, Jody, there are. Many go back to the time of Egypt, then the Greeks, then the Romans, then the Arabs, not to mention the Vikings, the Germans, the Spaniards, French, and most recently, the Germans. There may still be hidden artillery batteries with all kinds of guns, for both air and naval action. I know for a fact that Amalfi was a prime target."

"How do you know so much?" asked Julie, with a tinge of admiration.

"Michael, maybe your brother could give us a guide," Umberto suggested.

As there was no focus to their conversations, let alone on Sunday dinner, Fafa suggested they should all go to the local restaurant, up the street: *Il Tarî*. "Afterwards," she added, "We can stop by the Paper Museum. You know, it's the oldest active paper mill I know of."

At the restaurant, the attention of the adults fell on the two boys. Mom and Dad took a back seat, watching and enjoying the scene wherein their children were appreciated; they were of great importance. In any great civilization, children have always had center stage.

"I am having *spaghetti marinara*," the Captain said while looking directly into the boys' faces. "Do you know what my challenge is if I order *spaghetti*?"

The older answered with a smile on his face, while shaking his head from one side to the other.

"And, how about you?" the Captain asked the younger of the two? Receiving the same gesture, Fracastoro replied: "See what I am wearing? My white uniform. You're wearing white shirts. Our challenge is to eat *spaghetti* without getting any red sauce on our clothes."

No one laughed as much as the adults. Julie was exceptionally pleased to see *her* Captain being the center of attraction. Even Jody approved.

"I'll give the blessing," Don Paolo volunteered.

Immediately after everyone made the sign of the Cross, dinner was quickly served. All eyes, especially those of the boys, were on the Captain's chest. Having placed a large fork-full of dripping pasta into his mouth, he slowly sucked on the last strand, squirting the marinara sauce all over his uniform. The boys laughed hilariously, their own mouths filled with half-chewed pasta.

Having completed their dinner with sips of locally-produced *Limoncello*, the group leisurely walked to the Paper Mill and then in the lemon grove, full of Amalfi large, supple lemons famous throughout the world. When the group broke up, Captain Fracastoro took Michael to one side.

"I want you to know that your work is being cited. I am very happy for you. At first, I didn't know what to make of you. Congratulations."

Chapter 7
The Cathedral

As planned, Michael and Jody walked into the sacristy of St. Andrews. Don Paolo had asked Michael to go over inventories in the vault containing the reliquaries of various important individuals going back to the time of Jesus himself.

Michael was no scholar in this field; he claimed no scholarship in any field. By nature, he was always inquisitive about everything, to the point that he got into trouble because people assumed he knew when he didn't. And he was well aware of his weakness.

"What do you know about these things?" Jody asked.

"Only what I read in publications, that's all. And, by the way, I don't even remember 10% of anything."

"Michael, we need to go to the inner vault," his brother said.

Spreadsheets in hand, a special key for the main heavy door, he opened it with some difficulty, only to be in front of another door. It had no keyhole, only an electronic keyboard.

"Michael, Jody: please look the other way," Don Paolo asked.

Inside, there were all kinds of bones in respective boxes— their potential provenance clearly marked. At the end of one shelf there was another box of bones; but, without markings.

"Michael, please analyze these as best you can; and, give me your assessment, or, speculation, if any. I have to go back to my office. On leaving, just shut the doors behind you. They have automatic locks. I trust that you both will not divulge anything to anyone."

"Yes, Don Paolo," Jody answered with a nod.

There was a secret and tacit understanding that those

bones may have been those of Jesus.

During the Fourth Crusade, conducted mainly by the Condottiere of the Republic of Venice, its sailors and soldiers laid siege to the opulent city of Constantinople under Ottoman rule. The siege was completely successful in that the Venetians not only defeated the Ottoman forces, its naval forces brought about the complete destruction and subjugation of the people. Plundering of all type became the rule of the day. Churches were no exception.

Supposedly, this was the time when the remains of St. Andrew were confiscated and transported to Amalfi. Other reverential bones were also confiscated and brought to Amalfi; but these were never completely identified or categorized. Secretly, however, there was a belief, by very few people, whose identity has not been known, claiming that the bones belonged to Jesus. The following was their rationale:

(In the Deposition of Jesus, Joseph and Nicodemus received the body of Jesus.) They were the main two characters; Magdalene may have been another potential recipient. Jesus, together with two other men, died on the cross according to procedures prescribed by the Roman laws—not anyone or anything else.

"The question," Michael asked peremptorily, "why would the Romans give up the body of Jesus, specifically, and not of the others?"

"I have never heard this kind of stuff. What are you getting at?" Jody asked quizzically. "Are you challenging the Gospels?"

"No one in his right mind would do that. Belief in something is just that: belief! And science: it never proves anything other than to disprove it the following day. No, no: my interest is to learn what the Romans did. For instance, we know that the Romans, except for one time only—and that's never been very clear—released one body that had just died on the cross from being displayed for a long period of time after the successful crucifixion. All the others—we have to assume—by the thousands, were left standing on the cross until their bodies decomposed. The bodies—their bones were then gathered together and collected in certain areas—ossuaries"

"Why that procedure?"

"The Romans believed in deterrence. They wanted the people to see for themselves the value of obeying the law, especially thieves. That the Romans were ruthless execution-ers, there is no doubt in that. Jesus was not like the others, however; they were criminals. Jesus was a victim of circums-tances, as much the target of his own people as that of the Romans who would not allow any type of rebellion."

"Wait a second, Michael: Are there any actual records kept by the Romans on those proceedings? It seems as though there would be."

"Yes, Jody. The Romans kept very good records, and in great detail—ledgers and ledgers. Yet when it comes to the Prefect, Pontius Pilate, there are no official court records to speak of. The story of Jesus is not told by the Romans, who were in charge."

"So, what is your job, in this matter? This is somewhat scary. You're freaking me out."

"No, no, Jody: not to worry. Here, let's look at these bones. They do not look any different from all others. I cannot tell one from another," he commented nonchalantly, as he glanced at each.

"So, what is your conclusion?"

"Status quo: Come, let's go. We have better things to do."

He shut the lights. Just as his brother had ordered, the doors automatically shut as they left the heavily fortified reliquary. Out on the floor of the immense cathedral, they walked towards the central door. At the corner by the holy water font—a marble cherub, with its wings spread open, offered the holy water to the church goers. With one hand to one side, Michael extended the other toward the water basin; with the other, he grabbed Jody and pulled her into his arms, in a prolonged kiss that became more than passionate.

"We'll need double dipping of holy water to cool down," Michael said. Both smiled, made the sign of the cross, and walked outside.

From the top of the stairs, they could look across to the mountains to the east and north. The erratic walls were replete with tunnel entrances and un-attended battery sites. By the foot of the mountains, there were groves of lemon trees together with scattered grape vines. "You promised me you'd take me there," Jody reminded him—the memory of the kiss still present.

"May we go now? I know a few cozy places… Let me send a message to my brother first. I promised him I would."

While Jody analyzed the wide panorama—her eyes were mesmerized by a scene of transcending mountain ranges, landfill in full agriculture, leading down to the Tyrrhenian Sea waters below. Michael stood to one side inputting his message into his cell phone:

Looked at bones. Recommend analysis by professionals. Nail and rope marks visible. Spear marks also visible. Great hunch. Tonight with Jody.

"I can't get over how beautiful nature can be," Jody revealed to Michael as he brought his arm around her waist. "I may be too sentimental. But, I feel the embodiment of, "*She walks in beauty…*"

Sometime in the past, she had read Lord Byron's poem.

He, of course, wrote many poems about Italy. Subconsciously, though, Jody remembered the last two lines of that poem, and now, she was not sure why. Why she was remembering the two lines remained un-answerable:

> *A mind at peace with all below,*
> *A heart whose love is innocent*!

There was no doubt about her love being innocent and true; but was she at peace with herself? Did she have a premonition of impending splendor? Or was this a premonition of impending danger? She placed her hand tightly over his hand, and pressed both into her side. She walked off with him with optimism in her heart.

In absorbing her present state of emotions, she may have been like similar couples sharing the experience from the following similar lines:

> *Here they are; here they are,*
> *The God-made couple.*
> *He brought his hand to her breast,*
> *And there beheld paradise.*

Having taken one of several pathways, Michael led the way; Jody followed behind. Having reached the bottom of the mountain, he began climbing the steep wall along a path which had not seen human feet for a long time. Carefully, Michael avoided rocks and tree branches blocking the way. Finally, midway up, the first opening appeared large and dark, for the most part blocked by undergrowth and by rocks and dirt from running water.

"What do you expect to see around here?" Michael asked, discouraged by the impasse ahead.

"I don't know. Maybe I wanted to get a feel of those who had to be here, as if fulfilling a job or a duty. Not because they wanted to be here. On the other hand, what would those do if they were here of their own volition?"

Looking along the ground, to be sure no wild animals were there, he noticed a semi-open space with a lot of fresh underbrush—a perfect place to rest: complete silence, complete privacy, only chickadees noisily roaming around.

"What do you have in mind?" she asked in a sultry tone.

"I want to make passionate love to you, like we've never made before."

Without giving any thought, she began to take her clothes off. Having done the same, Michael lined himself up on the soft leaves, his eyes on her resplendent breasts.

"Come, darling," she asked, feeling his hands over her breasts. His mouth full as a hungry baby, he suckled on both.

"Please, please, Michael: Come into me."

Their mouths together, Michael gently slid over her body. In a second or two, they were unto each other as one. Remembering her wishes from their previous love-making, Michael continued in a slow assiduous rhythm. She responded with continuous kisses, clutching his head down to her mouth.

"I love you, Michael. I love you and I don't know why," she whispered. Let's stay like this. It is the only harmony in this whole universe. Please, yes, darling: don't stop!"

Except for time, everything or action comes to an end, only in the sense that nothing is ever static, that everything is always evolving. In some, the change may take the form of a groan or a cry: uncontrolled sharp cries, invocations to God, weeping, negation, ecstasy in having created something new but beyond their reach at the same time; in others, the change may make them taciturn—unable to express themselves due to their inability to comprehend what took place.

Out of breath, Michael held Jody's face tight against his face, his mouth open breaching for air.

"I don't want this ever to stop until I get into your heart—completely. Yes, complete happiness: With you and no one else!" Jody said, drawing him tighter to her.

"Wait!" he implored, almost out of breath. "Please, lay back." As she did, he placed his face next to hers. "I need time to re-coop."

"Yes, darling," she answered as she gently pulled him closer to her. "Yes, darling, yes," she repeated as though she knew the limitations of another human being.

"Are you sure, you still want to be the mother of our child?"

"Without a doubt, Michael: I wish it were already so."

"Why?"

"We're sure of this moment only. I would want it now, if it were possible."

"As the eternal optimist, we will have either a boy or girl."

"Of course, Michael, we will have twins. That explains why you were so exhausted."

Both smiled. Happiness had grabbed their souls.

The next day, Michael picked Jody up at the apartment. On entering, she said a special *hi* to her mother with a gentle hug.

"That's very nice," Julie commented on his gentleness. "We have a meeting, as you may know."

"Was I invited?"

"No, you were not. Captain Fracastoro will be presenting the results of a few tests. He seems proud of your work…"

"Mom, do you mind? We're going to explore a few of the caves in the Amalfi area. I'll tell you about them when we get back. Maybe we can have supper together? Would you like to?"

"Of course we would…right, Michael?"
"Yes, oh yes."

Back in Amalfi, Michael drove to the marina where he had a small outboard boat. Jody quickly asked why he had such a boat. She also observed on the fact that Michael—such an expert with transmitters and receivers—it seemed odd that he would be living in such a small apartment without the means to pursue his beloved hobby.

"Yes to both, Jody. Today, I will show why I need the boat. Promise one thing!"

"What's that?"

"That it stays a secret. Too often, I've been misunderstood. So, I keep things to myself. Agreed?"

"Of course, Michael: You have my word, no matter what," she pledged, her conscience tugging, realizing the immense commitment she made in light of her consent to being a US agent—especially to General Miller. Regardless, she would betray neither: first, because she was a responsible and patriotic human being; second, because she was in love with a strong desire to be a mother before it got too late. Besides, she had finally understood true love; and she owed it to Michael. Now, she wanted to experience motherhood—life's vehicle of generation. On seeing Michael pull the boat from the slip, she quickly turned her attention to him.

"This is a new experience for me."

"You've been on a boat before?"

"Not like this one, or in this way."

"I can just see you: holding on to the rail with one hand; with the other trying to control your wind-blown hair…"

"But, I'm not a blonde. Isn't that the typical image?"

"You're for real, however, and authentic."

Indeed, Jody dressed for the occasion: short shorts, braless with loose blouse, her hair in free fall. To be sure, she wore shoes appropriate for rock climbing. After a long curve northward, on picking up speed, Michael looked back at Jody in disbelief. In a million years did he believe this was the scene he was seeing, and, happening to him! Was he part of a plan and he not aware of any of it? In those moments, however, he was operating the boat, his mission to bring her to his secret place without mishaps or accidents. Certainly, she made it difficult for him to keep his eyes foreword. In addition, he was about to reveal to her a secret he had not shared with anyone. Surely, if they were alive, he would have shared with his parents.

The question: what brought him to this decision? Capitulation to love: If so, at what and at whose expense? Did love have to have a victim?

Driving the boat, one would not imagine this man having those kinds of thoughts.

On reaching his turn-away spot, he de-accelerated. Slowly, he proceeded into a coastal inlet with a backwater that led into a cave behind large protrusions of boulders and layered rocks. There were no trees: just huge walls of rocks. Making his way around a couple of boulders, he finally brought the boat to a specific rock. On tying the line around it, he looked at Jody.

"Are you alright," Michael asked; there was some hesitation on her face. The place was wild looking and certainly not welcoming to human beings.

"I'm fine. Where are we?"

"We're at a special cave, the Mussolini Cave. You'll soon see why. By the way, this is not to be confused with the Emerald Grotto. Having gotten out of the boat, he stood on a precarious flat rock, barely large enough for one person. "Come," he said as he extended his hand to hers. Be careful; this is not easy."

Her hand firmly in his, she stepped off with no trouble. Moving to one side, with one hand poised on the jagged rock, she took the bag that Michael had retrieved from the boat. On giving it back to him, just as they began trekking, she asked him.

"What you got, here?"

"Just some basic things and a bottle of white wine: Remember, we're not here on a picnic."

"Where's your bag? I've seen you with one before. Come to think of, I've also seen you with a phone, and no jewelry except for a bracelet which you seem to wear almost all the time."

"Should that be a clue to you?"

"A clue: Maybe that I should get you some jewelry?"

"How did I get into this? On the other hand, your point is well taken. I'll call Richard; he's our family jeweler. Anything you have in mind?"

"No! Let's get going!"

Having walked precariously around the rock pathway, they moved around into an opening with water pounding up and down a large bolder on top of which stood what looked like a monument. Light seemed to be coming from an opening at the top.

"What does—no, who do you think that looks like?" Michael asked as he pointed toward the higher part of the natural rock formation. Doesn't that look like a face of a politician?" he suggested.

"Actually, it does seem to have an image—of a human face. But, I don't have the slightest."

"Look at the chin—the jawbone. It's similar to that of Mussolini. Don't you see it?"

"I am glad you do," she answered, making fun of him."

"Oh, well: Come this way."

They walked under and around an overhead extruding rock formation. A path—only one who had been there before would call it such. Before Jody knew it, they were above the rim overlooking the water and well on their way upward, zigzagging, between one side and another. At a point they crossed from one mountain side to another; then they passed a few trees. A dark upward tunnel lay ahead. Once inside, Jody could see the path was man-made.

"What's with this?" Jody asked, a little out of breath.

"Here, let's sit and rest; we don't have too far to go."

Jody kissed him on his cheeks, thankful they had stopped. "I don't know where you're taking me; I am only glad that you know where you are going. Who in his right mind would come here? And what's this tunnel doing here? And what's the reason behind all this?"

"You will see. Before you know it, we will be at the very top of this mount—the very top! You will see spectacular sights, wide panoramas, extended un-obstructed views: line of sights everywhere."

"'Line of sight!' What's that? What's the purpose?"

Michael could not wait to reach the top to surprise her. He was sure she would be impressed.

"Do you see this path? I do not know how I found it. And, by the way, you are the only other human being that's climbed it up to here. From here on up, we will go through tunnels dug or built by ancient people, certainly some by the Romans and some by the Germans. You wanted to get the feel of these tunnels. Well, this is the beginning of a network whose locations are practically unrecorded."

"I see, but: what's possessing you in coming here?"

"Be patient; we'll get there soon. We'll celebrate over a *panino* with a glass of white wine," he promised with a smile.

"A 'glass' you said? You have glasses in your back pack?"

"No, Jody, I do not. I want to surprise you. Remember, I've come this way many times. I promise you will not be disappointed. *Forza; andiamo* Come on; let's go."

After having crossed a few other tunnels, they finally reached the very top. To the north, there was one more trail which showed human activities. On reaching it, Jody was surprised to see it was a type of bunker. Sure enough, it was Michael's secret hideaway—much more than a hideaway, however. He took her inside by a door only he knew it was a door. With a type of crowbar which he retrieved from a hole, he placed it under the right side of the stone slab. On lifting it, he pulled a roller out from the bottom. Then, placing the bar on the left side, he pushed up to insert the same roller. With a slight push, the slab rolled to the right, and, there, the cave was open.

Once inside, he showed the little kitchen. It had a wooden stove, one storage cabinet containing two plates and two wine glasses. There was no bathroom, however.

"So, when you have to go to the bathroom, where? And, is there water? Don't tell me you have water."

"Outside: I'll show you later." He had put together a canvas below the boulder that captured rain water that spilled into a row of plastic gallon containers, some of which he kept outside by the 'bathroom'—two parallel logs about 20 inches high, with a plastic container that sloped away into a recess which allowed the water to flush to the rear.

"Electricity: You don't have any?"

"We just got here; you'll see. I have generators. Are you ready to have our sandwich? Here, let's go out. There is a bench. I'll open the wine. Come; come on," he said in an affectionate voice.

He saw she was incredulous to what she was seeing. Her eyes were as wide open as her mouth! She could not imagine being all alone on a corner of the earth unreachable by other human beings. In addition, she surmised she was going to see much more: Michael had suggested that a network of tunnels led directly south to the Cathedral, and that many were used for storage of weapons and other items such as food and supplies.

Now she knew she had gotten into the heart of Michael. She had never expected anything like that.

The wind was mild. They sat in complete sunlight. The air couldn't have been clearer. Michael opened the bottle after having placed the *Panini* on the rough stone slab.

"To us, my love," Michael toasted, his eyes reverentially looking into her eyes.

"To our love; it will last forever. I feel it will. Michael, I love you so much."

After having eaten, Michael showed her around. In another space, hidden from view either from the air or from any other peak, he opened another make-shift door. Inside were a decent-size FM transmitter, one AM transmitter and two appropriate receivers. In a corner there were two gas-driven generators.

"Later, I will start one. You will see how effective it is. It also lights my bunk bed space."

"Who helped you put this together? You couldn't have done it alone."

"All by myself—everything: Brought all up on these shoulders—piece by piece, part by part, component by component, which I then reassembled. Everything works like a charm."

"Where did you get the stuff? Some of it looks military."

"If you know Naples, you know where to go. You can buy everything there. If they don't have what you want just place your request. By hook or crook, sooner than later, your wish will have come true. You may have to pay a little more. This equipment—all of it is American. I am sure it came from some NATO supply network.

"So, you also have connections."

"Not, hardly: I don't even know how I got my present job. I'm so thankful, though. It pays well. As a result, I am able to do all kinds of things. With this place here, no one has the slightest idea about what I do."

"Not even your neighbor? By the way, as I look around, I am able to verify that you are a real *Robinson Caruso*, if you know what I mean. How about your brother; he's never been here?"

"Least of all, my brother. He's a man of the cloth."

"How did he become a Deacon? No, no: Why. How come you don't seem to be a steep follower of our religion?"

"It's a long story. But I think that, while he was teaching at a prestigious school of music in Boston, he fell in love with one of his students—a beautiful black girl. That love affair ended tragically for my brother. He was fired. Unable to cope in Boston, he decided to make a new life in Amalfi. I soon joined him, having had my own problems. I can tell you this: my brother, Paolo, always said that upon retirement as a professor, he would become a deacon. Well, here it is: his dream has come true; and, he is doing such a good job. Do you know that sometimes ago, I believed Paolo to be truly a Saint."

"Michael, I had no idea about any of these things. In any event, when do you think we should be starting to get back home?"

"I thought we were going to spend the night here. It will be the only time I will have been here with someone else."

"I did not tell my mother I was going to be away. She'll be worried."

"Here's my phone. Do you want to call her? Or, would you prefer to pack up and go back?"

"What is your wish?"

"That we stay and go home tomorrow."

Phone in hand, she dialed her mother, somewhat hesitant to have to tell her mother about her overnight stay with Michael.

"Hello, who's this?" the mother asked, as she had never received a call from that phone number.

"Mom, it's me. I'm with Michael. I just wanted to tell you I won't be home this evening..."

"Where are you? Are you all right?"

"We decided to spend more time on Vesuvius. I wanted you to know what it is like to spend the night in this area. We're having a great time; please not to worry. I'll call you in the morning. How about you: what are you doing? I hope you won't be alone."

"Domenico and I are having dinner; we were hoping you could have been with us."

At that point, Michael realized he had made a mistake: he may have unwittingly given away his location.

After handing the phone back to Michael, Jody said with a sense of relief: "What's next?"

"Canned beans and more wine..."

"I thought we were on our honeymoon... What else have you got to show? For instance, there have to be antennas."

"Very observant: Let no one under-estimate your intelligence. Let's go. I think you're going to be surprised. I am very proud of my rig."

Jody followed him through a very narrow opening to the other side of the transmitters. Sliding through the opening, he pulled her through. There, he had screwed a wooden platform against the wall. A type of pulley with a handle stood out. As she watched, he began to turn the handle. From behind, a plastic pipe began to move upward. Though it had come to a stop, Michael continued to turn the handle until he came to another stop.

"That's it for here. Let's go outside."

Pushing her out, they quickly surfaced above to a site of two antennas standing tall.

"My, I would have never known. Very ingenuous! I can see why you went to the trouble when you could have installed and be done with them."

"But, why do you think I did it this way?"

"Because airplanes fly above, whether any one is here or not here."

"And because of drones; they're all over the place. Drones are both instruments and weapons. The industry has already become so vast. Reconnaissance is the least of their deployment. They can deliver minute chemical and biological attacks like never before. I believe that before too long tactical nuclear war heads will be delivered by drones. They will even deliver artillery rounds. You'll see: the next generation of these weapons will be the drone."

Jody had heard enough speculation on the drones. Her interest was to know Michael's communication system, first; then, she was going to look for the answer to the original question: Was he able to piggy-back a CBRN (chemical-biological-radiological-nuclear) weapon onto a radio frequency to be transmitted with the capability of targeting a specific individual with a corresponding receptive chromosome? Thinking about the whole made her uneasy: she was enjoying a honeymoon and did not want to spoil it for anything else in the world.

"Maybe we should stop talking about these things for now. I am not sure whether I understand what you're saying, anyway. Can I help prepare the beans? And you can open some more wine. Do you have any more?"

"Oh, I forgot to show my wine cellar."

"Surely, you jest?"

"Let's see," he said. "Come here." Behind another rock there was an indention with two natural shelves filled with several bottles of red and white wine.

"You surely know how to please a woman in love."

"Wait till we go to bed. I have sox for you to wear. The cubicle is hardly large enough for one person."

Around seven, the temperature was still mild and clear. The surface of the sea was calm; no waves were visible other than the reflection of movement in the very blue water, creating an almost natural link between the water and the sky. Even the sun, as it was getting ready to set well beyond to the west, was gathering its rainbow of colors reflected in slivers of see-through clouds, its colors liquefying into the shimmering water.

Michael and Jody stood up, their eyes fixed on the mesmerizing site of the sun beginning to set, neither being able to express or describe what they were seeing, and both standing in deep silence.

"Come, to our C Rations," Michael said with a smile.

"What's that?" she asked, knowing he was fooling around.

"Beans, darling: beans."

"How often do you come here, and for what purpose? I see you also have a computer. Have you also mastered the computer?"

"To the latter, I have basic knowledge; but I know a lot thanks to my young friend, Chris, from Boston. I just let him into my computer, and he fixes what ails me. The second part: We came today because in the morning I have a task to complete."

"I thought we came to celebrate a kind of honeymoon."

"I haven't given you a ring. Besides, I haven't asked you

to marry me yet. I haven't proposed. But, will you marry me, Darling? I don't know what I would do without you."

Jody, noticing Michael's sincerity in his voice, quickly confirmed acceptance. "I don't need a ring: just you!" She moved to kiss him.

Supper, indeed, was a can of beans, large enough for two. He had some *grissini*—by now well dried, and some crackers. The wine, on the other hand, more than made up for everything else. Jody actually enjoyed herself: Simplicity was enjoyable.

"So, Michael, what's with all this sophisticated equipment? Why such in-accessibility? Anyone else seeing this place, he or she would conclude without a doubt, that you are doing some awful subversive stuff. I know you're not; but, please tell me so."

"Nothing subversive, Jody; I assure you."

"So, why is there so much secrecy and obfuscation?"

"Mainly because of the site. The height of the place is like a radio relay site with line of sight advantages necessary for FM radio transmission."

"Who do you communicate with?"

"Ironically, I talk with no one—at least, not yet!"

"Can you explain why you're here when you need not to be here? But, you don't have to tell me anything, if you wish."

"First: If I need to send a radio message to any one, the transmission would be immediately picked and the location of the transmitter revealed.

"Secondly, I can receive all kinds of radio messages and no one would learn the whereabouts of the receiver.

"More importantly, I never need to transmit a message; I transmit a signal—only a signal. And I am nowhere near doing that because I do not have a specific target; more importantly, I still do not know how to arm the signal."

"Please, Michael, you're over my head. You do not have a

'target' and you do not know how to 'arm' a signal. Are we talking science fiction?"

"It won't be as soon as I will be able to arm the signal."

"Against...?

"...Against tyrants," interrupted Michael. "Yes, against terrorists, against all those who keep on killing while alive, because they are protected and no one can get to them."

"In other words, you could have taken Hitler out."

"Yes, a similar operational system would have made it possible. That would include Stalin, and many more. In today's world, it would include all those committing suicide, and those capturing and enslaving young girls."

"But, you can only know after the fact."

"Yes, unfortunately: But, they would not do it a second time."

"Woe, Michael. I don't know if I am overwhelmed or scared."

"You need not be scared. I would not hurt a fly. You need not be scared because in all these years, of one experiment after another, I have been a total failure: Hence, unproductive even as a work of science fiction. I am a total failure. You can see how I live."

"Tell me, in your words, how this would work; then, I would ask my second question."

"The basic idea: every living organism on this earth has a DNA of its own. Our finger prints identify and distinguish us one the other. I would say the same thing for our voices—no two voices are alike. My idea is to get true voice prints—like a finger print, which is physical. A voice print would be electronic, meaning, frequencies. Often, it is referred as a spectrogram of the human voice. If I were to make a copy of your voice, and store it on a device, I could use it without anyone knowing about it. Now, I can transmit that spectrogram to another individual; it would do nothing other than for that person or entity to have a copy. But, as I may have tried to explain another time, this system could be significant if I were able to arm it—that is, to attach something so that the recipient of the transmission having that specific voice could be infected as to create a type of cancer or other form of infection that would cause his or her death…"

"I understand clearly. Now, my second question: At what point are you with this invention—Am I right to call it a potential invention?"

"You can call it what you may. For me, it is a total failure, a thought which, in exploring its possibilities with a chemistry colleague of mine, may have caused some misguided individuals to believe that I had succeeded in harnessing radio waves.

"I wish I had. There would be fewer villains on this earth."

"Michael, when did this all happen?"

"At the school where I taught: Those were for the most part, terrible days for me. On a personal level I fell in love with a woman who turned out to be the opposite of any idealism of mine. A fool, I fell for her. I have never forgiven myself for having been such a fool. Why didn't I see it? Is that what love does? Do I have to think about that, now that I am so in love with you? I am sure; yet I am not sure. Do you understand, Jody, the burden I have borne over these years?"

"Yes, darling, I understand. I have had my ups and downs. I have never felt like this before. You are my only true love. Till death!

"It sounds juvenile, but I am convinced it is true."

"By the way, the reason we're here together is because in the morning I want to try to record the voice of one of those wanton killers. Supposedly, he will be talking on a special radio to his supporters. I want to see if I can succeed now, as I have failed all along in the past. So, tomorrow morning, I will be aiming the antenna southeast with the hope of getting some type of streaming.

"In any event, after that, we'll begin or trek back to Amalfi.

"I am going to take some tape with us. In any disaster, be it from nature or man-made, I always thought that if I were to survive, I would be able to do it only in this place—unless it were a nuclear attack, in which case, radiation would make me a fatality. So, the tape: I will mark our root by placing markers as needed, so that you can easily follow the directions. Once we're down, I am going to have you learn how to secure the boat and drive back to Amalfi. In the best of time, we should be here, together; in the worst of time, you should be here. I would want to be remembered by you. Do you think you would want to do it?

"Ominous! Regardless, the answer is yes. Yes, my love."

"Tell me, why are you choosing one and not another?

"I have to be sure that person has to be evil in body and soul. He or she has to be the one with genocidal predisposition."

"So, as not to make a mistake?"

"Definitely: Otherwise, I wouldn't be able to live with myself."

The evening had finally engulfed them in darkness which made the sky the brightest they had ever seen. A canopy of an infinite number of stars pulsated above; it proved there was infinity—just eternal immensity.

"We are part of it," Michael claimed, as he drew her closer into his embrace. As the bunk bed was already small, there was no way they could have been closer.

"It is a miracle we are here, like this, on this peak. Please let's stay like this. I want to fall asleep like this, in your arms."

Michael continued to gently stroke her, his movements

particularly soothing to her soft moaning. After several minutes, her moaning turned to silence. He dared not move, not even after the horrid thought that came to him: had he been unwittingly responsible for placing her in danger?

With that frightful thought, he eventually closed his eyes. Both the sea below and the stars above continued on their immeasurable routes to fulfill who knows what destiny. In the morning, was no darkness; those stars were no longer visible. But the water below churned itself into waves visible from above.

Assisted by Jody, Michael geared up his FM receiver having made sure its antenna was oriented in a southern direction. He turned it slowly from one side to the other for optimum reception of his input frequency. After having tried for about 45 minutes, he looked into Jody's eyes, commenting while raising his shoulders: "It was not meant to be: Not this time, not ever. Isn't that something?"

Finally, Michael had realized the futility of his efforts. After all that time, he had gained nothing on behalf of himself or on behalf of others; most probably, he had raised the ire of those whom he wanted dead. In retrospect, he had have empowered those very individuals to greater acts of terror. Amidst this was the biggest irony: having fallen truly in love, it seemed that he may have doomed that love to a tragic end. Unaware of that potential destiny, love, became an entity unto itself, attaining its own reality.

The two scaled the mountain. Having taken over the boat, Jody was on the open sea. Suddenly, she turned the motor off. The boat floating gently from one wave into another, Jody stood up.

"What are you doing, honey?" Michael asked.

"I've never done the waves," she answered, one breast

already out of her blouse. Michael, seated, she bend down. Pulling her down to his level, he took her breast to his mouth. Now completely undressed, she pulled him down to the floor of the boat, making sure not to fall as the waves were rolling in different directions. On lying on two cushions, she took Michael in.

"Don't rush," she urged, her mouth open to receive his lips. "Let the waves do the work," she continued as she pressed his mouth into hers. "Yes," she exclaimed when the waves tossed the boat from back to front and vice versa.

After about thirty minutes, Michael acceded to his orgasm; Jody was wildly ecstatic. Meanwhile, the boat had drifted out to sea. On getting up, Jody was suddenly startled. No land was to be seen in any direction.

"Oh, my God!" she exclaimed. "Which way do we go?"

Michael looked at the sun setting. "Veer to the left. In a while you'll see land and Amalfi south on your left."

"Oh, you're good, even in giving direction."

Jody was a fast learner. To his surprise, Jody quickly mastered driving the boat. Having reached the Amalfi port, with Michael giving her instructions on docking, she brought the boat into its slip. She nimbly jumped off the boat and secured the line onto the cleat. His pack secure on his shoulder, Michael took Jody's hand and walked up the stairs to his apartment. Once inside, he saw his brother working at his desk.

"Good morning," Michael said.

"Good morning to you, and to you, Jody. You look very happy. I am assuming you spent the night together."

"Yes, we did, Paolo. I think we have some good news for you: I think we're engaged…"

"Engaged! My, you two work fast." He got up and hugged Jody. "This calls for a celebration: And, how about the ring? Shall I call our friend, Richard, the jeweler?"

"I am marrying Jody; not you," Michael answered, a smile on his face. "I am so glad you approve. Now, your job is the ceremony at church. I will plan for the engagement party—something very modest. We will invite our relatives and closest friends. I will have to get going with this. As you know, Jody is due to go back home with her mother. We want to get married so she will stay here, with us. Do you mind?"

"Is she a good cook?"

"Thanks for your kindness, Don Paolo…"

"Never mind the, *Don*. From now on, Jody, it's just *Paolo*."

"Last night, the evening of our supposed engagement, your brother—here—served me beans from a can. And some white wine. What do you think of that?"

"Under similar circumstances, I am sure that *happiness* trumped everything else. I am so happy."

"Come on. Let's get some *prosecco o*pened. What do you say? I know it's early."

"I will never say no to it; it has to be better than last night. Michael, I am not berating it," she said without a trace of sarcasm. "But I do want to go tell my mother. Do you mind, Michael?"

"Let's shower and be on our way."

Prior to their leaving for Castellammare di Stabbia, with the two brothers sitting at the table outside, Jody took her phone from her bag and left a quick note for General Miller.

Wrong target
For sure

The message quickly disappeared. On replacing it into her bag, she went to join the two brothers, about to finish their drinks.

"Would you like more"? Don Paolo asked.

"No, dear... Michael, can we go?"

"Will you be back for supper this evening?"

"I doubt it. I'll call you," answered Michael.

Before long, the two reached Castellammare. Her mother was home, as expected. She had prepared a light lunch, and seemed very happy. She was extremely jovial toward Michael. On being told the two had made a commitment of engagement, she turned towards Michael:

"That explains why I am so happy."

While leisurely eating their *panini con prosciutto,* Jean told them that she and Domenico were going to the *Teatro San Carlo* and asked them whether they would like to go as their guests.

"We can stop for dinner at the Square. There are so many good restaurants, including your friend's," she suggested to Michael. Domenico will be driving; he's so good at it."

Jody and Michael looked at each other, looking for approval or refusal.

"What's the Opera?" Michael asked.

"A rare work by Gioachino Rossini: *Maomet II.,* maybe the Battle of Lepanto."

"What's that? I never heard of it, Mom. What's it about?"

"The war between the Venetians and the Turks. I don't know more than that," she added defensively.

Jody quickly pulled her phone from the bag nearby. On pulling up the blurb, she read it aloud.

"Typical of the continued struggle between the followers of two religions at odds with each other: one always on the offensive; the other always on the defensive, except for the Crusades," commented Michael.

"So much for the history. Are you coming?"

"Yes, or course, Mrs. Villa," Michael answered.

"Oh, enough with this 'Mrs. Villa'. Please call me, Julie. Besides, I am about to become your mother-in-law… Jody, that is simply wonderful. I thought you'd never do it!"

"I'm glad you are happy."

"Well, are you coming to the Opera, or not?"

"Of course, Ju-Julie," Michael assured her. A wide smile on his face complimented the smiles of the two women.

At the agreed time, Domenico arrived with his *Lancia* four-door sedan. He was surprised to find Jody and Michael there, and was happy to learn that the young couple had agreed to join them at the Opera.

Over cold *prosecco*, the four chatted about current events, all critical of the various terrorist attacks taking place around the world. Of particular interest were the many claims emanating out of the newly established Caliphate.

"Nothing bodes well here. I am reminded about the siege of Malta. The Saracens gave a new meaning to anal Crucifixion," Domenico commented, a severe frown on his wrinkled forehead.

"Domenico, what are you saying? We're going out for a good time!" Julie lamented, her typical smile now absent.

"I know what he is talking about. The problem is that the Christians fared no better. But, I agree with Julie. We should change the subject," Michael suggested.

"Here's the thing," Domenico insisted, a serious tone to his voice. "I cannot bring this up at our regular meetings. But, this Volcanic thing which we're all experts on in one way or another, if it blows when it wants to, either because of pressure from below, or because of man-made activity: What can we do? Unfortunately, the fact is we know how and why eruptions take place; but we cannot control them one way or another. The problem is, and this is the main point, we never talk about man-made intervention which can be more devastating than that of nature itself. What if a nuclear warhead had been exploded on Mt. Saint Helen? What if, for some diabolical reason, a nuclear device was to be exploded on Vesuvius: What would be the role of your communication network, Michael?"

"There wouldn't be any, Captain…" Michael began to comment.

"Let's cut out the niceties. Just refer to me as, Domenico."

"Yes, Domenico, we would not be here to tell about it. Truly, when I see the topographical landscape, I see nothing but disaster, from Monte Carlo, to Amalfi, to Sicily. That huge rock formation overlooking Monaco may become dislodged. I am more preoccupied about man-made activities than those of nature."

"I knew I liked you for a reason. You're absolutely right. We have to worry about our fellow human beings, those whose conscience—their very soul has been taken away from them. No, I take it back: they have allowed themselves to be stripped of the natural human conscience: By whom; no, by what? By a man-made document intended to keep people under control, by prescribing every aspect of behavior, at all levels of the physical evolvement of each human being. No other man-made document comes close to equal the tight control this document holds—not the Bible, not the Vedas, not the *Egyptian Book of the Dead*, not the *Tao Te Ching*, not the *Upanishads*, not the *Bhagava Gida*, not the *Buddhist Sutras*, not *The Prince*, for sure, not *The Holy Bible*, except for the *Quran*! Only the *Quran* controls the human being—body and soul, almost without exception. Its grip is complete to the point that no one can escape from its dictates. Just about every organized religion allows co-existence, except for Islam. According to its fanatics, one is either a faithful follower or doomed to death in whatever form, preferably by beheading. If it were possible, on this earth, we would all be born Muslims."

"Come on, guys, you're overdoing it. You've taken away the desire to go to the opera," Julie commented, knowing that the conversation would extend beyond Rossini's opera.

"I have a recommendation," Domenico advanced.

"By all means, Julie implored.

"Why don't we go down to the port? We'll have an *aperitivo;* after which, we'll stop at the fish market and I will get some salmon. I will cook it: *salmone al nonno* grandfather's salmon. What do you say? And we will not talk about all this terrible stuff. By the way, we need a couple bottles of *prosecco*. Do you have it, or do we need to buy a few bottles?"

"We have it," Julie affirmed with pride.

The four took a table on the sidewalk. Across from them, on a small podium, a small group of singers and musicians intoned typical classical music, to the delight of the many clients. Domenico was especially happy listening to the songs. He asked the waiter to bring four *Campari* with a few munchies.

Sipping and chit-chatting couldn't have been more delightful; everything was just great: they noticed the gentle waves coming ashore, and could already see the early stars.

"This is the way to enjoy life," Domenico commented, his glass in hand. Everything is so beautiful… Jody, can I tell you something?"

"Certainly, Domenico."

"You may not know Sicilian poetry…"

"I do not."

"Well, when I first met your mother, I recited—mainly to myself, the following:

"Rosa fresca aulentissima ch'apari inver' la state,
le donne ti disiano, pulzell' e maritate:
tràgemi d'este focora, se t'este a bolontate;

per te non ajo abento notte e dia,
penzando pur di voi, madonna mia…

"Now, let me give you my translation:

O most fragrant rose, born from a summer's day,
Married women and young ones all desire you.
Let it be your wish to assuage my pain
For I can no longer sleep—night or day
Because I'm always thinking of you,
Madonna of my heart.

"This is the stanza I recited to your mother. Not having words of my own, I borrowed the words of a poet to speak to your mother. I hope you liked the poem. I hope you do not disapprove my having fallen in love with your mother."

"Wow, all these beautiful things! How evocative! Can this earth support it all?"

"You're wonderful, Domenico, in sharing the beautiful poem with us. Yes, I love the poem. I am happier loving a human being like you."

With several songs sung by this Neapolitan young man, he paused to announce the next song: *Santa Lucia Luntana*, a song sung by all the major tenors on the world stage, including Caruso, Tito Schipa, Beniamino Gigli, Pavarotti, and Andrea Bocelli. This young singer, though at the local port, through the lyrics of the song he knew he would bring tears in every person's eyes. All immigrants, having departed from the Port of Naples to America, were affected by that day of departure. The song depicted scenes that repeated themselves under the very eyes of Captain Fracastoro.

"Partono i bastimenti pe terre assai luntane,…

Ships are leaving for far-away lands;
the passengers aboard are singing their songs:
they are Neapolitans..."

Although Domenico was from La Spezia, now that he had been working in Naples for so many years, he knew what it was to be Neapolitan. More important, he knew, because he felt it—he knew the emotional attachment that the people had for their popular songs and to that city specifically. They were not just popular songs that belonged to an era; they were songs which spoke to the heart of a place, to the Neapolitan people, more appropriately, to the heart of the human being.

Un-expectedly, the young singer announced the title of the next song: *O Sarracino* The Saracen. Everyone clapped enthusiastically. Apparently the lyrics tugged at the hearts of the present guests. It did so to Domenico. The song made him happy. On listening, there was a genuine smile on his face, even though the song was about a young Neapolitan man of Muslim background. In other circumstances, a similar song would evoke anger; in this circumstance, it evoked joy:

"*O Sarracino, o sarracino*
Bellu guaglione...

Oh Saracen, Saracen
You're so handsome.
Oh Saracen, Saracen
You make maidens swoon;
You.re good looking
With a great heart...

"That is very pretty, Domenico," Jody observed, reacting

to the expression of happiness on his face, as if he were wishing there was a better relationship if not better acceptance of disparate human beings regardless of where they lived or whatever religion they practiced. Certainly, in the song, there are no references on the behavior of those past wars whether in Europe or in the Middle East. "Isn't your neighbor, Umberto, a descendant of the Muslims?"

Julie noticed the same expression on Domenico's face. "I'm very proud of you."

"We should go now. Remember, we need to stop at the fish market."

At the market, Domenico took the lead on choosing the salmon: it had to be wild, a particular cut and even throughout, enough for four people. He had a family recipe—a grandfather dedicating it to his granddaughter, Alessia.

1 Half fresh lime, its juice mixed with slivers from its pulp
2 Two large spoons of Original Barbecue Sauce
3 Six large spoons of vegetable oil
4 Two large spoons of Lemon-Pepper Seasoning

Place all ingredients in a bowl; stir briskly; spread evenly over the Salmon fillet; pour a little water to rinse the bowl, and pour under the salmon. Marinate for about one hour. Broil for about 15 minutes or until the top of the salmon becomes dark red. Let it rest and serve after 10 minutes.

In the small kitchen, Julie gathered the proper utensils and placed them by the sink. Domenico took over from there. By himself, he prepared the sauce to dress the salmon. After covering the fish, he added a bit of water to the bowl. He swirled the bowl a few times. Lifting each side, he poured the water evenly under the fish. Half-hour later, accordingly, he placed the broiling pan in the oven. He also prepared spinach and a tossed salad. Julie had already bought bread and a sponge cake for dessert.

"My, Domenico, the kitchen looks cleaner than before. You're so neat," she congratulated him.

While Jody helped set the table, Michael watched a soccer game on TV, sipping on *prosecco*. He particularly liked Lionel Messi.

"Michael, what's the score?" Domenico asked.

"Messi is winning," he answered.

"Yeah, but who's playing?"

"Does it matter?" he asked with both his hands stretched out, causing the two women to laugh.

The four enjoyed a simple, but delightful dinner. Their conversation ranged from current events to literary references. Nothing serious, however, impacted negatively on their togetherness.

The evening came to an end when Jody and Michael left for Amalfi. Not for Domenico and Julie, however; they spent the night together.

Unbeknown to Michael, his brother was waiting to finalize the engagement and marriage plans; and, unrelated, Umberto was also waiting to talk with Michael.

"Good morning, Paolo, how are you?"Michael asked as he entered the apartment followed by Jody.

"Everything just fine," answered Don Paolo. "I've made some tentative dates for your betrothal and wedding' I want to make sure to reserve the time at church. The other thing is that the Bishop has approved my *requiem mass*. I have already begun to enlist musicians and singers. Everyone seems to like the idea. I have chosen three tenors and two baritones to render *Mary, did you know?* They will sing as single voices or in duets, or as chorus. I can't wait to hear this part, as each will sing separately in different areas on the floor. We're beginning our rehearsals this week. What do you think, Jody?"

Thinking he was talking with Michael, Jody fumbled for a second: "Fine, fine," Don Paolo, "just fine! I am fascinated by the song about Mary. Several popular singers sing it differently. But, I like what you just said. It sounds great! How about, *Shepherd me, Oh Lord?* For some reason, I always thought that was your favorite," Jody said in a laudatory voice.

Not expecting that question, Paolo cleared his voice. "Yes, glad you asked. I had planned a couple of comments later. But, here they are: A duo of one tenor and one soprano will sing the entire score. Several choruses will sing only words of the title, from *sottovoce* to *crescendo* alternatively. Toward the end, the whole floor will come in with a thunderous sound glorifying the leadership of God in enhancing the humanity of mankind."

"Well, all this is because of you; you're making possible. Here we are, two brothers well advanced in age, and neither married. That's awful. So, I am so grateful. To think we may have a child of our own soon. You two make a great couple... Michael, are you in agreement?"

"Yes, Paolo, of course: By the way, before it slips my mind, what is the disposition on the inventory of those special bones in the reliquary chamber?"

"I have not told you, I know. Three specialists are conducting a thorough examination. While they haven't finished, they seem to be excited over the fact that our assumptions may be proven correct. But, so much for that, Jody: Are you both here for dinner this evening?"

"Yes, we planned to stay over. Do you mind?" she asked straight forward.

Don Paolo remained expressionless. Modern times had arrived even within the household of a Deacon.

"That's why you are a Deacon, not a Priest," interrupted

Michael, knowing what was on the mind of his brother... Jody, I am so looking forward to this evening."

Umberto had been waiting on his deck with the hope of seeing Michael. He had a worried look on his face.

He had been visited by a couple of hoodlums, supposedly from the Middle East—somehow affiliated with the guy that had sold him the illuminated Quran. They wanted to know his relationship with Michael. On being told that he hardly knew anything about Michael, the two did not believe him. Feeling threatened, he told them to leave and to never come back. Regardless, the problem was that they ordered Umberto to get information on Michael right then and there, especially information regarding Michael's radio experiments. With this, he ordered them to leave, lest he call the police. Umberto was anxious to tell Michael what had happened. Finally, late morning, Michael and Jody walked onto the deck. On seeing Jody with Michael, Umberto's facial expression changed. He seemed relieved.

"Good morning, Michael. How are you two doing? Nice to see you this beautiful day," he said without much enthusiasm.

"Well, Umberto," Michael said, pulling Jody by the hand into the foreground. "Jody and I are engaged, and we should be married soon. What do you think?"

Umberto hesitation became very evident, as he stumbled to answer.

"Michael, what great news: I kind of thought you two were a number. Even Fafa commented on you two. She thinks you make a great couple. She even said that, as far as she was concerned, you both look genuinely in love.

"Yes, the reason I wanted to see you was this: Fafa and I wanted to invite you for dinner. Now, we want to have you

over to celebrate your engagement. I am sure the boys will also
be very happy. Congratulations! How about this Saturday? Can
you make it? And yes, we also want to have your brother. Will
you ask him?"

Michael and Jody looked at each other with happy expressions on their faces. "Certainly," Michael said as he
extended his hand to Umberto. After shaking hand, he went on
his way toward the square. In walking down the stairs, Jody
paused for a second to look at the sea water below softly
rolling against the retaining wall.

"It's so nice. What a beautiful day!" She exclaimed.

At the office of the cathedral, Don Paolo waited for his brother.
He had made an appointment to meet with the Bishop to
receive his approval for the production of the High Mass for
the up-coming high mass. At the agreed time, the two brothers
waited by the door of the Bishop. A Monsignor opened the
door and asked the two guests to enter. The Bishop was waiting
on his feet. On seeing the Deacon, he extended his hand. Don
Paolo took the Bishop's hand and kissed it. Michael did the
same thing.

Seated in three separate chairs, the Bishop quickly began
to ask questions of Michael. He had heard good things about
him especially relating to the Alarm System. For, he too was
concerned about the next eruption—the havoc it could cause in
lives, and to a lesser extent, to property. While the first century
eruption had killed thousands of people, any modern explosion
would kill by the hundreds of thousands.

"We are grateful for your dedication and diligence. Captain Fracastoro has spoken well of you," he said. "Congratulations!" the Bishop added. "Now for the Solemn Mass: What is
this about?"

"Yes, Most Reverend Bishop: Basically, the inspiration

came from observing the sacredness of human life, in a scene that took place nearby. A young couple of two children, one being breast-fed, show how parents care for their children, being sure they are cared for under all kinds of conditions. Well through music and lyrics, we want to portrait the transition, as from darkness to light, as from noise to sound, as from sin to redemption, as from brutal barbarity to enlightened wisdom, from dependency as a child, to independence as an adult.

"There will be instruments placed at different stages around the Cathedral; likewise, choruses will all be placed at different places. The bulk of the main singing will be done by the people themselves sitting or standing in the center—from the back to the front, and from left to right. Need I say more, Most Reverend?"

"You've said it well. You have my approval. I am sure that once again, the Church will take a leading role in creating another masterpiece. Who does not enjoy the works of Vivaldi, Palestrina, Gesualdo? Not to mention Gregorian Chant.

"Anything else, my dear Brothers in Christ?"

"Yes," Don Paolo added humbly. Michael is engaged to be married."

"You have my blessings."

About five feet 10 inches, weighing about 200 plus pounds, this burly-looking man entered into Umberto's restaurant and went directly to the office. On hearing the knock, Umberto saw himself face-to-face with a threatening and cruel face. His neck was large. Long, thin-like sausage muscle-like layered his entire neck above his wide muscled-shoulders.

"I am Mahmud and I am here on business. We need to speak in private, in your office…"

"Why in my office and…"

"In your office!" he reiterated pushing Umberto inside and shutting the door. His threatening tone was backed by obvious and deliberate action. "We have to have access to your friend—Michael's apartment. You have to make it possible. Is that clear?"

"I don't have a key to his apartment. We respect each other's..."

"We're not talking about respect. We need to know from you when the priest, Michael and his woman friend are away. We need about three hours in the apartment. Is that clear?" Mahmud asked, his eyes closing, his forehead creased like the layers of his neck muscles. "So you don't think this demand is not for real, I need to remind you that your life is as important to us as your wife and your two boys."

"My boys! What are you talking about? Are you threatening me and my family?"

"If you know what's good for you, you will adhere to our request without further comments. We only have one week's window."

"'Window!'" What do you know about windows or anything else, for that matter? I haven't known anyone of you being famous for having invented anything or created anything other than death," Umberto raved. A gun in his desk's draw, he continued: "People like you need to be eliminated to save the rest. Yes, the rest of the Muslims—the good one you're defiling every day. By killing them left and right by killers like you: butchers with no respect for life, be that of your own or of my own. Look at you! You're the picture of Satan. Why do you have to commit genocide on Christians? In this modern world, you and your ilk have done just that. Let me tell you what's worse: the deep silence of our political and religious leaders. In the old days, they had the courage to launch crusades; today, we launch platitudes.

"As for you, whoever you are: get the hell out of here now, or you'll be seeing Satan sooner than you think."

Mahmud listened without comment. Knowing that Umberto may well have a pistol, he decided to retreat. "That's alright, Sire. I am leaving," he said in a controlled voice. "Unfortunately, the order to you did not come from me. I am only a conduit, and a zealot at that. Not to worry; I am out of here. But remember: you received your order."

"I've dealt with bullies all my life. No one was as low as you. I can't even compare you to a pig—pigs have nobility of their own. You, you! You are a derelict human being. Go kill yourself; it's the only good you could do. But you won't! Because if would require the courage of a human being of which you have none."

Mahmud opened the door and quickly walked out into the street. Umberto rushed to the window to get a last glimpse before he disappeared out of sight. His gut feeling, though, told him this was not going to be the last of that man.

"Why me!" he exclaimed to himself, his heart pounding. "What have I done to deserve this?"

What drenched him was the sight of Fafa and their two handsome boys. That thought almost paralyzed him to the point he almost staggered on his feet. One of the waiters saw him and walked over to assist him.

"Mr. Saracino, are you well? Can I help you?"

"Thank you; thanks. I am going to my office. To think that my bloodline intersects with that bastard: Look what that bloodline has created! A new breed of soulless murderers!" he commented in anger. He knew this was not the last of that man; he was sure of it.

After checking the working condition of his pistol and found it to be operational, he felt the need to procure an unobtrusive side arm.

About 15 minutes from his restaurant, he walked to the *mercato nero* the black market; there he could buy or order anything, from drugs, to machine guns, from the *De Vulgata Bible* bible to illuminated copies of the *Qu'ran*. The place bustled with people walking by vendors singing praises of their products—a real cacophony of the Neapolitan dialect sounded off by disparate voices of boys and girls, and older men and women. "What a place to bring up a family," he said to himself in a congratulatory way; he had made the right decision to move to Amalfi for a better life for his kids.

Umberto approached the man from whom he had bought the pistol. Recognizing his old client, he yelled: "*He, Umber'! Come stai?* How are you, Umberto. *E che te pozz' fà* What can I help you with?"

"I need a good pistol I can carry in my pocket and not be noticeable. Do you have such things?"

"Do I have such things? Me, *o capo rei capi camorristi!* Come, let me show you."

Inside his flimsy store, he opened a bag full of small arms. "This one would be perfect for you also because you can find rounds practically any place. See, it's a Beretta! Here, hold it; it's not loaded."

Umberto held it in different positions. Feeling comfortable, he decided to buy it.

"How much do you want?"

"*Pe tè*, for you, whatever you want to give me. After all, you always treat me at the restaurant, especially when I bring my favorite dates, he said with a genuine smile, and twisting his fingers to the left of his left cheek, which meant he approved the food, the entertainment and the looks of his date.

The pistol in his right pocket and several cartridges in his bag, after slipping him an undetermined amount of cash, Umberto walked out to the noisy street, feeling more secure and even more worried.

That night, after closing, and the personnel gone, Umberto decided to walk around the building to his car in the back— an old Fiat 126 with several rust spots with appropriate scratch marks, a rusted muffler, and bumpers that have seen their day. His Fiat was the same that served the Russian people behind the Iron Curtain for decades. The same car was issued as the 124 Spider, now a new model. Looking at Umberto's car, no serious thief would want it, especially if parked on the streets of Naples. The car, however, was transformed by a private firm, and it had all-around bullet-proof glass, reinforced doors, theft-proof doors on trunk and hood, an antenna that received more than typical AM-FM signals, a four-speed transmission, heavy duty breaks, anti-sway bars, acceleration almost equal of a *Testarossa,* re-enforced suspension, and special adaptors for offensive weapon fire. On turning on the car, the engine sounded more like a modern red 124 spider than a pea-green Russian 124 family sedan.

He pulled out onto the main street, on his way to Amalfi. It was past midnight. The streets were practically deserted. As he drove past the first street on the right, he noticed a car pull out behind him. Having gone more than five minutes, he saw the car was still behind, staying at a reasonable distance. To make sure the pursuit was not by design, he took the coastal road south toward Amalfi. The road was slow to drive due to all kinds of construction work and heavy natural curves. In many ways, this little frequented road was not much different than the famous Amalfi Drive itself.

In a section of straight road, Umberto accelerated to about 70 miles an hour. Looking at the back mirror, he saw the car in hot pursuit. At a heavy curve ahead, he came to an abrupt left turn—to about 10 miles an hour. The other car slowed down accordingly. A couple of kilometers ahead,

Umberto remembered heavy construction, at the intersection east to west. The extension to the west was blocked. Knowing this, he accelerated to about 80 miles an hour. On reaching within a couple hundred meters, he turned his direction for a right lane entrance. Immediately thereafter, he turned the signal off and made an abrupt turn to the left lane. The driver took the bait and went rough shod onto the right. On seeing the block, the driver swerved to his left, into the side of the steep cliff. In a second, the car went careening down the cliff, turning upside down several times and bumping off of sharp rock formations. In no time, the car took a last dive directly into the water. Having come to a stop, Umberto ran to the precipice, just in time to see the lights still on the car as it sunk. He shook his head, recited a quick prayer, and went back to resume his drive. As no one was there to witness the accident, he decided to proceed on the road instead of taking the *autostrada* to Amalfi. Now, more than ever, he wanted to be sure that no one else would be able to pursue him—very possible in exiting the highway. Finally, he got home without incident. Parking his car in the garage, he walked up the steps in complete circumspect, making sure the doors were locked and not tempered with. Inside the usual dark made the night light shining brighter. He walked to the boys' bedroom. Seeing them both fully asleep, he breathed a sigh of relief. He placed his hand on the boys and kissed their heads one after the other. On entering the bedroom, he also saw Fafa, sleeping as usual—another sigh of relief. Once in bed, he extended his hand over her breast and pulled her back into his belly. Before long, he fell asleep, as though nothing had taken place.

In the morning, Fafa served breakfast on the deck. Umberto never mentioned a word of what had happened to him the night before. The boys did their own thing, mainly playing with each other. If ever there was a picture of human harmony, the four individuals on that deck was proof that such achievement was obtainable by other human beings. However, Umberto was obviously self-absorbed.

"Fafa, I want to show you that I decided to carry a pistol on me. You know, the restaurant business brings all kinds of clients. We never know who may come in. For sure, we do not know how many of our clients are—just standard clients; they come to eat, to drink, and to be entertained. If they get their money's worth they are fine; otherwise, they will complain. Others, on the other hand, may become clients to fulfill their personal, professional or political agendas; these are dangerous. Because of them, I got this small pistol which I carry in my pocket. You need to know because you may want to clean my trousers as you normally do. I have it here; I'll show inside, out of sight of the kids."

"Yes, darling; I will. Not to worry. But, Umberto, what's bothering you?"

"Honey, the only thing you have to know is that I have enjoyed our love for all these years. I am a very lucky man. And, these two boys: We're so lucky. Please listen: I am worried about what's happening in the world. It seems to me new hordes are breaking out. The Dark Ages may be replacing our Age of Enlightenment. Please, keep your eyes open. We need to be vigil at all times."

As he was uttering those last words, Michael walked out of his apartment. "Good morning!" he exclaimed enthusiastically.

"Yes, Michael, good morning: Where's Jody?" Fafa asked with a smile on her face.

"She'll be out in a few moments. We're on our way to the Cathedral. My brother is well advanced in his High Mass. It looks very good, indeed. I see the boys are having a great time together."

Unaware of Umberto's predicament, Michael and Jody walked across the busy square, up the wide marble stairs to the main entrance. Don Paolo was standing with several musicians and vocalists by a side altar to the right. On seeing his brother and Jody, he yelled for them to join the group. Prominent in the group were: the composer, the *Maestro*, two writers, and the arranger. Because the production was envisioned to be large, the AV director and technicians were also there.

After the introduction, wherein everyone was full of smiles, Don Paolo continued with his concept. First he gave the outline; then he gave his rationale behind each point; lastly, he asked for questions and suggestions. This was his outline:

1 Reduced percussion behind the main altar;
2 Two sets of woodwinds, brass, and small chorus—
   at side altars
3 Full orchestra: woodwinds, string, percussion, brass,
   full chorus—to the rear, in the center
4 The audience spread throughout with freedom to move
5 Sheet music of various parts given to audience at doors

After about one and a half hour, Don Paolo dismissed the group, and each person took off in various directions. They all seemed very inspired.

"What do you think?" Paolo asked his brother.

"I never understood the involvement when you first described it. Now that I am here, I can feel the effect. Except that there is no stage here; the whole floor of this vast cathedral is the stage. I am curious to see how the people will react; I am sure they will turn their faces according to where the music comes from. Cleverly, they will all be looking at the altar first—to the percussion behind the altar. Then as the score proceeds, the music and chorus from the side altars will create some confusion. The big part of the prediction will be with the last movement with the full orchestra joined by all the musicians, choruses, and church participants... What do you think, Jody? Am I making sense?"

"Don't ask me! Ask your brother," she answered with a twinkle in her eye. "Nevertheless, I do have a question: Where is the light technician? After all, by your own account, the theme is to go from darkness to light, from night to day? Isn't that right?"

"I told you, Michael, you have to bring Jody around more often."

"Wow? I can just see the expressions on the people's faces—from dark to light! If you don't mind, I want to be in the very center with all those people," Michael answered in a resolute and cheerful tone.

"Michael, Paolo: I have an announcement to make, and I would like to do that at dinner..."

"Is your answer, yes, or no?"

"Of course it's yes," answered Paolo. "What is you pleasure?"

"The *Tarì* will be fine."

"Seven!"

Michael had no idea on the announcement, and was curious. At one point, he thought it may have had to do with her mother, possibly deciding to get married with Domenico. Although he tried several times, he never got a clue from her. Finally, at the *Tarì*, after a great meal, Michael ordered dessert with *prosecco*.

"Jody, you have to tell us your announcement. You promised."

"Yes, darling," she answered, raising her glass. When the two brothers raised theirs, she continued: "May our first child be a boy like you, Michael! I am so very happy."

Michael was blown away, and Paolo likewise. Jody had pulled a fast one, and the announcement could not have generated a higher joy. The three drank. Their glasses on the table, Michael embraced Jody, quickly to be embraced by Paolo.

At this point, the restaurant guests understood the reason for the commotion, and they all shouted their congratulations to the would-be mother.

At the apartment, that evening, while Michael was in the bathroom and Paolo in his room getting ready for bed, she opened her bag, picked up the phone, and placing it on her bracelet, sent a one-word message:

Pregnant

As the screen turned black, she rubbed her fingers alongside the pocket containing the pistol, and placed her bag in its special inner compartment.

For Michael, that evening was unreal, full of happiness the likes he had never felt. In bed, he kissed Jody. Then, he rubbed her belly, kissing it many times. Jody was awed at getting so much attention. She believed in the miracle of life. Now she was part of it, and it was more than enjoyable. She had not really expected it to be so fulfilling. Extending his arm over her side, he placed the palm of his right hand over her belly. Finally, they fell asleep—her back into his, no longer aware of their bliss, or of anything else.

Domenico asked Julie to have Michael plan to visit the site overlooking Monaco, in conjunction with the wishes of their Committee. It was felt that the area needed to be better surveyed and analyzed. Specifically, they wanted to know whether the single antenna erected at the suggestion of Michael was enough, or whether the situation may demand an additional unit locate in a different spot.

Michael and Jody had already reached the outskirts of Genoa when RAI interrupted its classical music program with special news:

> *A car was lifted out of the water south of Naples. Two men strapped to their belts were found dead. In the car, there were also three assault weapons, side arms, and ammunition. The dead men carried no personal identification. The police are asking for help in identifying the men. First indication: these two men were terrorists working in the area of Naples, but not necessarily connected to camorra-type organizations...*

The expression on Michael's face changed. "What could this mean?" he asked—a frown on his face.

"What is wrong, darling?" Jody asked, successfully hiding her own apprehension. By the time we get back, I am sure the investigation will reveal the details... Look, there's a Bar-grill ahead. Let's stop for a *cappuccino*. I can really use one..."

"With a warm *sfogliatella*?" Michael added with a satisfying smile on his face. He realized he had overacted on hearing the news.

Upstairs, they sat by a table above the passing lane of the *autostrada* below. Cars sped as high as 140 kilometers an hour with hardly any encumbrances.

"The difference driving in America is that slow drivers pigheadedly insist on driving slowly in the passing lane. In Italy, that does not seem to be the case," Jody commented.

"Look at that red car—it was a Ferrari *Testarossa*," exclaimed Michael. Look: It's already gone.

With the pastry and coffee on the table, the two looked at each other with puzzled expressions on their faces. Each wanted to broach their concern on the news, but neither could find a way to do it.

"When I'm in Naples, I always stop at any *pasticceria* for breakfast. I have never been dissatisfied," Michael stated.

"What about this *ndrangheta*? What's that all about?"

"Every society has individuals who organize themselves to commit crimes for personal gains and to the detriment of the citizens at large. Naples has its own, of course," Michael explained.

Jody quickly joined in: "You know. My mother always talked about the Boston gangsters: how they were and are portrayed in the newspapers. When criminals have Italian names, the editors almost always identify their Italian ethnicity with connections to the Mafia, Cosa Nostra, or the underworld. When criminals from other national, ethnic, or racial groups appear in the media, the editors simply list them as criminals. Among the worst scenes are those in Boston. Non-Italian-Americans committed the least number of crimes. But to judge from the newspapers, they were the biggest offenders."

Michael listened, but showed no interest in pursuing that theme.

Jody pressed on that possibility: "Do you really think it had nothing to do with those two guys?"

"I don't know, Jody. But, I tell you, this: *sfogliatella* does not taste good to me. How is yours?"

"As great as ever, and the coffee just as great!"

"Jody, we've got to go back. I don't feel good about any of this," Michael interjected, an aura of concern pervading his face. "Now more than ever, we need to be more circumspect about our surroundings. We have a baby. Our responsibilities are different now."

"Of course, honey, I understand. I feel the same way. I am so happy both of us have assumed this responsibility. Our baby is lucky indeed to have us as his parents."

"You said *his*. You already know it's a boy?"

"Michael, I don't know. Would you mind a baby girl?"

"Only if she didn't look like you or was not as bright as you."

"Well, darling, that will get you everywhere. What time are we getting home?"

At about 9:30 in the evening, a few days later, Umberto received an urgent call from Fafa: a strange man was appearing at the bottom of the stairs, peering into the apartment door. He would stand for a minute or two, disappear and return again. On telling her to be sure all the doors were locked, he asked her if the Michael and Paolo were home. On hearing that they were not, he told her that he would be returning right away, and to keep the phone handy.

Having instructed his manager to close the restaurant as normal, he rushed to his car. His right hand making sure his pistol was in his pocket, he sped off as if he were at the front of a Formula One car race.

Averaging about 180 KPH, shifting regularly between fourth and fifth gear, his engine at the highest RPM, Umberto reached his apartment in not time. Unfortunately, he arrived too late.

As he climbed the lit-up stairs, at the same time Mahmud had just stepped onto the deck. On seeing him go for his pocket-knife, Umberto lunged forward, tackling him as a fullback of an NFL team. On the ground, Mahmud quickly got up, looking for his knife. Once again, Umberto dove with his head right in Mahmud's chest, causing him to stumble against the railing. Off balance, he fell with his face down, his neck between the broken railings. On seeing Mahmud struggling to lift himself up away from the chokehold, Umberto jumped with both his feet onto Mahmud's gross neck. Holding the top railing firmly with his hand, and with foot heavy on the neck, he pushed down with all his might, he screamed:

"This is how barbarians need to die," Umberto yelled at the top of his lungs as though he were the real Saint Michael: His foot pressing down on the Devil's neck while holding the spear ready to drive into the heart of the Devil. Then, as he pushed himself up and down to press harder on Mahmud, he realized the man had almost stopped pushing upward with his hands. His eyes wide open and still, Mahmud finally stopped moving altogether. There was no way Mahmud could remove Umberto's heavy foot on his neck.

In a rage, Umberto almost flew to the top of the stairs. He rushed into his bedroom. There, Fafa laid on the bed, her neck slashed, blood still bleeding.

"No!" he yelled in desperation as he ran into his sons' room. There on their beds, they laid dead from wounds to their neck. "God, God! Why! Why them; they never did anything to anyone! They never did anything to anyone," he repeated in between sobs and screams, even as he held the boys to his chest, and kissing their heads. For some unexplainable reason, suddenly he stopped crying. After gently placing the boys on the bed, he ran downstairs in a fury. He grabbed one of the steel replacement rods he hovered over Mahmud's body, and began to push the pants off the dead man. The rectum uncovered, Umberto began to place the tip of the rod into the man's rectum. As he was about to push it through, he stopped.

"No, No!" he yelled desperately. "No, No! An animal would not do this. No, No! And I am not a barbarian. There's still a God for me and in me," he repeated to the top of his lungs. "I am a human being. I was born redeemed," he continued, sobbing even more. He threw the rod over the railing and fell down onto the floor, his mouth open—saliva gushing out to a stream of tears. "We've gotten beyond the Siege of Malta!" he exclaimed once again; immediately thereafter, Umberto passed out.

Once again, the Police were unable to identify *Mahmud*. Even the name was not for real. Newspapers and other media outlets continued with all kinds of speculations—suppositions at best. There really was no good information available. The authorities, however, confirmed their efforts on the investigation.

Meanwhile, Amalfi committed itself to a city-wide funeral, with the Bishop administering to the funeral Mass, on Monday. Cemetery plots had been already reserved at the Monumental Cemetery of Amalfi. Even the City of Naples made a special commitment on behalf of Umberto's contribution to the city; it sent one team of its traditional specially manned coach-hearse.

As one could imagine, the St. Andrew was jammed packed. A single highly-polished walnut wooden casket with colorful drapery was at the center of the church. The Bishop, followed by Don Paolo and the rest of the staff, led the ritual. Altar boys stood at the ready with their incense dispensers— light wisps of smoke-spread all over the church. Many in attendance put their fingers to their noses; others just cleared their tears from their eyes.

Flanked by Michael, Jody, Julie, and Domenico, Umberto sat dejected. His eyes looked caved in; his demeanor: deep and taciturn.

The Bishop exchanged a quick glance. He immediately knew there was nothing he could say or do to assuage the man's utter desolation. Nevertheless, he went on as planned. The liturgy was full blown; the music in consonance with sadness. Over words of optimism on behalf of Fafa and her children entering Paradise, and therefore participation in eternal bliss with God himself, the Bishop walked around the casket covering it with the wispy incense. The chorus sang an early Palestrina piece; trumpets sounded as well.

In the end, the pole bearers prepared the casket to be taken out. Umberto stood up as an automaton having no human life. Michael placed his arm around him. Umberto did not turn his face; his eyes stayed on the casket.

Outside, the team of Neapolitans placed the casket gently in the hearse. On command, the horse began its sad trek to the gates of the cemetery. The brass ensemble with percussion played its typical funeral music. Even the young people, especially those of the two brothers' ages, remained silent, many with tears rolling down their faces.

At the burial site, attendants at the large structure awaited for the casket. After placing it on a proper shelf, they hermetically closed the door. The Bishop turned to the people for his last prayer. Then, after leading the people in the sign of the cross, he asked them to return to their homes in peace.

Once again, Michael held Umberto with his hand. Feeling no real response from his friend, Michael looked in desperation at Jody. Domenico, sensing the problem, moved to the other side of Umberto. With difficulty and frequent stumbles, they returned to their apartment.

In similar events, family and friends would meet for a repast. This time, there was no such meeting.

In the next few days, Umberto did not leave his apartment, Both Michael and Jody did their best in bringing food and drinks. However, Umberto, though grateful, did not eat any food in their presence. He had decided not to eat at all. Falling in a coma, Umberto died. Apparently life was no longer bearable.

Jody's emergency number sounded and immediately stopped. It meant for her to read an attached message. She looked at the phone with an awful premonition. Hesitantly, she placed the instrument on the bracelet, but had to pull it back because she had not matched the correct notch. "Oh, if only Michael were home!" she said to herself. In a couple of seconds, she made the right connection:

> *leader dead*
> *throat complications*
> *retributions alert*

As before, the screen immediately went dark. Placing the phone in her bag, she made sure to check on her gun within the bag. Specifically, she made sure she could shoot from the outside by inserting her finger into the hidden hole of the bag. Her concern was on how to tell Michael. Her biggest concern, however, was their individual safety, because, whereas the threats were real, the reasons for the three of them were without rational foundations. She did believe that Michael had unwittingly contributed to that situation: But, where to go? Under those circumstances, where could one go and be safe? Her head was full of references:

In America, with its 911?

In France and Belgium?

Worse, in any of the so-called Muslim nations—all riddled with daily brutal attacks by terrorist armed only with bomb-producing mini massacres? Which God do they follow: The one that orders them to kill? Or, the God of those who are killed? Where does the rational human being come from? Does he come from the Bible? Does he come from the Quran?

Once in the bull's eye, how does one evade it?

Michael had finally returned home. He had gone to a special meeting on the Vesuvius Committee. On entering the apartment, he automatically felt something was wrong. On confirming he had heard a brief report on RAI that an important leader from rival Muslim tribes had died from complication of the throat, he too became apprehensive.

"We'll just go on with our activities. We need to be vigilant: that's all. Nevertheless, I think we should take another trip to the mountain. I want to be sure you can get there on your own, if you need to. Besides, we should want to spend another night together up there. What do you think, Jody?"

Packs on the back, in shorts for both, Jody carrying her back pack with the strap around her neck, they walked downstairs along the walkway leading to the slip. The water was clear and gently rolling its smooth small waves against the retaining wall. A steel railing allowed them to maintain their balance in walking.

At the slip, Jody took charge, including picking the line. Having started the motor, they were quickly on their way, leaving behind what looked like a tranquil city. At the cave, she secured the boat inside at the prescribed place. Thus far, Michael was pleased in seeing her do everything just right. They walked around the natural statute of the *Duce*, and up the meandering pathways, clinging to rocks or undergrowth when needed. Further up, they began to see the markings they had placed on their last visit. After walking in or around the man-made tunnels, they were able to see the top of the mountain.

Taking a break, they sat on a slab or rocks overlooking the Tyrrhenian Sea. The blue water reflected vividly into the sky and vice versa. Both were prone to seeing the beauty in nature, marveling over the infinity of colors and forms of all kinds encompassed within their eyes. They were even more impressed in noting that nothing stood still; nothing in nature was static, including the slab they were sitting on. However, they analyzed everything from a poetic point of view. They even referred to God at one time.

"How does this all come about?" Jody commented in a low voice.

"You are right in the question because you said, 'How does this all come about?' not, 'How did all this come about?'"

"What's the difference?"

"Just think how many new life forms, new trees, different chemical formulas are coming into being every moment. It's just that we are not privy to these things. We think, as scientists, that we have discovered just about everything there is to discover. This observation would stand if nature—this earth and sun were static, non-changing. God has neither come nor gone."

With Jody leading, after about another 45 minutes of climbing, they reached the summit. Both made 360 degree turns in awe of the continuous panorama. After the brief pause, they continued until they reached their headquarters. Everything was exactly as before. Jody pulled out the crow bar, inserted it at the bottom to the right, and took out the roller. Then, after inserting it to the right, she re-inserted the bar, and the slab rolled open. "*Voilá!* Magic, thanks to you."

Michael turned on the power. With the antenna orientation fixed, he turned the receiver on.

"Why is that so important, Michael?"

"I want to know the chatter coming from the East. I want to know if there is any substance to the report on the supposed death of this individual. I need to know if I ever recorded his voice."

"And what would you have done had you made that recording?"

"Nothing, nothing: As it turned out, I was never able to

do anything because I got nowhere close to achieving the goal of my experiments. Otherwise, Jody, I am sure I would have tried to kill those guys, including individuals the likes of those that killed Fafa."

"Yes, I believe you would have…"

"That's why, Jody, we have to be careful now more than ever. I cannot let anything happen to you," he said looking at her belly. Levels of responsibilities have risen drastically. This is the only place where you and I have a chance of being safe, of surviving. I want to think of this place as our alternate abode."

Michael explored the surrounding, with Jody in tow. They walked in many directions in and between outcrops of solidly anchored rock formations and big boulders spread throughout. Only here and there were remnants of underbrush.

"I guess if we were to keep walking south we'd reach the top of the mountains surrounding Amalfi."

"Yes, Jody, this is the direction. By the way, there are many tunnels that go in many directions especially in the Amalfi area. You know, I don't think there is any kind of report with a listing of their locations. Who knows what's still there," he wandered aloud.

While Jody stood to one side, Michael, with his earphones on his head, listened to radio signals with the hope of verifying the report on the death of the prominent tribal leader. Finally, he heard his name.

"Do you recognize the name?"

"I do not."

"So, what does that mean, Michael?"

"It means two things: One, I have failed with my experiment; Two, another person may have succeeded. Either way, I am a total failure because on one hand I had nothing to do with his death (although I wish I had, especially when I think of

Fafa); on the other hand, I am being blamed for something I didn't do. Worse, some believe I have a secret to some new weapon when it is only an imaginary one."

"Michael, I have a suggestion."

"Yes."

"I'll get the *panini*; you get the glasses with the wine."

"*Va bene, amore.* Very well my love," he responded. On saying the word *amore*, he felt his heart quicken. He was still very much in love.

Sitting on two folding chairs, facing the Mediterranean Sea to the west, the two just chatted as they ate.

In Washington, General Miller called a meeting of his leaders together. The buzz among each was: "What the hell is she doing on top of a mountain?"

"Gentlemen, we have confirmed the death of the Wahhabi leader. We also know the cause of death—cancer of the throat. It is insinuated that this cancer was caused by some sort of radio transmission having frequency-specific intelligence which recognizes the oral apparatus within the mouth and infects some specific organ. It is science fiction to me; it doesn't matter, however. It is for real to those who don't know any better, who want and need scapegoats for their actions.

"I am afraid that Jody is in danger, and that she, together with Michael Capoverde, are looking for a safe haven.

"We need to send a Special Forces detail to Amalfi and to this specific mountain top. The reason is we have reports of sporadic FM and AM radio transmissions from that point that make no sense whatsoever. We need to find out more on what's going on.

"Have the Italian authorities been contacted?" The Commanding Officer of the Navy Seals asked. Are we to expect military-type confrontations? Do you have more information?"

The General answered in the positive to the first and in the negative to the second and third. Then he asked to be shown the results of the drone's surveillance. Sure enough, photos showed human activity—even spots with possible antenna activity.

"Is the only route to the top through climbing?" The General asked.

"There are several routes to the south and east: not easy ones, however," commented the Officer.

"Do we have agents on the ground?" the General asked. On hearing a positive response from the CIA, he continued: "First, neither Jody nor Michael is a target. Second, the three dead men were terrorists. Third, Michael is their target. Fourth, indirectly, Jody is their target as well. Implement appropriate courses of actions to keep them safe."

The meeting adjourned, General Miller was back in his office. Having glanced at his family's picture on the desk, he turned to the window. Looking across the busy streets, he remembered Jody's kiss. His eyes opened and closed gently. He felt as though he was in a cloud.

Around ten thirty Saturday morning on the floor of the cathedral, several small groups of visitors (a few with professional guides) moved about with ease. On seeing a wedding ceremony about to begin in one of the side altars, out of curiosity, the groups moved close to witness the event.

Jody was dressed in a light blue silk dress while Michael wore a blue blazer with a small American flag on the lapel. Her mother, Julie, wore a similar dress in dark green; her consort, Captain Fracastoro was in full white navy uniform. Don Paolo wore his vestments, with a typical collar around the neck. Except for the unexpected visitors, there was nobody else representing either the bride or bridegroom. In a way, Don

Paolo was practically fulfilling the ritual of a civil marriage ceremony.

The highlight, of course, was assuming the promise to love one another till death, to support one another throughout their married life, to be faithful to each other, and to raise their children within the Catholic Church.

"At this point," Don Paolo observed, "Jody and Michael will exchange their wedding bands. You will note that Jody does not have an engagement ring because it hasn't come, yet." They all laughed, especially the visitors some of whom chuckled as being the best part of the ceremony. "Now, the groom may kiss the bride."

Michael first kissed her hand; then, his hand tightly clutching hers, he kissed her on the mouth. He finally stopped when the visitors burst into a large and loud applause.

"Are we invited to the reception?" one younger boy asked with full smile.

As planned, the wedding reception began around seven in the evening at Umberto's Restaurant. The celebrants were those on Professor Villa's committee with their spouses, plus the *geezers* connected to the *Octos* belonging to Captain Fracastoro, and their spouses. The singer was their favorite: Roberto Spaccacuore.

"*Stasera si celebra.* This evening we celebrate the wedding of Mr. and Mrs. Michael and Jody Capoverde. Please note: Michael has a full set of black wavy hair. How he was name *Capoverde* I don't know…"

Everyone laughed. Jody pushed her fingers through Michael's thick black hair.

"*Brindisi!* Toast!" shouted the Captain, to which everyone stood up with their glasses full of *Prosecco*. "This wedding is truly extraordinary. No finer couple, no more than two wonderful human beings could have made this evening possible. We are sure of one thing: no couple will have as good looking children as Michael and Jody. To your happiness, to your joy; and may you both live in joy!"

Everyone stood up—cheering and drinking. The newly-weds crossed their arms and drank. Michael, of course, kissed her passionately.

"Hey!" old-man Vinci shouted—his glass already empty. "My turn!"

Julie stood up to toast her daughter…

"Wait," Vinci yelled. "My glass is empty."

"Domenico, I thought you, as their Captain, you would have them under control. What kind of Captain are you?" she said to his delight and that of the *Octos*. "To you, my darling daughter: you have been the joy of my life. Michael, you married the most beautiful and the smartest woman in this whole wide world," Julie stated. Everyone cheered, especially Domenico; he stood up leading everyone on.

While they were sitting, eating *antipasto*, and drinking appropriately, Don Paolo stood up.

"May I have your attention," he said in a loud voice.

"Wait one second please. *Cameriere*, please fill my glass," Vico asked, a twinkle in his eyes. He knew exactly what he was doing.

"Of course, Don Paolo answered. I am so glad you're here. But, ladies and gentlemen, I want to toast the newly-weds, and reiterate the fact that they truly make a wonderful couple. You know, I am Michael's older brother. I know him since he was born. In my eyes, I cannot imagine a better, more loving brother. Michael, you've been everything to me. I know you will be everything to Jody. Now, if I may, my friends, I am going to reveal a secret… May I? Michael and Jody, may I?" On receiving their positive nod, Don Paolo continued. "Jody is with child."

Pandemonium broke out. "Two glasses of *prosecco* yelled Vico as he laughed hysterically. Michael stood up. Then, taking Jody by the hand, he pulled her up, turned her facing their guests, he said: "Look: she is also beautiful."

Roberto took to the microphone and began to sing songs from the Renato Carosone repertoire. Everyone was delighted as they chatted, ate and drank leisurely. After having sung a few songs, the orchestra began to play Naples' most famous *tarantella*. After a quick glance to his Captain, Vico stood up, took Julie by the hand, and took her to the floor. In no time, he was jumping up and down as though he was a teenager. To his surprise, Julie held her own. On being turned to the right, she flipped her arm into the air. When he flipped her to the left, she did likewise, with apparent joy on her face. The end came amidst a crescendo of music to which the couple responded in kind. After the music stopped, the two stood side by side, Vico somewhat bending toward Julie. She extended her arm, and he stood up straight.

There couldn't have been better entertained.

Not even the solo dance of Michael and Jody that followed came close to matching the performance of Vico and Julie.

"*Signò*" Vico asked of Berardino's wife, during a lull in the music, so that everyone could hear him, and in perfect Neapolitan: "*É vere che marítete non ce la fa chiù ra garibaldino?*" (Is it true your husband...)

"*Mio marito?*" she answered back. "*A mugliera dovesse esser accussì fortunate.*" (Your wife should be so lucky.) A bragging smile on her face told everybody that old age hadn't reached Mr. Berardino yet.

"*Berardì, e che te race a mangià?*" Vico asked mischievously. (Bernie, what does she feed you?)

"Non songhe fatti tui!" (None of your business.)

Out of the clear blue, Vico extended his neck over Berardino. *"Che stai facenno?"* (What are you doing?) Berardino complained, pushing Vico away.

"Puzzo?" (Am I smelly?), Vico asked"

"Peggio de nu puzzolente. Ma, pecchè? (Worse than a skunk. But why?)

His eyes wide open under extending eye brows, he told Berardino about the incident he had had over a week ago. He had taken his wife to a comedy show, which they enjoyed very much. Because they had had such a great time, Vico thought that maybe this was the time to get into bed to make out. But, when he made a move of extending his hand to her breast, she told him he smelled like a pig.

"E che facisti?" (And what did you do?)"

"Niente, proprio niene. (Nothing, absolutely nothing.) Vico, you are so many things; and you may be a pig. A stinking pig you are not. "

With that confirmation of solidarity, Vico became serious.

The main menu: *spaghetti marinara,* followed by *vitello al prosciutto* with various vegetables, and lastly before the wedding cake, various cheese *bocconcini.*

Vico reflected on the word, *bocconcini,* small mouthfuls as opposed to *bocconi*, regular size mouthfuls. "So," Berardino interrupted. "What are you trying to say?"

"See that woman, there at that table?"

Before he could say another word, Domenico stepped in: "Remember where we are and what we are celebrating…"

By about nine thirty, most of the *Octos* looked tiredly happy. Noticing it was getting late, Michael asked that the cake be brought out.

The usual ceremony: knife in hand, Jody placed the blade

on the center of the large and beautiful cake. When Michael placed his hand on hers, they pushed down for the first slice and to an appropriate applause.

"*Prima me!*" First me!" yelled Vico.

"*No, prima mio marito, Berardino!*" (No, first my husband, Berardino,) Mrs. Berardino yelled in fun.

"Darling," interjected Jody," I will always put you first. I want you to be good till the very long, long, end."

"You can bet on it, Jody. But," he continued, speaking into her ear, "I can't wait for the reception to be over."

Before the reception ended, Don Paolo took to the microphone for a last announcement: he invited everyone to make an effort to go to Amalfi to hear and participate in the High Mass Requiem.

At that point, the Orchestra began to play its last piece— the *tarantella*. Except, this time, Domenico and Julie were already at her apartment. She had felt re-energized doing the *tarantella;* now, she was more than ready to show her womanhood to her lover. Meanwhile, Vico was already in bed, snoring.

Jody and Michael returned to Amalfi soon thereafter. When Paolo went to bed, they decided to do the same. But, not because the novelty of their love-making had worn off. They just kissed, went into their bed, snuggled, and fell asleep. They were too tired.

Domenico and Julie were the new *kids* on the block except for their body sizes and age maturity. They were full of energy and eager to make up on activities the otherwise had lost. Among them was the San Carlo opera house. This building has been very famous for its many productions. Gioachino Rossini, the rock star of his day, had a lot to do with this *Teatro di San Carlo.* The season's repertoire included a new production of *La*

Traviata by Giuseppe Verdi. The story was about a sickly Violetta and her young lover, Alfredo. As expected, their love was doomed by fate itself. While alive, though, they loved each other to the fullest of their potentials. Remarkably, Julie and Domenico were not outwardly conscious of the parallel between the protagonists in the opera and themselves until the story unfolded. Then, suddenly, Julie envisioned the lives of Jody and Michael. She began to cry.

"What's the matter, Julie?" Domenico asked?

Julie took his hand and pressed it close to her cheeks. On feeling the tears dripping down, he pulled her face toward him. "It is a love story unlike ours. We will live a long time and we will love each other throughout that time."

"Yes, yes, darling: we will," she affirmed, keeping the secret to herself.

During the intermission and after the performance which drew repeated applauses from the audience, the chit chat centered on the leading soprano, Sylvia Friedman, an American who had studied at the Conservatory. More importantly, she was African American, now as popular in Naples as any similar soprano.

"We'll have to tell Michael and Jody. They might want to come see this opera," Julie commented. "On second thought: maybe not!"

Jody having gone to spend the day with her mother in Castellammare, Michael and Paolo sat on the deck having breakfast. As usual, they brought each other up-to-date on their personal activities, as well as other items that needed their personal attention. Among others, Paolo had observed that lately, Michael was walking with his side pocket slightly bulging.

"Michael, what are you carrying in your pocket?"

"Oh, oh," he remarked slightly embarrassed. "Here, let

me show you." To his brother's bewilderment, he explained it was the gun that Umberto had given him before dying, and that he had decided to carry it when leaving the apartment. "Besides, so many things happening around here; I feel better carrying it with me."

"Be sure not to take it to church!"

"No, of course not! On the other hand… never mind; I will not definitely take it there. However, you are aware of the fact that terrorists—Islamic terrorists—are hitting mainly un-armed groups, both in their own territories and abroad."

"I know and pray every day, that good sense and respect for life will take over their lives. Oh, I cringe when I read those reports. Nevertheless, we have to stay the course. You know that I am basically an optimist by nature."

"Have you gotten the report on the ossuary? It should have come by now."

"Yes, it came and I destroyed it. I put it through the machine—the shredder!"

"You didn't tell the Bishop?"

"No, because it's my own personal project."

"And why didn't you tell me?"

"I am telling you right now. We just haven't had private time to do that."

"What was on the report?"

"Mainly, what we surmised. One strange comment was in the form of an observation on the fact the only Crucifixion with a large following of people was that of Jesus. Furthermore, there was only one set of bones with special scars. In any event," he added, "at times it is better to leave well things alone."

At that point two men walked upstairs toward the next door apartment. As they approached to turn, Michael greeted them.

"Good morning! May we help you? The apartment is closed," he stated with a slight apprehension. Michael was already feeling the heat being around strangers.

"No, no. We were to have fixed the railing a long time ago. We understand the apartment is up for sale and the real estate office wants the railing fixed."

"Very well," Don Paolo inserted. "Let us know if you need anything. We have cold water inside.

"Many thanks, Father," the repairman answered on seeing the priestly collar. They then quickly moved to the part of the railing needing fixing, having no clue of what had taken place at that exact spot.

"The other thing happening is that the committee's work is coming to an end in a few days. Everyone will be off, including Julie. Guess who's going with her?"

"The Captain!" Paolo answered surprised. "I knew it!"

"Well, he has taken a leave of absence from his port position, and should be back—I think. Jody is staying with us.

"I have meaning to ask you: Are you comfortable with us here with you?"

"Yes, Michael: you and Jody have added great joy to my life. I am very thankful and grateful. You are my brother in every sense of the word."

In about an hour's time, the two repairmen completed their task. "*Abbiamo finito,*" (We have finished) the leader reported to Don Paolo, who in turn asked both to join him for refreshments.

Michael served some chilled white wine from Amalfi.

Honored for having been invited, the man commented on the high quality of the wine.

"Do we have *grissini*? (Bread sticks)?"

"We do; I'll get them," Michael answered.

While Michael was inside, Don Paolo beseeched the two

to join the Sunday High Mass, telling them to be sure to bring their wives, their children, and, possibly grandchildren, not to mention, friends and relatives. When Michael brought the bread sticks, Don Paolo only repeated his recommendation to the two men. The problem with the *grissini:* It forced Michael to fill two more glasses of wine.

The two men having left, Don Paolo expressed serious concern over several newspaper reports of terror activities in the area. Differentiating between the acts of terrorism in the other nations of Europe and in Italy, he could say that Italy was lucky. Nevertheless, he was troubled.

Michael hardly said anything one way or another. He certainly had his own feelings on the matter. Besides, he did not want his brother to have to worry about his younger brother's involvement in these matters. For that reason, Michael changed the subject.

"Jody and I are thinking of taking a one-day trip to Capri. What do you think?"

"She's never been?"

"She will now."

Michael had two options to Capri: go with his little boat, or, go by car to Naples, visit at the Port with Captain Fracastoro first, and then take the boat to Capri. If he went with his little boat, at Capri, he would be able to explore the very erratic coast of the main island and the other extraordinary rock formations in the area; but he would be allowed to go into the Blue Grotto with his boat, for instance. Going with his boat, however, he might be able to do it if the sea level were flat for both directions: Strong chance he and Jody would not make it alive. A few seconds later, he decided to go by car. Instead, he could spend the morning at Pompeii and the afternoon at Herculaneum. He presented his thoughts to Jody.

"Capri!"

In less than an hour's drive, the two arrived at the Port. On telling the guard he was visiting Captain Fracastoro, Michael was given directions to park his car next to the office.

"What a pleasure," Domenico said aloud, as he extended his arms in embracing Jody. Then, on shaking Michael's hand, he asked: "What are you two doing here? Is something wrong with Julie? She was well when I left her."

"I don't know about that," Michael interrupted with a grin on his face.

"Stop it!" Jody interjected with a slight scolding, because it was not true.

"Well, how can I help?" he asked."

"I would love to see your operation. I've never been in the office of a Port Captain," Michael said in a serious tone.

"My pleasure..."

After calling his assistant to take over, Domenico took his two guests around the various parts in the building. In one room, there were many monitors lit up all at the same time."

"Where does your surveillance begin?" Michael asked?"

"With that monitor, right there," Domenico pointed with his hand. It covers the traffic coming and going through the Strait of Gibraltar. We follow the routes of each vessel whether it goes to Portugal or Spain, France or Italy, or, whether the vessel goes to any other port of North Africa.

"When it comes to the Middle East, we have a separate office—for that only. We created it as a separate office because of all the upheaval brought about by Muslim home-gown terrorism. Our hope is sooner than later, we can come to some agreement amenable to all sides, and limit if not diminish the on-going senseless carnage."

"How about the various coastlines: How do you manage

surveillance?" Michael asked, causing Domenico to pull back a little. Then, remembering that Michael used to express himself the same way during the Vesuvius meeting, he quickly resumed his stance.

"We have many capabilities. Our newest potential is the drone. By the way, Italy is fairly well advanced in this field, notwithstanding DaVinci with his helicopter."

The reference brought a smile to Jody's face. She quickly took advantage of the pause: "Enough of this stuff. I want to go to Capri," she interrupted. All the while, she had taken the information to heart.

"*Capitano!*" Domenico called out. "These two *young* people are very close friends of mine. You are the expert on the geography west of Naples. Please stop whatever you are doing. Take our office boat, and bring these two love birds to Capri. Make sure they go into the Grotto, and let them see those natural vertical structures shooting into the sky. To think that sometimes ago, the landmass was connected to the mainland. By the way, his first name is *Gregorio*."

"*Piacere,*" Jody said, extending her hand to his.

"*Grazie,*" Captain Gregorio answered in a kind and appreciative voice. He was rather handsome even though he had one hair grown out of the lobe of his ears, and two hairs growing out of the tip of his nose. Though he knew the waters in the region like the palm of his hand, he was also well read in the literary classics.

"*E, io mi chiamo Michele…*And, my name is Michael. I am Jody's husband."

"Very well: Now that you've all met, let's go to the boat so that you can be on your way. You have a lot to do and to see," Captain Fracastoro," interjected. "Gregorio, here are the vouchers for lunch on Capri. Jody, we're having dinner at my apartment. Your mother will be there. I would recommend stopping for an *aperitivo* at the *Caffè Caso* in the center of the Square. And, by the way, when you're in the taxi, don't worry about crashing; just keep yourselves tied to your seats."

"I heard the rides are wild," Jody commented.

"Indeed they are! You're going to Capri: don't you have a camera?"

"We do, here, in my bag. It takes a great shot even if it is 35 mm."

Once comfortably aboard, Captain Gregorio started the engine. That it sounded like a race car would be an understatement. The boat was used to career speedsters and drug runners, among others.

Once out of the Port, Gregorio ran full throttle. While effortlessly separating the still waters at the bow, the stern continued to sow streams of white foam rising high into the sky. Jody, wild eyed, clung close to Michael. In less than one hour, they were within the main port of Capri.

After docking, Captain Gregorio gave them his cell phone number. "You are on your own. Up ahead is the taxi station. Take anyone—you can only go one way: up or down. When you want me to join you, call me. Within 30 minutes I will join you. *Ciao*."

Having walked to the stand, Michael and Jody climbed aboard an open candy-colored Fiat-made taxi. A smile on the face of an obvious young Neapolitan driver, he asked, in English: "Is this your first time in Capri?"

"Yes," answered Jody, with an unexpected trepidation.

In a couple seconds, Jody was holding on to Michael—her heart in her mouth. She gave out shrills when the taxi almost collided with another taxi coming down from the opposite direction. It got worse when the taxi seemed to be veering off the cliff, stopping in a split second at the very edge—obviously a very well-rehearsed act. By the time they got to the Center, Jody was drained of energy.

"Did you like my driving?" the Neapolitan asked, a grin on his face.

"Never again," she answered with a forced smile.

"How else are you going to get back?"

At the *Caffè Caso*, both ordered the famous *aperitivo* of the house—a Campari blend, served with *patatine,* very much to Jody's liking.

After about a half hour of respite, they once again were in line for a taxi to Anacapri at the very top. Ahead of them was a group of teenage girls already in the vehicle. After receiving notice of take off, with the taxi defying gravity, as though Chuck Yeager were behind the wheel, the only sound louder than that of the car was the shrieking of the girls.

"Taking off," the driver of Michael and Jody said. With that, he took off. Falling back onto Michael, Jody swore never go back to Capri especially when the oncoming taxi intentionally almost collided with the taxi conveying the screeching girls, and then that of Jody and Michael.

"Jody, I've checked it out. These guys are almost accident-free for the past ten years."

"I don't care, unless you more than make up tonight."

"It will be my pleasure," he answered with a sweet but moist kiss. "Besides, after we've had our lunch at the Monzú, you will want to come back."

Michael called Captain Gregorio. As predicted, the Captain was there, at the restaurant. When he arrived, the two were already seating at the outer edge of the dining room with a wide open panorama into the western sea. After ordering the *aperitivo* of the house, each also ordered the specialty of the day as the main dish.

"Remember," the Captain emphasized, "lunch is on Captain Fracastoro."

"I'll have another drink… No, no, I'm only kidding, Jody said, her face one big smile. "By the way, Captain, "what can you tell us about famous people that have come to Capri?"

"Really a lot, if you wish. Like, major Roman emperors spent time here; Tiberius built his famous villa. My favorite Italian author that spent lots of time here was Torquato Tasso, who, by the way, was born in Naples—Sorrento, to be exact. He wrote the *Gersusalemme liberata…*"

"Yes, yes, I remember the name. Mom told me that her colleague, Tony Oldcorn, I believe, translated it for his thesis. Have you heard of Tasso, Michael?"

"Yes, I know of his works, but not in depth. He wrote two epics on the Crusaders. He also wrote lots of poetry. But, unfortunately, I know little of him."

"In my opinion, Tasso presented a well-balanced account on the fight between the Christians and the Muslims. Neither of the two factions was the villain nor the hero, unlike so many renditions wherein one is purposefully made the villain at the expense of the other. For instance," Captain Gregorio continued, "even in the art of jostling, Tasso represented that type of combat as no one before him or after had ever done. Critics have been even in their praise for Tasso's expertise. Certainly, the Muslims of those days had a different view of the Christians for the simple reason that the *Madrasa* had not yet been invented by the Turks. The method of teaching, through repetition and memorization, the Koran to the masses wasn't even in the cards. Remember: even the Koran was not allowed to be printed for more than a couple of centuries after the printing press had come about. This so-called holy-book was reproduced by hand and mostly in vellum…"

"My friend had a couple of them," interrupted Michael.

"Where are these copies; they're worth lots of money,"

the Captain added.

"Unfortunately, I don't know. The owner died in the most ruthless way… Oh, look, they're coming with the main course. Let's eat. I'm hungry!"

Over a couple of glasses of white wine of local vintage, the three leisurely consumed their food in obvious delight. The Captain enhanced the repast by drinking to their health. On learning Jody was pregnant he ordered a special *prosecco* to go with the house *Torta caprese*. In the meantime, at the request of Jody, the Captain ran off a list of renowned men and women who had either worked on the island or lived there: John Singer Sargent, Benedetto Croce, Somerset Maugham, Graham Green, Rodolfo Valentino, Greta Garbo, Sophia Loren, Jackie Kennedy, Jane Russell, and on and on.

"Now, the question is: How are you, in getting down, so we can go to the Blue Grotto?" Michael asked of Jody.

"Michael, you need to allow women to act capriciously from time to time. You just be sure to stand firm in front of me, darling, when we're in the taxi."

The drive down to the port was more eventful than the ride going up. Jody stood closely to Michael, and was not as afraid. She had understood that the ride was part of the charm of the Island. Everywhere they went people on the other crafts—yachts or canoes—everyone always waved at each other, or said *ciao*.

At the port, Jody and Michael took the special boat that took to northeastern part of the island. After about 30 minutes, the boat full of tourists stopped in front of a hole that looked like an entrance. The captain of the boat stopped briefly to tell everyone to duck and stay down while going through, and not to sit up until they were well inside—not until he told specifically to re-take their seats. After several pushes by the captain, the boat floated from rough water to a complete smooth surface of refracting blue water. Its suffused color permeated onto the huge closed ceiling of the grotto to give the feeling of a sky. As the captain moved to the center, he told his guest to have their cameras ready. In a minute, he put his full hand into the water. In an instant, he pushed his hand across the surface. The hundreds of water droplets fell to the surface mimicking cascades of falling stars. The tourists felt as though real stars were falling over their heads, in a luminous blue light filtering into the grotto from the sunlight outside.

Jody felt dumfounded. She had never been involved in this type of what was for her a true natural miracle. She was overtaken, and whispered her feelings to Michael, who drew her close to him.

In leaving the grotto, the captain once again urged the tourists to crouch down until they got outside. There, everyone clapped in excitement.

At the Port, Captain Gregorio was waiting. Aboard his boat, he asked, a smile on his face indicating he already knew the answer: "Well, did you like it?"

"Like it?" repeated Jody incredulously. "It was nothing short of startlingly beautiful. It felt as though the stars were falling from the sky on top of our heads."

"Well, what I am going to show you next very few if any tourist see. We're going to stop at various places along the coast line, and take pictures by the two tall structures still standing above the water. We will come close, but not go through the opening at water level. It may remind you of the California Sequoia with a man-made hole at the bottom to let cars drive through."

The trip for both finally did come to end. Jody was both ecstatic and tired. She began to feel the new demands of pregnancy, and began to act accordingly.

"Are you both ready for supper?" the Captain asked. "By

the way, I want you both to know that, even though Captain
Fracastoro is taking a leave of absence, you can call me
whenever you need," he told them. "I am grateful he chose me
as his replacement for the time being," he added unaware he
was pulling his hair from his ear.

"Grazie, no; I am full," Jodie said, thanking him with
humble gratitude.

On their way to Amalfi, Jody extended her right hand to
Michael, who drove quietly and defensively on the *Autostrada
del sole* The Highway of the Sun that took them home. The
successful trip to Capri tuned out to be more than an enjoyable
highlight in her life, another gift to cherish. Nature, however,
had bestowed upon her the greatest gift of all. Although she did
not express that sentiment to her husband, he felt in the clutch
of their hands.

The City of Naples was bustling with activity. Traffic moved
fast and erratically. It was even more so at the Port. Several
luxury liners and passenger ships were already loading; other
vessels waited in queue. Cargo ships of all sizes also filled the
port. Like millions of passengers before them, passengers,
family members, and friends gathered in the reception halls to
bid their last farewells. Countless tears shed over the centuries
in these places.

Julie and Domenico were in line to board. Jody, full of
tears, held her mother's hand. Michael, instead, walked
alongside Domenico, stopping for the last handshakes and
embraces. For so many, this was the point of beginning and
ending.

"Mom, we'll see you soon in Boston. I am going to miss
you," Jody said amidst a torrent of tears.

"You take care of that baby, honey. I can't wait for the
Baptism!"

With that, the two older couples turned foreword to their liner; Jody and Michael, instead, receded to go back to Amalfi.

In the car, on the highway, Jody received a message. Placing the receiver inconspicuously by the bracelet, she opened the screen:

Alert
General

The screen automatically went blank.

"What was that all about?' Michael asked.

"There should be a law against solicitation and crank calls," she answered putting the phone back into her bag.

Regardless, the message was ominous. Always told not to draw specific conclusions until better information was forthcoming, Jody's hunch that, despite the many international crises being reported, and there were indications of possible nuclear activities in the East and in the Middle East, from North Korea to Iran to the newly established Caliphates. The preoccupation, among the leading countries as China and Russia, as well as the countries of the American continents, let alone Europe, was that an armed missile attack was more than possible by some runaway entity tied to religious fundamental-ism—neither Christian, nor Buddhism, nor Hebraic.

Notwithstanding the media coverage on individuals committing catastrophic actions against other, innocent human beings—always planning the destruction of fellowmen without realizing the real potential of their own demises, Don Paolo worked feverishly in mounting his Opus for the Sunday High Mass, as though those manned forces either did not exist or their leaders would come to their senses and stop.

Together with his collaborators, he was well on his way

in giving body to an idea based on the simple basic theme, in no particular order:

From dark to light, from noise to sound, from death to life, from chaos to order, from incipient life to organic life, from chemistry to biology, from tyranny to presidency, from one to many, from Goliath to David, from the singular to the collective, from sound to symbol, from symbol to words, from words to intelligence, or, from sperm to the human being, from un-evolvement to evolvement, from the simple to the complex, etc.

Don Paolo had ideas of his own on how the earth was created; he kept to his belief without actually sharing his concept with anyone especially with those who knew about science. Secretly, as a man of religion, in his short life, he came to find more assuredness in his belief in religion than in science. His basic reason was that just about every scientific discovery eventual was proven either wrong or defective, starting with Aristotle himself, the Ptolemaic Universe in ancient times, or Darwinism in modern times. And, certainly, not all the discoveries of Galileo proved to be true. Regardless, Don Paolo considered science having the dual potential of enhancing life in the sense of daily living, or of destroying it collectively as with nuclear, biological, and whatever other weapon system capable of producing mass destruction.

His basic premise was as follows: Whether the action began from within the Sun itself, or due to another object colliding into it such as another planet or another star, that action caused the sun to spill over its boundaries in the form of solar eruptions or sun flares. These—when they take place, which is almost constant as in the surface of water boiling in a caldron, shoot out away from the surface of the sun and then pulled back by the sun's gravity. When, however, these flares being too large and heavy, go beyond the sun's own gravity range, those same flares, through a process of circularity, find their own orbits and eventually establish themselves as single planets or other entities, including solar systems, in particular or specific orbits.

In the case of the earth, Don Paolo believed that the earth was created in that way—from the flares in the form of living lava. Now, in its own orbit and within a different environment, the earth evolved more or less as follows. With its outer sphere solidifying at various levels and degrees, it enclosed or encapsulated its active core. Within this phase, the earth retained all its original elements as exist in the universe such as life: hence, life to biological forms. When water came onto the earth (Paolo had no opinion on how water came to earth except that it did not come with the original flare-flares themselves). The water being a conduit, it broke down solid matter thus releasing its chemistry. From the breakdown of solids, the soil amassed, biology began to take the role in the emerging biological forms: hence, chemistry to biology.

Unlimited forms of life began to emerge on a continuous basis; entire species came and went according to the commands of fate: like the earth itself, no living form being static, every living form cycled and re-cycled for the duration of the earth, even after the earth is reclaimed by the sun itself—impermanence within permanence.

Because of his brain, the human being was born craving answers to his own questions. There being none, he created a God in his image. Satisfied, he created a society to manage his human weaknesses so that both the single and the collective individual could survive to enhance both—the single and the collective unit, under the guidance of God's awareness—accentuating the higher degree of awareness of a closer bond between man and God.

The Requiem, therefore, had to depict these various phases and conclude with the participation of musicians, chorus, and especially the people receiving the mass—all establishing their intimate connection to a living God.

The baby growing within—without signs of anything going wrong, Jody, now a team with Michael both became husband and wife, with new responsibilities being obvious for both. She decided that she had to sit down with Michael and tell him about why she was in Amalfi in the first place, the reason for her dual role. That she should have fallen in love was by fate; it has saved her life by giving her meaning, and by giving her happiness. With Michael having made all these things possible, she could no longer be carrying her *jeweled* bracelet, a *phone* that was not a regular phone, and a *gun* hidden in a bag which she would have used to kill him if warranted. Her compulsion stemmed also from concluding that Michael, in so many ways, was a dreamer on behalf of his fellow human beings except he was no *Superman.* The difference was that Michael never really thought he could recycle the courses and cycles of the Universe. He abided by and believed that like life of any biological form, everything moved forward and nothing ever moved backward. Whatever actions were or are committed cannot be erased or be entirely corrected.

"Michael, honey, please take the coffee outside; I will bring the brioches," Jody asked, her mind made up on her revelations. Her bracelet typical on her wrist, she also brought her bag with her, which was very unusual. Outside, coffee cup in hand, she continued. "Michael, darling…"

"What's with the bag? Are you going to…?" Michael was being humorous. Instead, he suddenly stopped short of finishing the sentence. He knew what was in the bag but never let on. "Are you going to shoot me?" was the original question he never finished. "Yes, Jody, what are you going to tell me about our baby?"

"Other than being fulfilled? No, I have some confessions to make…"

"You do? Don't we all? And, is it really necessary?"

"To me it is. Please listen. I am not a graduate student doing research on the employment market. I work for the Federal Government as a CIA agent. I put my life on the line every day. Although I enjoy my work for its challenges, I can no longer continue with it. I have resigned. You're to be blamed. I fell in love with you, and, now look," she said pointing to her tummy. "I have been investigating you because our government believed you invented a new weapon with the potential of high casualty results. It all sounds good. Even though we really did not believe it could be done, we had no choice but to investigate if not for ourselves, to be sure that others did not get it, especially our enemies. The fact that terrorist organizations have secretly believed that one of their leaders was killed rather than dying naturally from cancer, still worries us. Those people will use anything as excuses for what they do."

"Yes, Jody, I know all that. You need not go any further. I did not know for sure what you did. But never for one second did I believe in your faculty research story. I fell in love with you because you needed to be loved, as I did. It happened that we needed the same thing. Thanks to your employer, on your part, and thanks to my being a bubblehead: we met. Now, we have a life together, and I couldn't be happier. What else, darling?"

"See this bag? See this phone?"

"Yes, both are odd to me. But, you have your own things, and I would never pry into them. I figured you would want to tell me if it were appropriate."

"Well, the phone is special and I cannot tell you more;

the information is classified, even though I have resigned. By the way, classified information remains so until it is declassified. Intention of use or misuse, one way or another, was always considered a criminal action."

"Your bag—your bag: tell me about the bag," Michael asked, more to confirm his gut feelings about the content.

"Well," she answered with some hesitation. "You see, it has a side pocket almost undetectable to the untrained eye. It contains a specifically designed firearm, a pistol that can be activated through this space. I can simply push my finger through to the trigger. If I fire, the bag automatically opens the opening to the front for the bullet to flow through. It's a powerful little gun. I wouldn't want to be at its end."

"What else?" Michael asked, satisfied that he had had the right inkling.

"That's it. You think there could be more? I have a few questions about you: Who was Miss Robin?"

"Miss Robin? Wow! Miss Robin: She was such a nice person. I had many conversations with her. Actually, I used her to bounce off my ideas on phonemics. But she never really knew where I was coming from. I loved her face. One late morning, we were seating at our desks by ourselves. I don't remember what she said. Whatever! I just got up, bent over, and gently kissed her on her mouth. I still remember it. She didn't push me off. She simply gently pulled me closer. In fact, I pulled back and apologized. 'Don't apologize;' she said, 'we should do more off of school grounds.' Of course, we never kissed again and never met anywhere. I still remember the kiss because she enjoyed it as much as I did. So, why would you know about her?"

"I interviewed her, and she told me the same story. It was her description of your kiss that made me fall in love with you. I knew right then and there that you could not have been a criminal, even though I had no choice but to investigate you."

"What else, Jody, did you find out about me?"

"Yes, I would like to know what happened to the old woman who survived a car accident—which was not reported by her bald husband; she later died unexpectedly and without an autopsy?"

"What about it?"

"What do you mean: *What about it*?"

"I don't recall such an incident."

"They were involved with another couple and spend lots of time together. The wife would trim the hair of the other husband—he was semi-bald—in the bathroom with the door closed. He would return to the kitchen with a grin on his face, like the cat that had eaten a canary. To be sure, the squatty old woman knew that her friend was naïve. Her inability to warn him that her husband was having an affair with his wife doomed her. On her dead bed, her husband never left her alone because he knew that she knew her husband was giving it to her trusted but naïve friend's wife, and made sure she would not be in a position to tell her naïve friend about the affair."

"So, are you saying that the husband killed her?"

"That was the story. Can you verify it?"

"Yes, I can, provided you can tell me more because I still don't remember any of it."

"I was told by one of those people that you are the one who had told that story."

"So, now, I am also the inventor of a story I know nothing about. Between my *scientific* research, which has been a complete disaster, and *storytelling*, of which I know nothing—I can keep on concluding that I am indeed a failure—a num skull. How am I going to be seen in the eyes of our child?

"As a man of the world, one full of idealism, who understands nature and the nature of man, who, meaning me, is kind, who would kill a fly only if it were a mosquito biting into the softer part of his soft skin, who never made love to another woman because he waited for me all of this time, a man who truly fell in love and will be the proud father of a *real love child*: how do you like that? Ours is the result of a real love child! How do you like that?" He repeated.

"Very much, a lot actually: Can you tell me more?" she asked with a mischievous smile on her face. "You're so much fun to be with. Now, you just made me realize that I spend a lot of time without sex. I need to make up for all the love-making I've lost..."

"I thought you were never going to get to this point. What are we waiting for?"

The two brothers went to the cathedral to work on the rehearsal. Don Paolo was rather satisfied with the progress; the *Requiem* was well structured. Those having participated in giving it a working form, they were in agreement that they were creating something unique. In fact, looking at the topography alone, they realized that there was no similar work of art on record. Michael liked the music as it was distributed throughout the church, although he had reservation on its title; he did not feel that the work was really a Requiem. Nevertheless, he liked the pervasive theme of reverse entropy.

Meanwhile, Jody had stayed home to prepare sandwiches for lunch. Unexpectedly, the door bell rang. Shaking her head, she paused for a moment. Then, with her bag in hand, she proceeded to the door. Outside was a well-dressed black woman. Taking no chances, she kept the bag in her right hand while opening the door with her left.

"May I help you?" Jody asked, keeping the door semi closed.

"Yes, good morning. My name is Sylvia Friedman. I am a

graduate of the Conservatory in Boston. I knew Paolo Capoverde. In fact he was my professor. I believe he lives here. I
would like to talk with him, if I may."

With that, Jody opened the door, asking her to enter. On
placing the bag in its special place, Jody asked Sylvia to sit
down.

"May I give an *espresso*?"

"Yes, it it's not too much trouble."

"No trouble at all. What brings you to Amalfi? Not Don
Paolo, I hope!"

"Don Paolo—what do you mean? Maybe I have the
wrong person."

"Paolo was a professor. You have the right person and the
right place. So, why are you here? And, yes, he has become a
man of the cloth—a Deacon but not a Priest. Presently, he is
involved in producing a Requiem Mass to be produced as part
of Sunday's High Mass. So, what brings you here?"

"Yes, of course. May I ask your name, and who you are?"

"I am Jody Villa, now Jody Capoverde. I am married to
Michael, Don Paolo's brother. Originally, I come from
Boston."

"It's so nice to meet you, Jody; you seem to be a wonderful person. I am sure you are very happy. As to why I am
here—on this, a surprise visit—is that I have the leading role in
La traviata now at the San Carlo in Naples. I thought it might
be good to get away for a bit, and surprise Professor Paolo—
now Deacon? How do I address him?"

"That, depends," Jody answered, not letting on the fact
that she knew about Sylvia and Paolo, that she was the cause
behind his having had to leave the Conservatory. "Certainly,
Don Paolo might be appropriate."

"Yes, I guess so. As I recall, he always wanted to be a
priest…"

"How would you know this?"

"Paolo and I were very close."

"Weren't you his student? I believe you said that."

"Yes, of course, Jody. We'll talk about that another time. Is it possible to see him? Or: Should I go right back to Naples?"

"No, my dear Sylvia: Let me finish with my chores, here, and we will walk to the cathedral and surprise him. By the way, the coffee is ready. Would you like it now?"

"Yes, please, Jody; thank you."

"My mother went to see the opera before she left for Boston; she did not tell me you had the leading role."

"Your mother does not know me, does she?"

"Apparently not, even though she teaches at Harvard."

"Is that so? I went to a few lectures on DaPonte at Boylston Hall."

"What a coincidence! I went there myself a few times. Do you mind my asking? You are very good-looking with a presence—I am reminded of *contralto* Marian Anderson. Succeeding in Italian Opera is not easy. I am sure that times have changed. You must be pretty good. I mean, not just any *soprano* gets a leading role at the San Carlo."

"You're very kind, Jody. Maybe we can arrange for the three of you to meet with me in Naples. I would love to have you in the audience."

In less than half hour, Jody finished her chores. Typical, before leaving the apartment, she secured her bag, taking only her cell phone. On letting Sylvia out the door, she made sure to lock the door.

They walked down the stairs to the common sidewalk running parallel to the water, in the direction of the square and the cathedral. There were many people in the square. On seeing Sylvia, several men did a double-take, also because she was so good looking. Few older men brought their hands to their forehead, bending their heads. Sylvia smiled back.

"I'm jealous," Jody commented with a smile.

Inside the Cathedral, several groupings of singers and musicians were gathered in respective places. Jody could see Michael next to his brother in the center, near a make-shift podium.

"Come, come with me," Jody said, taking Sylvia by the hand. Let's join that group," she suggested.

They walked so as not to be seen by either of the two brothers, who were taken-up in answering questions. After giving Sylvia the score, Jody told her to sing with the group. Surprised, Sylvia asked for a rationale behind this behavior.

"Not to worry. I want to see the expression on his face when you sing—if he can distinguish your voice."

"He had better be able to; he was my professor..." she answered.

"You stay here. Introduce yourself. See you after," Jody said. As she walked away, she had wanted to ask what other things he might be able to distinguish beside the voice. She didn't for fear of being a typical bitch. Knowing better, she smiled at the thought.

"*Ciao*, darling," Michael said on seeing Jody. "How are you two doing?" he asked, his eyes on her stomach, He embraced her and kissed her gently.

"We're at a rehearsal," Don Paolo commented, a smile on his face. His colleagues laughed.

"Yes, and I am sure you have the singers well super-vised," she said.

"'Well supervised'?" Don Paolo said to himself. Howev-er, he quickly took the baton in hand, and began directing, his plan being to bring each group in without any breaks, both as single units or collectively. An expression of approval was evident on his face as he brought each group under his baton. The passage dealt with Isaac: When Abraham replaced his son, Isaac with a ram on the sacrificial altar he brought forth the first step of the new civilization—from barbarity to civility.

When that group, together with Sylvia began to sing—her voice being very strong, the expression on Don Paolo's face began to change. Something was different. On emphasizing a *crescendo*, and hearing that voice, his heart picked up in its beat. Yet, he could not tell the difference, and the name of Sylvia was not in any corner of his mind. Jody, to one side, standing next to Michael, was able to discern the change on her brother-in-law's face: from smiles to frowns.

With the rehearsal having come to an end, Don Paolo lifted his head in the direction of that chorus. Suddenly, he saw Sylvia walking toward him—his heart was in an uproar. He looked into the eye of Michael; then, beseechingly, he looked at Jody. Don Paolo seemed in shock—silently in shock. Jody placed her arm around his waist.

"Not to worry, Paolo. She may still love you. She just wants you to see what has happened to the student you formed, for which she has become a star."

There she was. Sylvia extended her had to him, a slight smile on her face. "Hi, Paul, you look different with that collar."

"Hi, Sylvia, you look so mature," he said, wanting to differentiate between her looks as a student at the Conservatory and now, several years later as a *diva Prima Donna*. Un-be-known to those around him, except for Jody, no one knew the emotional turmoil within the Deacon. No one knew the background and the relationship between the two.

Paolo had agreed to marry her; it was Sylvia who said no. He remembered her words: *You're a wonderful man; our love-making un-matched. Not enough reason to get married. I will always love you and desire you. I am sorry about you losing your job.* On the bright side, he felt some vindication over the fact that if he had not left the Conservatory, he would not have come to Amalfi and be a creative Deacon. In addition, if it had not been for Sylvia, neither Michael nor Jody would have found each other and gotten together. Most important, he would not have become and uncle to his brother's child. For every action, there is a reaction, he thought, and the result is the offspring of that reaction.

"Michael, please take Jody home for our repast. I want to stop at the sacristy for a couple of minutes... Sylvia, please come with me; we'll join them in a few minutes.

With Sylvia to his left, they walked to what was his office. After she was seating comfortably in her chair, Don Paolo began to talk, with a slight stutter: "This is a huge surprise. I still don't know what to make of it."

"I didn't know what to expect, either. But, please, Paolo, I have not agendas of any kind. I have no reservation about what we did: It was the best time in my life, because I loved you deeply, and I knew that you loved me as much. I never expect that you would be sacrificing yourself, however. And I have loved you more for it. I never told you how much I cried. But, you gave me strength, and I have become the better for it..."

"Yes, Sylvia, I truly loved you," Don Paolo said, standing in front of her. He placed his left hand over her head, and blessed her with his right hand, in the name of Jesus. "And yes, Sylvia, I still love you..."

"Paolo, now I know: we should have had a child. It's my fault."

Before leaving the church, at the door, Don Paolo dipped his fingers into the Holy Water and blessed himself. Sylvia simply stood by looking on. "Why do you do that?" she asked.

"Catholic churches have holy water at the entrances. We have the opportunity of personal initiative, that we can bless ourselves without the presence of a priest. By so doing, we confirm our belief in Christ."

Sylvia moved back, placed her fingers in the holy water and asked him to say the words, which she repeated after him. With smiles on their faces, they left the church with expressions as though they were lovers. Not few people stopped to greet their Deacon walking side by side with a beautiful black woman. No one recognized her as a *Prima Donna*; every man was visibly envious of their Deacon.

At the apartment, Michael had prepared a couple of bottles of *prosecco,* and Jody was ready to serve her *panini.* The four celebrated Sylvia's visit as the artist that she was and as a human being with a great personality. Glasses in hand, Michael called for a *brindisi*: "To Sylvia, welcoming you to Amalfi, and with best wishes with a successful career as a *diva.* Please invite us all to your premiere as Aida at *La Scala* in Milan…"

"Complementary tickets!" added Paolo, causing all to laugh.

"*Grazie, grazi...*" Sylvia answered, a little unsure about her Italian.

Throughout the afternoon, Michael continued to have reservations, but never let on.

"We do have some four hours of daylight," Jody observed. "Why don't we go to Michael's secret hideout—the four of us, and stop at a restaurant on the way back. I am assuming you're staying overnight," she added, her eyes on Sylvia.

"I did not make plans. I do have to be back in Naples tomorrow.

Borrowing practical clothing from Jody, Sylvia was happy to have fit in so well. Of course, she had no idea about the hideout. It was a revelation to Paolo. Michael did not complain in any way or other. Having divulged his secret to Jody, he no longer could presume the place his secret hideout any longer. He did believe that taking them to the top of the mountain would be a memorable experience.

Each wearing sneakers, the four walked the stairs down to the boat. Once again, under the guise to show how good Jody was handling the boat, he asked Jody to be the *captain* of the boat. By so doing, he wanted to assure for himself that she could take care of herself in case of an emergency.

Sure enough, everyone expressed praise for the way she had navigated the waters of an open sea. Inside the cave, Paolo and Sylvia marveled at the verticality of the space. He even made fun of the Mussolini-like natural sculpture at the base of the cave.

Adhering to Michael's instructions, the three followed in his footsteps, pointing to specific natural and man-made landmarks. Paolo was especially intrigued by the labyrinth of tunnels running in so many directions. During a rest period on the western façade mid-way up, Paolo asked of Michael:

"I see many vertical openings having lateral tunnels. If there is a huge tsunami or hurricane with huge waves running into the cave below, are these tunnels impacted by the water?"

"What 'ya mean, Paolo?" Sylvia asked—a slight bewildered expression on her face. She had never been on any such trip in her life, and was successful in hiding her fears.

"Yes, Paolo, there are records that show tunnels almost all the way to the top of being inundated—by sea, not rain water. So, it can happen. Remember that Old Amalfi was destroyed by a land slide caused by water. The top of the mountain just collapsed. But, here's the lesson to be learned. Notice that most of the tunnels take a sharp turn either left or right? That's to diminish the force and velocity of up-ward moving water forced into the lateral caves. So, as I will show you later in my *hide-away*, I kept that principle in mind so that—and of course it will never happen in our life-time, in case there is a surge of water upward, the water will go out the top without inundating my space… Well, enough of this. Jody, you take the lead from here. I will bring up the rear."

With the two women in front, the group cautiously walked up the various paths. Paolo and Sylvia made no bones on showing how impressed they were with Jody, who remembered the various marks they had posted. On reaching the top, Sylvia was obviously out of breath but mesmerized. "How did you do this?" she asked, wide-eyed. "Wagner never came close to this kind of setting in his, *De Walküre.*"

"I never saw the *Opera*," said Jody, "But isn't that about how women decided which men should be soldiers and which soldiers should be rejected?"

"I don't know. I just sang a brief role a long time ago."

"When I was deciding on moving to Amalfi, I discovered that Wagner spent lots of time between Ravello and Amalfi. He wrote some of his operas while living there," Paolo said. "I like his music, specifically his overtures more than the text of his operas."

The four sat on the special chairs, all sipping on semi-cool *prosecco*, all looking and enjoying the view of the Tyrrhenian Sea. Sylvia asked rhetorically: "Aren't those two columns south of Capri in this direction?" she asked, her arm pointing west.

"Yes," answered Michael. "Maybe we should take a boat ride there."

"On our boat?" asked Jody in a disapproval tone.

"No, no: We can rent a boat or take a cruise."

In front of the stone slab, Jody, by herself, moved the slab open with the crow bar. Sylvia was literally incredulous.

Don Paolo had other concerns, and was hoping someone would bring up the subject on where Sylvia was going to sleep the night. In noting the big interest in exploring the area before going back, he decided to let go and join his brother. He was surprised in seeing the array of communication equipment, especially the contraptions supporting the antennas. He hadn't had a clue about his brother's activities, and was flabbergasted in the implications of his brother's network.

"Michael," Paolo observed, "are you saying that you would kill a human being?"

"Of course, *brother*, if it meant saving your life, or Sylvia's, or Jody's and her baby, or, for that matter, or of all those Christians obliterated because they were Christians. I would have killed those terrorists before they could have killed as they did in the West and in the East."

"Of course, Michael: I understand... Sylvia, what plans do you have for tonight?"

"I don't..."

"Michael and I have decided to sleep on the couch. Sylvia can sleep in our bedroom. Is that alright, Sylvia? I am sure Paolo won't mind. Sylvia, remember: Paolo is a Deacon." The three laughed, and Paolo felt relieved despite his re-awakened manhood. "Before we leave, Michael, can you show me how you keep your place from being inundated? No, no: first tell me if water has come up this high in our lifetime?"

After insuring them that such a phenomenon had not taken place in recent memories, he assured them that it was not likely to happen probably ever again.

"So, why the precautions?" Paolo asked.

"I know. However, as I may have already said, there is proof in the lower tunnels of inundation from water being pushed upward... Now, let me show the solution—not full proof, to be sure."

The cave was designed such that its entrance to be to the right, with a rock slab easily moveable into the frame to block any of the natural elements of intrusion of either man or wild animals. As the three listened, Michael referred to Jody on the use of the crow bar to open and close the slab door.

In a moment when the two women were alone, Sylvia asked confidentially: "I don't understand why Michael is so intense on showing you everything. Does he know things you and I don't?"

"He is different, alright; he's very different. In certain areas, I do not understand him at all; in other areas, he's a genius. Above all, he's a wonderful human being. That's why I love him—so very much."

Jody first, followed by Sylvia, Paolo, and Michael, they walked back down the various paths. Once again, Jody seemed proficient in navigating back to the bottom of the huge cave. They even walked across the _solid_ head of Mussolini. Having backed the boat out of the cave, Jody took a sharp left. Revving up the engine, she took off in a flurry.

At the apartment, Michael suggested to go to Ravello for dinner, perhaps to visit Gore Vidal's cliff-hanging villa.

"Who is Gore Vidal?" Sylvia asked.

"Gore became famous for his appearances with William Buckley, Truman Capote, and many others. He was sarcastic, critical, and contemptuous. He became popular and very wealthy. He lived in Ravello, as I just said."

"What was his connection with Ravello?" Sylvia asked out of curiosity.

"He inferred being of Venetian blood because his last name was popular in Venice and in the Friuli area in northern Venice. He was a progressive and an avid Democrat. Aside from his personal idiosyncrasies, he was a humanist of the

Renaissance type. Because of his sarcasm I never liked him; I gave him credit for his erudition, however."

Michael drove the picturesque road from Amalfi to Ravello, being sure to drive defensively. He had had a lot of experience related to the Amalfi Drive.

The men dressed in trousers with light jackets; the women dressed in reserved elegance, each wearing blouses and skirts. In getting dressed, Jody began to notice the change in her body and was pleased to notice the difference.

On coming into the city, Michael passed by Vidal's multi-million dollar estate. The women were really impressed, especially to learn how many famous people had lived there while Vidal was alive.

"It's for sale, Sylvia," Michael commented.

"Ya, ya: I'll buy it tomorrow, because, tomorrow, I will be free from being indentured to the Federal Government—as ex-slaves we have history behind us. I will have paid off my student loans! Alleluia, praise the Lord."

"It is a travesty on how our government has butted into an otherwise great educational system with the claim of helping students on one hand and on the other making them owing to the government. I prefer what Michael and I did: we worked and paid our tuition. As a result, we owed 'nobody nothing,' he said with a purposeful smile.

"I hear *ya*," countered Sylvia, causing everyone to laugh.

As Michael drove to the streets looking for a restaurant, he stopped to survey it; then, moved on to the next. On reaching the next restaurant, they all agreed to have dinner there, mainly because of its location with its view of the panoramic view of the sloping city.

"*Buona sera*," the waiter greeted. "*Benvenuti!*" he added with a smile.

"*Grazie*," answered Don Paolo, his collar drawing attention.

From across the large dining hall, however, unbeknown to Sylvia, she seemed to have been recognized by the Maître D'. Discretely, he called the waiter over to him, spoke in a low voice for a few seconds, and released him back to the four guests.

"This way, please. I have a suitable table for you."

With everyone, nodding, they walked through the crowed hall to their table near the wall, positioned in the center so that they could practically see the full activities of the entire floor. Michael was quick to note that despite the many guests, the hall was rather quiet. Jody and Sylvia, on the other hand, observed how well-dressed the women were:

"Young and old!" she commented. "What do you think, Paolo?"

"I think the food looks great!"

Happy with their table, especially with a feeling of semi-privacy, at the suggestion of the waiter, who moved the chairs to accommodate the women into their seats, the four were more than just content. They never wondered why they had been seated that way: Sylvia was seated with her back to the wall looking at Jody and into the dining room; the men were seated on each side. Two male waiters in white uniforms quickly approached. Seeing Don Paolo with his collar, the waiter deferred to him with a reverential bow.

"*Buona sera. Preferite ordinare dal menu , o, essere serviti a nostro gusto* (Good evening. Do you prefer to order from our menu, or, be served by our traditions)?"

"You are our guest, Sylvia. What is your preference?"

"I don't know. I am the adventurous type, however."

"I'd go with the house," Jody interjected.

"*Va bene* (Very well, we'll go with your suggestions. Does that include the drinks?"

Having received approval, the waiter left. In no time, another appeared with a bottle of *prosecco* on ice with appropriate glasses.

"In your honor, Sylvia," Jody said, quickly joined by Paolo and Michael.

Another waiter arrived with a tray of *bocconcini* little bites—cold and hot, served at the request of the patron. Accordingly the waiter served as asked and as many as requested.

"These are great," Sylvia said. "What makes them better is the wine—*prosecco*, I mean."

The waiter quickly moved to fill their glasses. Having had enough of the first offering of *antipasto*, another waiter arrived with another set, mostly baked items—all individually prepared and very light in body. Once again, the four approved. The next offering included baby artichokes, asparagus, and similar vegetables. With this, the four moved to a second bottle of *prosecco*.

"This stuff is very good. Do I have to be concerned with how much I drink?"

"Yes, if you were Native American," interjected Paolo with a smile, doing a great job containing himself. Sylvia was still his great secret love, and there she was, in full body and soul, and he, the stronger in controlling his lust. Across from him, Michael reached the conclusion that his brother was in full control of himself.

"Did we agree on the accommodations for this evening?" Jody asked.

"Of course, we have," assured Paolo.

Quietly, Jody asked of Michael: "Heaven or Hell?"

"What are you talking about?" he asked slightly irritated.

"The two of them: Do you think they're going to abstain?" she asked with a rather wicked smile on her face but without any malicious intent. "Because," she continued in a sultry tone, "it could be Heaven and more Heaven."

"How do I know?" he answered in kind irritation.

"We'll have to wait till morning," she stated as though she knew what Michael did not. "Remember the custom in some small villages: the sheet display the morning after?"

"Ha, ha, ha!"

"What are you two talking about?" Paolo interrupted.

"We were just wondering on the next course. So far, so good," Jody added, lifting the glass to her lips.

The four were really enjoying their conversations; more so, they were enjoying the food elegantly served in morsels, from fish to meats, from *pasta* to *risotto,* in any amount, but really limited to not more than two pieces. Otherwise, they would not be able to continue. Rumor went that only very few individuals went beyond ten separate servings.

The four were well into their sixth. Among other, they ate rabbit in white wine wrapped in thinly sliced pepper in vinegar. Considering their sustained drinking, they were somewhat unaware of the activities taking place around them.

The sitting of arriving guests, for example, was being conducted, very discretely, to facilitate an orientation toward the main wall.

When the four reached six choices from the courses, and knowing the dessert was on tap, Jody complained that her skirt was getting too tight around her waist.

"That's because you're pregnant—lucky you!" Sylvia commented. I know we're having fun; but, what about the *conto*?" She asked, defraying thus the reference of wishing she were pregnant with Paolo's child.

"Not to worry, Paolo. I have it under control. However," Michael added, "I've had it. There room only for dessert. Cheers!"

The extravagant desserts were also matchless. Sylvia especially out did the rest. She was the last to quit. "This is it for me," she said but not without emptying her glass.

"*Cameriere! Conto, per piacere,*" Michael asked the waiter for the bill.

In a couple of minutes, the waiter presented the bill listing all the items the four had consumed. However, there was no price neither after each item nor a total amount at the bottom of the bill. Instead, the Total Amount a large Zero.

"What's going on!" exclaimed Michael. "This does not belong to us. Please give us the correct bill," Michael told the waiter.

"Please read the other side," the waiter said in a soft voice.

Michael turned it over: *Compliments of the house, in honor of our Diva, Sylvia Friedman. Grazie.*

Apparently, the Maître D' had read about Sylvia, and he just wanted to show his appreciation. He had been at the San Carlo and had been more than pleased by her performance.

"May I speak to him, *per favore?*"

Shortly thereafter, the Maître D' was bowing his head to Sylvia. "*L'onore* The honor is mine, and of our staff, and our wonderful guests. We are honored," he repeated humbly.

"*Come posso* How can I repay for your generosity?" Sylvia asked. Her face was filled with an obvious expression of gratitude."

"You could sing an aria," injected Michael.

"*Cosa meravigliosa* A marvelous thing, *Signora* Friedman. As you can see, we arranged the tables with the hope you would do just that," the Maître D' answered with approval.

Sylvia looked at Paolo. On seeing him shake his head in approval, she answered: "*Va bene* Very well."

She stood up, her back against the wall, the Maître D' quickly turned to the guests.

"*Signore e signori* Ladies and gentlemen, your attention please…"

With that, Sylvia began to sing in a lush, vibrant voice: "*Mi chiamano Mimì,* They call me Mimì, although my name is Lucy…" (from Puccini, *La Boheme*)

Needless to say, on finishing the aria, the guests stood up in total pandemonium.

Few Non-Neapolitan men clapped, invoking the Virgin Mary: "*Madonna mia!*" The men were especially taken by her sensuality.

Several Neapolitan men exclaimed, "*Marònn…*"

Nothing of the sort had ever happened to Sylvia; impromptu as it was, she felt triumphant. Nothing of the sort had happened to restaurant guests either. They were beside themselves.

"*Grazie, grazie*" she repeated. Shrills of joy ran up and down her spine. The women took the flowers they were wearing and threw them at Sylvia. The men followed by throwing the flowers on the table center pieces.

On sitting down, Sylvia turned to Paolo and kissed him on the mouth. She then turned toward the Maître D' and gave him a hug. Meanwhile, Michael and Jody remained baffled; they did not know what had hit them. Jody, however, got up and gave Sylvia double and triples hugs.

Back at the apartment, the four were still high. They were finally inebriated from the *prosecco;* each realized having reached new levels of inebriation, except that, the inebriation-- it had come about, thanks to Sylvia.

The four sat in the living room just trying to relax. Finally, Sylvia asked to be excused. Paolo immediately followed suit, except he went to his room. Jody and Michael, on the other hand remained on the couch. After covering themselves with sheets, Jody queried:

"Well, Michael, what are you predicting? Hell or heaven?"

"Oh, stop it, please! No need to be gossipy. They're mature, and they will do whatever is right."

"I am betting on, 'heaven'."

In no time, the four were fast asleep. The only sound to be heard was that of Michael. His snore was more evident as a result of having eaten too much food, and imbibed too much *prosecco*.

All awoke in the morning. Jody cleared the couch of the sheets. Sylvia soon appeared with a hearty good morning and more hugs from Jody. Soon, Paolo also appeared, fresh-looking and ready to go out for breakfast.

"How did you sleep?" Jody asked of Sylvia.

"Right through without getting up once," she replied, a disappointing expression on her face. She turned to Paolo: "Good morning, honey. I am going to miss you."

In witnessing the exchanges, Michael felt vindicated, but said nothing, although he looked at Jody with a chastising frown on his face.

Her bag in hand, Sylvia walked side by side with Paolo, who wore his collar. Jody and Michael were ahead, not within listening range. "Why didn't you come last night? I really missed you, now more than ever. Paolo, I really love you."

"Sylvia, I almost did. I hardly slept a minute. Memories tore me apart. I realize how much I loved you, and yesterday you gave me proof once again on how wonderful you are. I have to live with and in that memory."

"I understand, Paolo. You did the right thing, my love."

At the bar, they sat at a table outside. The waiter quickly came with a sparkling *buon giorno!*

"We'll have four *cappuccini* and four *sfogliatelle*.

In no time, they were enjoying their last breakfast together. Jody seemed the sadder.

"We will miss you, Sylvia. You brought delight to us all.
Last night was memorable. Keep up the good work; you're
going places, honey."

"Thanks, Jody. You're my newest *bestest* friend."

"How about us?" Michael asked humorously, his hand
extended toward Paolo.

"Of course," Sylvia added. "Paolo is the love of my life."

Paolo trembled from within. Nevertheless, he was able to
control his tears. He had succeeded in rejecting the devil who
had urged him to consummate his sexual prowess. But the real
challenge had come from the Siren within his own apartment,
who solicited him to go beyond the Pillars of Hercules, and he,
Paolo, had stayed behind.

"O.K., everybody, we had better get going. The train will
not wait for us," Michael said, more to lift the mood. Turning
to Jody, he whispered in a self-justifying tone: "Heaven for my
brother; don't you agree?"

At the station, they hugged and kissed. "With her lips
close to Paolo's mouth, Sylvia said her last goodbye: "I will
always love you."

Chapter 8
The "Requiem"

By ten o'clock Sunday morning, residents of the city of Amalfi and surrounding areas were all gathered in the Cathedral ready and eager to be living participants in the Requiem High Mass—a temporary title at best. Both Michael and Don Paolo were present; Don Paolo was the conductor.

Jody, on the other hand, had stayed back to do her chores She agreed to join them just before the Mass was to begin.

As she was in the process of wiping the table, she looked toward the door as a result of some unexpected noise. On looking up, she saw the silhouette of a man getting ready to ring the door bell. Her pocket book in hand, she moved cautiously toward the door. On hearing the bell, she cracked the door open.

"Yes, may I help you?" she asked, her voice subdued.

"I am looking for Jody Villa. I am told she lives here."

"Who are you?"

"I will be happy to tell you," the heavy-set muscular man said, a slight froth in his mouth. "But, I need to be assured who I am speaking with."

"Alright, I am Jody."

With that, the large man grabbed her by the hand and forcefully pulled her outside. "You're coming with me," he retorted. His voice truly threatening, he pushed her toward the stairway leading downstairs to the board walk by the water. At the bottom, by the rail, Jody asked in a very polite and innocent voice: "Sir, can you please tell me where we are going. I have no problem following you wherever you take me."

"I cannot tell you where we are going. Now, stop talking and keep walking," the man ordered threateningly, a slight accent in his words.

"I know where you are going: straight to hell." She pulled her bag up. A single shot went right through the man's heart. "No virgin will be waiting for you; no other woman with *burqa* will be waiting for you. Even the devil emancipated his women from *sharia*," Jody mumbled. With a grim expression on his face, the bully fell dead. Thankfully for Jody, he fell with his chest resting in a semi-erect position on the railing. In an instant, and being sure no one was around, she picked him up by his feet and heaved him over the railing, looking at his face as his body dropped into the water. Probably because he was heavily armed, he sank beneath the water and quickly disappeared altogether. Rubbing her hands for good riddance, she turned her head towards the square and began walking practically by herself to the Cathedral. Never in her life did she understand the meaning and the need to implement the theme "from the devil to goodness" as now. She walked fast, determined to see her brother-in-law's work go on as planned. On entering the Church, no one could detect her agitated state of mind, even though her heart was pounding. She had fulfilled the role of St. Michael, who slew the devil.

She made her way, one bump after another, to the center. To her surprise, Sylvia was standing along-side several solo singers, mike in hand.

"What are you doing here?" Jody asked. Evidence of shock was evident on her face.

"Jody, I couldn't let this go by."

"When did you get here?"

"This morning... Look: Paolo is on the podium. We're starting. Good luck!"

Hanging on the inside walls of the cathedral were many large screens appropriately placed either for the church-goers themselves, or for specific group of performers or soloists. Each screen lit up to give directions to the crowed and to display the dialogues or lyrics of particular songs. When the lights were dimmed, Don Paolo directed his baton to the percussion section. On dropping the baton, windy noises from all around the perimeter began to fill the church with all kinds of noises. Random drum beats accentuated the noise, now changing to depict volcano-type noises of lava moving and solidifying. Bursts of other noises continued to fill the church. The attendees were captivated. They all looked around in silence wandering what to expect next. A man's voice broke the noisy scenario: "The universe has resulted from God; our earth has been issued from the sun. No part of the universe is devoid of God's life potential." Subdued sounds from the brass instruments began to creep through the percussion-produced noises. In addition, chorus-produced fricatives filled the church at various lapses, in exchange between and among the various choruses, and at times tumultuously and dramatically produced noises joined by sibilance's—all at the same time. In addition, clicks without intelligence, forcibly popped up at random:

"In its new orbit, the outer edges of the planet solidified. Its crust, containing the smaller sun within, was further cooled by water arriving in abundance. It filled the lowest parts of the planet. Continents with land masses and mountains emerged. Breaking down the rocks into granules, from erosion, it created the soil. Together with the wind, the water spread the soil throughout the earth. Depending on local conditions—retaining whatever type of soil and temperature, an infinite number of formula-giving organic forms emerged. Among them: grass, trees, animal species, and human beings—all living forms, with each individual fated to evolve and to procreate according to one specific incipient formula. With all of us, God imbued each one of us with a soul. God gave us free will. If we follow negative principles, we will surely go to hell—eternal damnation! If we follow Christian principles, we will go to Heaven—eternal bliss with God himself..."

As the speaker spoke, Don Paolo directed the musicians and chorus to respond with appropriate music.

At one point, Don Paolo began consecrating the host. Due to the large number to receive the host, he made sure to have about 50 men and women to go deliver the host into the crowd. The conductor directed the orchestra and the singers from their positions from throughout the church. As soon as Don Paolo released to the servers the chalices filled with consecrated hosts, as they spread throughout the church offering communion to all those who wished it, the conductor brought the orchestra and choruses together in singing, repeatedly at different levels, *Agnus Dei, qui tollis peccata mundi, miserere nobis.* Each recipient was imbued with an expression of humble reverence to Jesus.

After completing that phase, Don Paolo took a brief pause. On seeing the audience silently relaxed, he directed his baton to the orchestra. With the instructions on the screens around the inside walls inviting everyone to sing, the lyrics of *Shepherd me Oh Lord...* appeared. And, on lifting his baton, the orchestra began together with audience. The whole cathedral vibrated with the fervent emotions of everyone. Then, at a given point, the specific screens in front of the special sections of baritones, tenors, sopranos and older children lit up to the lyrics of, *Mary, did you know....* Each group sang as directed both: as solos single groups, and then all at the same time. Don Paolo, though agitated in keeping control of the multifarious groups, kept his composure. The production was coming off better than he had expected. In his heart he felt that nothing better than what was happening in front of him could have pleased God as much. And to see all of those people singing with so much fate and dedication, he felt a sense of achievement and accomplishment he had never felt in his entire life.

Jody, who was intently participating in the performance, suddenly felt the phone vibrating. Turning to one side, she opened the screen:

ATTACK IMMINENT
SHELTER 10

The screen immediately turned blank. Jody was in shock. She moved toward Michael. He quickly ordered her to take Sylvia and quickly to take the boat and rush to his mountain hideout—not to procrastinate or stop, or to speak with anyone. He and his brother would join him soon thereafter.

The two women, silently, began walking toward the exit, Sylvia in tow. At the door, a detail of *carabinieri* had already entered the church. Its leader walked smartly to the podium. After ordering Don Paolo to stop the performance, he stepped on the podium. Microphone in hand, he asked the people to become silent and to listen to his orders:

"*Siamo in uno stato di emergenza* We are in a state of emergency. An attack on our city may be taking place, we do not know from where or by whom. You are all, without exception, and without panic—I repeat, without panic—to go to your homes, secure the strongest shelter possible, especially basements or behind any concrete enclosure. Stock it well with canned food and bottled water. Take flash lights—do not take bottled gas. Take blankets and sheets. As a precaution, only because we do not know the type of attack, I recommend bringing as many gas masks as you can without wasting time. Make sure you have portable radios and cell phones. Do not use the phone for chit chat; save its power.

"Now, in quick step, without running, walk out and go home holding hands especially with the children."

Michael approached Paolo. "I sent the women to the hideout. We can wait here. I know a tunnel beyond the reliquary. Let's bring as much as we can. Let's go!"

In a matter of a few minutes, the Cathedral emptied. Outside, the square was already empting of civilians and replaced by soldiers in positions with assault weapons. However, no one was expecting attacks either from the sea or by land.

In the port, naval war ships of all kinds were cruising in many directions, stopping civilian vessels whose leaders had not received the warning, and ordering them to seek immediate refuge.

Jody and Sylvia had already reached the top of the mountain and were at the front *door* to the cave entrance. From behind the ledge, she took down the steel bar and placed it under the right side of the slab. Then, after telling Sylvia to press down on it, she pulled the heavy plastic roller out. Then, after inserting the bar under the left side of the slab, Sylvia pushed down enough to allow Jody to re-inset the roller. With that, the slab practically slid to the right; to Sylvia's great surprise, the slab rolled to open. Once inside, they repeated the operation. Jody immediately turned the receivers on. The news was grim: A test missile, with a nuclear warhead, had indeed been launched from an un-confirmed site in the east and traveling west into Europe. While over Greece, the Allies attempted to strike it down, but succeeded only to break its course, because it could not be re-directed. Having passed over the southern booth of Italy, it fell into the deep waters west of Amalfi. When it reached a particular depth, it exploded.

Un-imaginable masses of water arose in the forms of tsunamis and typhoons, moving in all directions, especially to the west and to the east, destroying everything in sight. The first to disappear were the island of Capri with its surrounding columnar peaks; then Corsica and Sardinia disappeared. Slamming into the main coastline, the water pushed itself into every opening. Michael and Paolo, hiding in a tunnel, were sucked out and thrust upward at the other end, disappearing altogether from view. The Cathedral, already broken, its remnants were scattered into oblivion. Water already covered the landmass well beyond the mountains of Amalfi.

To the north, the gulf of Genoa was destroyed. To the West, the huge rock formation, above Monte Carlo, having dislodged, plunged into the sea.

The waters of the Mediterranean, having pushed out beyond the Strait of Gibraltar into the Atlantic Ocean, now were returning into the quasi empty Mediterranean basin with a vengeance. Ocean Liners were tossed about into oblivion as though they were toys. Corsica and Sardinia disintegrated. In reaching the remnants of Amalfi, the super massive tsunami all but destroyed the land to the south and to the east—all collapsing into the water as though land had never existed. Southern Italy disappeared, as did everything else. Although the waters had destroyed all living forms beyond memory, life, emanating from the Universe, nevertheless continued as if nothing had happened.

The storm over, at Michael's hideout, Jody and Sylvia stood silent, unable to reproduce human sounds. Their hair all but gone, their faces were going through a phase of Albinism. In looking south, if they could see at all, there was nothing but water in front of them. In looking in any direction, there was no land—also because they were unable to process or to analyze anything internally. Neither knew whether they were fulfilling the phase from life to death and vice versa. Because their brain stopped functioning, they were unable to engage let alone entertain invoking free will. They weren't even aware of their being alone on top of a mountain surrounded by an open sea. Certainly, neither of the two knew who was responsible for the present attack, which claimed Christians and Muslims alike, as well as millions if not billions of other innocent human beings, that potentially was doing away with the human race. More sobering, they were unable to ask the question on why those human beings responsible for the disaster were bent on wanting to destroy themselves.

Standing at the extreme peak, feeling a slight movement within her stomach, Jody responded by placing her hand over her belly.

However, she was unable to determine whether she was carrying the beginning of a new life form, or the end of ours.